THE
HANGED
MAN'S SONG

John Sandford

G. P. PUTNAM'S SONS
New York

PUTNAM
— EST. 1838 —
G. P. Putnam's Sons
Publishers Since 1838
An imprint of Penguin Random House LLC
penguinrandomhouse.com

Copyright © 2003 by John Sandford

First G. P. Putnam's Sons hardcover edition / November 2003
First Berkley mass-market edition / October 2004
First Berkley premium edition / January 2011
First G. P. Putnam's Sons premium edition / July 2023
G. P. Putnam's Sons premium edition ISBN: 9780425199107

Printed in the United States of America

"Hard-boiled computer hacker Kidd and his sometime girlfriend, LuEllen, make for a refreshingly roguish couple" (*Entertainment Weekly*). Now they're back in #1 *New York Times* bestselling author John Sandford's electrifying new novel of murder, intrigue, and revenge—Kidd style.

THE HANGED MAN'S SONG

When Kidd's superhacker friend Bobby is murdered and his laptop is stolen, Kidd knows it's panic time. The secrets stashed in Bobby's computer are enough to hang Kidd and everyone else in Bobby's criminally ingenious cyber-circle. It's up to Kidd and his partner, LuEllen, to track it down, find Bobby's killer, and save their own necks—because the secrets are downloading faster than anyone anticipated. And they're far more staggering than anyone imagined.

"A roller coaster of a read . . . Chapters ricochet and burst, erupt and twist."　　　　—*Providence Journal-Bulletin*

"Action as hot and twisted as a Mississippi back road."
　　　　—*Publishers Weekly*

"Smart."　　　　—*The New York Times Book Review*

"Fast-paced."　　　　—*The Cleveland Plain Dealer*

"Exciting."　　　　—*People*

continued . . .

*This one is for my fellow hosers
at the St. Paul Papers.*

You know who you are.

1

NOW THE BLACK man screamed *No!*, now the black man shouted, *Get out, motherfucker,* and Carp, a big-boy at thirty, felt the explosion behind his eyes.

Tantrum.

They were in the black man's neatly kept sick-house, his infirmary. Carp snatched the green oxygen cylinder off its stand, felt the weight as he swung it overhead. The black man began to turn in his wheelchair, his dark eyes coming around through the narrow, fashionable glasses, the gun turning, the gun looking like a toy.

And now it goes to slo-mo, the sounds of the house fading—the soprano on public radio, fading; the rumble of a passing car, fading; the hoarse, angry words from the black man, fading to inaudible gibberish; and the black man turning, and the gun, all in slo-mo, the sounds fading as time slowed down. . . .

Then lurching to fast forward:

"HAIYAH!" James Carp screamed it, gobs of spit flying, one explosive syllable, and he swung the steel cylinder as hard as he could, as though he were spiking a football.

The black man's skull shattered and the black man shouted a death-shout, a *HUH!* that came at once with the *WHACK!* of the cylinder smashing bone.

The black man spun out of his wheelchair, blood flying in a crimson spray. A .25-caliber automatic pistol skittered out of his fingers and across the red-and-blue oriental carpet into a corner; the wheelchair crashed into a plaster wall, sounding as though somebody had dropped an armful of pipes.

Time slowed again. The quiet sounds came back: the soprano, the cars, an airplane, a bird, and the black man: almost subliminally, the air squeezed out of his dying lungs and across his vocal cords, producing not a moan, but a drawn-out vowel oooohhhh . . .

Blood began to seep from the black man's close-cut hair into the carpet. He was a pile of bones wrapped in a blue shirt.

CARP STOOD OVER him, sweating, shirt stuck to his broad back, breathing heavily, angry adrenaline burning in his blood, listening, hearing nothing but the rain ticking on the tin roof and the soprano in the unintelligible Italian opera; smelling the must and the old wood of the house tainted by the coppery odor of blood. He was pretty sure he knew what he'd done but he said, "Get up. C'mon, get up."

The black man didn't move and Carp pushed the skinny body with a foot, and the body, already insubstantial, shoulders and legs skeletal, small skull like a croquet ball, flopped with the slackness of death. "Fuck you," Carp said. He tossed the oxygen cylinder on a couch, where it bounced silently on the soft cushions.

A car turned the corner. Carp jerked, stepped to a window, split the blinds with an index finger, and looked out at the street. The car kept going, splashing through a roadside puddle.

Breathing even harder, now. He looked around, for other eyes, but there was nobody in the house but him and the black man's body. Fear rode over the anger, and Carp's body told him to run, to get away, to put this behind him, to pretend it never happened; but his brain was saying, *Take it easy, take it slow.*

Carp was a big man, too heavy for his height, round-shouldered, shambling. His eyes were flat and shallow, his nose was long and fleshy, like a small banana. His two-day beard was patchy, his brown hair was lank, moplike. Turning away from the body, he went first for the laptop.

The dead man's name was Bobby, and Bobby's laptop was fastened to a steel tray that swiveled off the wheelchair like an old-fashioned school desk. The laptop was no lightweight—it was a desktop replacement model from IBM with maximum RAM, a fat hard drive, built-in CD/DVD burner, three USB ports, a variety of memory-card slots.

A powerful laptop, but not exactly what Carp had expected. He'd expected something like . . . well, an old-fashioned CIA computer room, painted white with plastic floors and men in spectacles walking around in white coats with clipboards, Bobby perched in some kind of Star Wars control console. How could the most powerful hacker in the United States of America operate out of a laptop? A laptop and a wheelchair and Giorgio Armani glasses and a blue, freshly pressed oxford-cloth shirt?

The laptop wasn't the only surprise—the whole neighborhood was unexpected, a run-down, gravel-road section of Jackson, smelling of Spanish moss and red-pine bark and marsh water. He could hear croakers chipping away in the twilight when he walked up the flagstones to the front porch.

RIGHT FROM THE start, his search seemed to have gone bad. He'd located Bobby's caregiver, and the guy wasn't exactly the sharpest knife in the dishwasher: Carp had talked his way into the man's house with an excuse that sounded unbelievably lame in his own ears, so bad that he couldn't believe that the man had been trusted with Bobby's safety. But he had been.

ANY QUESTION HAD been resolved when Bobby had come to the front door and Carp had asked, "Bobby?" and Bobby's eyes had gone wide and he'd started backing away.

"Get away from me. Who are you? Who . . . get away . . ."

The whole thing had devolved into a thrashing, screaming argument and Carp had bulled his way through the door, and then Bobby had sent the wheelchair across the room to a built-in bookcase, pushed aside a ceramic bowl, and Carp could see that a gun was coming up and he'd picked up the oxygen cylinder.

Didn't really mean to do it. Not yet, anyway. He'd wanted to talk for a while.

Whatever he'd intended, Bobby was dead. No going back now. He moved over to the wheelchair, turned the laptop around, found it still running. Bobby hadn't had time to do anything with it, hadn't tried. The machine was running UNIX, no big surprise there. A security-aware hacker was as likely to run Windows as the Navy was to put a screen door on a submarine.

He'd figure it out later; one thing he didn't dare do was turn it off. He checked the power meter and found the battery at 75 percent. Good for the time being. Next he went to the system monitor to look at the hard drive. Okay: 120 gigabytes, 60 percent full. The damn thing had more data in it than the average library.

The laptop was fastened to the wheelchair tray by snap clamps and he fumbled at them for a moment before the computer came loose. As he worked the clamps, he noticed the wi-fi antenna protruding from the PCMCIA slot on the side of the machine. There was something more, then.

He carried the laptop to the door and left it there, still turned on, then went through the house to the kitchen, moving quickly, thinking about the crime. Mississippi, he was sure, had the electric chair or the guillotine or maybe they burned you at the stake. Whatever it was, it was bound to be primitive. He had to take care.

He pulled a few paper towels off a low-mounted roll near the sink and used them to cover his hands, and he started opening doors and cupboards. In a bedroom, next to a narrow, ascetic bed under a crucifix, he found a short table with the laptop's recharging cord and power supply, and two more batteries in a recharging deck.

Good. He unplugged the power supply and the recharging deck and carried them out to the living room and put them on the floor next to the door.

In the second bedroom, behind the tenth or twelfth door he opened, he found a cable jack and modem with the wi-fi transceiver. He was disappointed: he'd expected a set of servers.

"Shit." He muttered the word aloud. He'd killed a man for a laptop? There had to be more.

Back in the front room, he found a stack of blank recordable disks, but none that had been used. Where were the used disks? Where? There was a bookcase and he brushed some of the books out, found nothing behind them. Hurried past all the open doors and cupboards, feeling the pressure of time on his shoulders. Where?

He looked, but he found nothing more: only the laptop, winking at him from the doorway.

Had to go, had to go.

He stuffed the paper towels in his pocket, hurried to the door, picked up the laptop, power supply, and recharging deck, pulled the door almost shut with his bare hand, realized what he'd done, took the paper towels out of his pocket, wiped the knob and gripped it with the towel, and pulled the door shut. Hesitated. Pushed the door open again, crossed to the couch, thoroughly wiped the oxygen cylinder.

All right. Outside again, he stuck the electronics under his arm beneath the raincoat, and strolled as calmly as he could to the car. The car, a nondescript Toyota Corolla, had belonged to his mother. It wouldn't get a second glance anywhere, anytime. Which was lucky, he thought, considering what had happened.

He put the laptop, still running, on the passenger's seat. The laptop would take very careful investigation.

As he drove away, he thought about his exposure in Bobby's death. Not much, he thought, unless he was brutally unlucky. A neighbor trying a new camera, an idiot savant who remembered his license plate number; one chance in a million.

Less than that, even—he'd been obsessively careful in his approach to the black man; that he'd come on a rainy day was not an accident. Maybe, he thought, he'd known in his heart that Bobby would end this day as a dead man.

Maybe. As he turned the corner and left the neighborhood, a hum of satisfaction began to vibrate through him. He felt the skull crunching again, saw the body fly from the wheelchair, felt the rush. . . .

Felt the skull crunch . . . and almost drove through a red light.

He pulled himself back: he had to get out of town safely. This was no time for a traffic ticket that would pin him to Jackson, at this moment, at this place.

He was careful the rest of the way out, but still . . .

He smiled at himself. *Felt kinda good, Jimmy James. HUH! WHACK!* Rock 'n' roll.

2

FROM MY KITCHEN window in St. Paul, over the top of the geranium pot, I can see the Mississippi snaking away to the south past the municipal airport and the barge yards. There's always a towboat out there, rounding up a string of rust-colored barges, or a guy heading downstream in a houseboat, or a seaplane lining up for takeoff. I never get tired of it. I wish I could pipe in all the sounds and smell of it, leaving out the stink and groan of the trucks and buses that run along the river road.

I was standing there, scratching the iron-sized head of the red cat, when the phone rang.

I thought about not answering it—there was nobody I particularly cared to talk to that day—but the ringing continued. I finally picked it up, annoyed, and found a smoker's voice like a rusty hinge in a horror movie. An old political client. He asked me to do a job for him. "It's no big deal," he rasped.

"You lie like a Yankee carpetbagger," I said back. I hadn't talked to him in years, but we were picking up where we left off: friendly, but a little contentious.

"I resemble that remark," he said. "Besides, it'll only take you a few days."

"How much you paying?"

"Wull . . . nothin'."

Bob was a Democrat from a conservative Mississippi district. He was worried about a slick, good-looking young Republican woman named Nosere.

"I'll tell you the truth, Kidd: the bitch is richer than Davy Crockett and can self-finance," said the congressman. He was getting into his stump rhythms: "When it comes to ambition, she makes Hillary Clinton look like the wallflower at a Saturday-night sock-hop. She makes Huey Long look like a guppy. You gotta get your ass down there, boy. Dig this out for me."

"You oughta be able to self-finance your own self," I said. "You've been in Washington for twelve years now, for Christ's sakes."

Pause, as if thinking, or maybe contemplating the balances in off-shore checking accounts. Then, "Don't dog me around, Kidd. You gonna do this, or what?"

WHEN ALL THE bullshit is dispensed with, I am an artist—a painter—and for most of my life, in the eyes of the law, a criminal, though I prefer to think of myself as a libertarian who liberates for money.

At the University of Minnesota, where I had gone to school on a wrestling scholarship, I carried a minor in art, with a major in computer science. Computers and mathematics interested me in the same way that art did, and I worked hard at them. Then the Army came along and gave me a few additional skills. When I got out of the service, I went to work as a freelance computer consultant.

Aboveground, I was writing political-polling software that could be run in the new desktop computers, the early IBMs, and even a package that you could run on a Color Computer, if anybody remembers those. I was also debugging commercial computer-control programs, a job that was considered the coal mine of the computer world. I was pretty good at it: Bill Gates had once said to me, "Hey, dude, we're starting a company."

Underground, I was doing industrial espionage for a select clientele, entering unfriendly places, either electronically or physically, and copying technical memos, software, drawings, anything that my client could use to keep up with the Gateses. The eighties were good to me, but the nineties had been hot: a dozen technical memos, moved from A to B, could result in a hundred-million-dollar Internet IPO. Or, more likely, could kill one.

All that time, I'd been painting. I can't tell you about whiskey and drugs and gambling and women, because those things are for amateurs and rock musicians. I worked all the time—maybe dabbled a little in women. Unlike whiskey, drug, and gambling addictions, I'd found that women tended to go away after a while. On their own.

As did the political-polling business. I sold out to a competitor because I was losing patience with my clients, with my clients' way of making a living.

Politicians fuck with people. That's what they do. That's their job. Every day, they get up and wonder who they're gonna fuck with that day. Then they go and do it. They're not of much use—they don't make anything, create anything, think any great thoughts. They just fuck with the rest of us. I got tired of talking to them.

So the years went by, with painting and computers, and now here I was, talking to Congressman Bob. I wheedled and begged, even pled poverty, but eventually said I'd do it—truth be told, I needed a break from the fever dreams of my latest paintings, a suite of five commissioned by a rich lumberman from Louisiana.

Then there was my love life, which had taken an ugly turn for the worse.

Getting out of town didn't look that bad. That's why, for the past two weeks, I'd been working in the belly of the *Wisteria*.

THE *WISTERIA* WAS a casino and hung off a pier on the Gulf Coast of Mississippi, between Biloxi and

Gulfport. Designed to look like a riverboat, it was the size of a battleship. Sweeping decks of slot machines, which would take everything down to your last nickel, sucked up most of the space. There were also three restaurants, two bars, and a poop deck for the low-return games.

Muzak, mostly orchestrated versions of old Sinatra sounds, kept you happy while you cranked the slots, and gave the place its class. All of it smelled of tobacco, alcohol, spoiled potato chips, sweat, cleaning fluids, and overstressed deodorant, with just the faintest whiff of vomit.

I was inside for six hours a day, thinking about painting and women, while throwing money down the slot machines. The job was simple enough, but I had to be careful: if I screwed it up, some bent-nosed cracker thug would take me out in the woods and break my arms and legs—if I was lucky.

Or, I should say, *our* arms and legs.

MY FRIEND LUELLEN had come along. She actually liked casinos, and I needed the help. She was also doing therapy on me: she referred to my lost love as Boobs, and had worked out a complete set of verbs and adjectives based on that root word. The day before, in the *Wisteria*'s fine-dining restaurant ("The best surf-and-turf between New Orleans and Tallahassee"), she'd held up a glob of deep-fried potato and said, "Now *there's* one boobilicious Tater Tot."

"You give me any more shit, I'm gonna stick a Tater Tot in one of your crevices," I said, with more snarl than I'd intended.

"You're not man enough," she said, unimpressed. "I've been working out three hours a day. I can kick your ass now."

"Working out with what? Golf? You're gonna putt me to death?"

She pointed a Tater Tot at me, a little edge in her voice. "You may speak lightly of my crevices, but do not say bad things about golf."

THE JOB: MISS Young Republican Anita Nosere—who was, from the pictures I'd seen of her, fairly boobi-licious herself—got her money from her mother. Her mother was managing director of a syndicate that owned the Wisteria. Congressman Bob had been told that the casino was skimming the take, thus shorting both the U.S. government and the state of Mississippi on taxes. The skim was one of those simple-minded things that are almost impossible to spot if the casino does it carefully enough.

It works like this: the casino advertises (and reports to the tax authorities) a given return on the slot machines. If that return is even a little lower than the rate reported, the income increases sharply. That is, if you report that your machines will return 95 percent to the players, but you really only return 94 percent, and a million bucks a night goes through the slots, you're skimming $10,000 a night. In a few months, that adds up to real money.

Of course, you have to be careful about state auditors. For a politically well-connected company, in Mississippi, that wasn't a major problem: "Them boys is crookeder than a bucket of cotton-mouths," Bob said.

The congressman could have hired one of the big independent auditing companies to do his research, but that would have cost tens of thousands of dollars. Me, he could get for free, and get a good idea if the charges were true. If they were, then he'd hire the big auditing company, do the research, and hang the Noseres, momma and daughter together, all in the name of truth, justice, and the American Way.

EXACTLY WHAT WE did was, we dropped dollars—and quarters and nickels—into slot machines and counted the return, and then ran the results through a statistics package. We wanted 98 percent confidence that we were less than half of a percent off the true return. We therefore needed to take a large random sample of machines and had to run enough coins through each machine that we'd get a statistically accurate return on each.

I'd chosen the target machines the first night, using a random numbers program in the laptop I carried.

We'd been at it ever since, dropping the dollars, quarters, and nickels, doing the numbers at night, avoiding crackers with bent noses, and generally dancing around the possibility of acts of unfaithfulness, if that's what it would have been.

Can you be unfaithful to a mood, to a sense of guilt? I mean, the woman was gone. . . .

But Marcy's departure had driven me into an emotional hole. A number of good women have walked out on me, and there's no way that I can claim it was always, or even usually, their fault. When the first bloom of romance fades away, they begin to pay attention to my priorities. Sooner or later, they conclude that they'll always be number three, behind painting and maybe computers.

They might be right, though I still hate to think so. There was no question that as I got older, I'd become more and more involved in the work. I'd sometimes go days without talking to anyone, and become impatient when a woman wanted to do something ordinary, like go out to dinner.

That was not a problem with LuEllen. I'd known her for a decade, spent hours rolling around in various beds with her, and still didn't know her real last name or where she lived. I knew everything about her but the basic, simple stuff.

At this point, we were not in bed. I don't know exactly what she was doing, in her head, but I was just drifting along, dropping coins, thinking about painting and sex and listening to the rain fall on the casino roof, the car roof, and the motel roof, thinking about getting back to St. Paul and the serious work.

LUELLEN AND I were staying in separate rooms at the Rapaport Suites on I-10, one of those concrete-block instant motels with a polite Indian man and his wife at the front desk, a permanent smell of cigarette smoke in the curtains, and a dollar-a-minute surcharge on the telephone. The place wasn't exactly bleak, it was simply *nothing*. I can't even remember the colors, which were chosen not to show dirt. My room was a cube with a can, a candidate for existential hell. And we couldn't get out.

Rain had been falling since the day we arrived. A hurricane was prowling the Gulf, well down to the south, but had gotten itself stuck somewhere between Jamaica and the Yucatán. The storm wasn't much, but the rain shield was terrific, reaching far enough north to cover half the state of Mississippi. We'd been kept inside, Noseres to the grindstone.

And life was looking grim for the mother-daughter duo. The numbers said they might be skimming two percent.

WE HAD JUST finished a three-hour session with the slots, and after freshening up—taking a leak, I guess—LuEllen came down to my room, pulled off her cowboy boots, and sprawled on the bed to read *Barron's*.

She's a slender dark woman with an oval face, a solid set of muscles, a terrific ass, and a taste for cocaine and cowboy gear, to say nothing of the odd cowboy himself.

"Numbers?" she asked, without looking at me.

"Yeah." I was sitting with my head thrust toward the laptop screen, the classic geek posture, and my neck felt like it was in a vise. "How about a back rub? My neck is killing me."

"You haven't been very attentive to me and I'm not sure a back rub would be appropriate," she said. She turned a page in *Barron's*. "Or any other kind of rub."

"You wanna do the fuckin' numbers?"

"I'm not getting paid the big bucks."

"Yeah, big bucks . . ."

She sighed and tossed the *Barron's* on the carpet; she was basically a good sport. "All right." She popped off the bed, came over and went to work on my back. She has powerful thumbs for a small woman. "Wanna go out for a hot-fudge sundae?"

"Sure. Keep working, let me check my e-mail." She was knuckling the muscle along my spine, right at my shoulder, and I rolled my head and punched up the e-mail program on my laptop, and went out, at a dollar a minute, to see what I could see.

An alarm came up for one of my out-of-sight e-mail addresses. Spam, probably, but I looked. No spam—it was a note from a man I didn't know, who called himself *romeoblue*.

The e-mail read, "Bobby down. Drop word. Ring on."

"Motherfucker," I said as I read it. I didn't believe what I was seeing.

LuEllen caught the tone and looked over my shoulder. She knew about Bobby, so I let her look. "Uh-oh. Who's *romeoblue*?"

"I don't know."

"How does he know Bobby?"

I knew the answer to that, but I avoided the question. LuEllen and I trusted each other, but there was no point in being careless. "Lots of people know Bobby. . . . Listen, now we *gotta* go out. I gotta make a call."

BOBBY IS THE deus ex machina for the hacking community, the fount of all knowledge, the keeper of secrets, the source of critical phone numbers, a guide through the darkness of IBM mainframes. As with LuEllen, I didn't know his real name or exactly where he lived; but we'd done some business together.

THE GULF COAST could probably be a garden spot, but it isn't. It's a junkyard. Every form of scummy business you can think of can be found between I-10 and the beach, and most every one of them built the cheapest possible building to do the business in. It's like Amarillo, Texas, but in bad taste.

We ran through the rain from my room to the car, then trucked on down I-10 to the nearest Wal-Mart. We made the call from a public phone using a tiny Sony laptop I'd picked up a few weeks earlier. Dialed up my Bobby number and got nothing. No carrier tone, no redirect to some other number, just ringing with no answer. That had never happened before. I made a quick check again of my e-mail and had a second message, from a person named *polytrope*. He said, "Bobby's gone. Out six hours now. Drop word. Ring on."

"Maybe they got him," I said to LuEllen, popping the connection. "The feds. I gotta make another call, but not from here. Let's go."

LuEllen's a professional thief. When I said, "Let's go," she didn't ask questions. She started walking. Not hurrying, but moving out, smiling, pleasant, but not making eye contact with any of the store clerks.

In the movies, the FBI makes a call while the bad guy is still on the telephone, and three minutes later, agents drop out of the sky in a black helicopter and the chase begins.

In reality, if the feds had taken Bobby, and had a watch on his phone line, they could get a read on the Wal-Mart phone almost instantly. Getting to the phone was another matter—that would take a while, even if they went through the local cops. In the very best, most cooperative system, we'd have ten minutes. In a typical federal law-enforcement scramble, we'd have an hour or more. But why take a chance?

We were out of the Wal-Mart in a minute, and in two minutes, down the highway. Ten miles away, I made a call from an outdoor phone at a Shell station, dropping an e-mail to two guys who, separately, called themselves *pr48stl9* and *trilbee*: "Bobby is down. Transmit word. Ring on." I sent a third e-mail to *pepper@evitable.org*: "3577." The number was my "word," and I was dropping it into a blind hole.

"THAT'S IT?" LUELLEN asked, when I'd dropped the word.

"That's all there is. There's nothing else to do. Still want that sundae?"

"I guess." But she was worried. We're both illegal, at least some of the time, and we're sensitive to trouble, to complications that could push us out in the open. Trouble is like a panfish nibbling at the end of your fishing line—you feel it, and if you're experienced, you know what it means. She could feel the trouble nibbling at us. "Maybe chocolate will cure it."

THE RING HAD been set up by Bobby. A group of people that he more or less trusted were each given one segment of his address. If anything should happen to him—if his system went unresponsive—we'd each dump our "word" at a blind e-mail address.

Whoever checked the e-mail would assemble the words, derive a street address, and go to Bobby's house to see what had happened. I didn't know who'd been designated to go. Somebody closer to Bobby than I was.

To keep the cops from breaking the ring, if one of us should be caught, we knew only the online names of two members of the ring. I didn't know until that day that *romeoblue*, whoever he was, was a member of the ring, or that he had one of my blind addresses. The guys I called, *pr48stl9* and *trilbee,* didn't know that I was part of it, and I had no idea who their guys were, further around the ring.

Nobody, except Bobby, knew how many ring members there were, or their real names—all we knew is that each guy had two names. Two, in case somebody should be out of touch, or even dead, when the ring was turned on.

And the *ring on* thing—if one of us *was* caught by the cops, and extorted into contacting the ring, a warning could be sent along with the extorted message. If the message didn't end with *ring on,* you'd assume that things were going to hell in a handbasket.

All of this might sound overblown, but several

of us were wanted by the feds. We hadn't been charged with any crimes, you understand. They didn't even know who we were. They just wanted to get us down in a basement, somewhere, with maybe an electric motor and a coil of wire, to chat for a while.

"YOU THINK HE'S dead? Bobby?" LuEllen asked. We'd been visiting a particular ice-cream parlor, named Robbie's, about three times a week. The place was designed to look like a railroad dining car, but had good sundaes, anyway. We'd just pulled into the parking lot, to the final thumps of the Stones' "(I Can't Get No) Satisfaction" on the radio, when she asked her question.

I nodded. "Yeah. Or maybe unconscious, lying on the floor," I said. That made me sad. I'd never actually met him, but he was a friend, and I could feel that hypothetical loneliness. "Or . . . hell, it could be a lot of things, but I think he's probably dead or dying."

"What'll you guys do? He's always been there."

"Be more careful. Take fewer jobs. Maybe get out of it."

"I've been thinking about getting out," she said suddenly. "Maybe stop stealing."

I looked at her and shook my head. "You never said."

She shrugged. "I'm getting old."

"Pressing your mid-thirties, I'd say."

She patted me on the thigh and said, "Let's go. We're gonna get wet."

THE GUY WHO ran the ice-cream parlor wore a name tag that said "Jim" and a distant look, as though he was wishing for mountains. A paper hat perched on his balding head, and he always had a toothpick tucked in one corner of his mouth. He nodded at us, said, "The regular?" and we said, "Yeah," and watched him dish it up. Lots of hot chocolate. The sundaes cost five dollars each, and I'd been leaving another five on the table when we left. Jim was now taking care of us, chocolate-wise.

In the booth, over the sundaes, LuEllen asked, "You think you could really quit?"

"I don't need the money."

She looked out at the rain, hammering down on the street. A veterans convention was in town, and a guy wearing a plastic-straw boater, with a convention tag, wandered by. He'd poked a hole in the bottom of a green garbage bag and had pulled it over himself as a raincoat.

We watched him go, and LuEllen said, "Drunk."

"Seeing your old war buddies'll do that," I said. "World War Two guys are dropping like flies now."

"Wonder if Bobby . . ." Her spoon dragged around

the rim of the tulip glass; she didn't finish the sentence.

BOBBY HAD A degenerative disease, although I had no clear idea of what it was. The ring had been set up to take care of things should he die or suffer a catastrophic decline. If he went slowly, the ring wouldn't know until the very end. At the last extreme, we would have all gotten files of information that he thought we might individually want—a kind of inheritance—and he would have erased everything else.

I had hoped that he'd go that way, in peace. Quietly. He apparently had not.

Of course, it was also possible that the feds had landed in a silent black helicopter, kicked in the door, and slid down his chimney and seized him before he could enter his destruct code, and that they were now waiting for us in an elaborate trap, armed to the teeth with all that shit that they spend the billions on—the secret hammers and high-tech toilet seats.

But I didn't think so. I thought Bobby was dead.

BACK AT THE motel, I tried to work on the casino stats. I had a feeling I better get them done, just in case the Bobby problem turned into something ugly. Trouble tapping at the line. Every few minutes I'd check my e-mail. Two hours later, I picked up an alarm from another one of my invisible addresses: "Call me at home—J."

"Gotta go back out," I told LuEllen. She was bent over the bed with a lightweight dumbbell, doing a golf exercise called the lawn mower pull. "Got a note from John."

"Is he part of the ring?" she asked, doing a final three pumps. She knew John as well as I did.

"I'd always assumed he was, but we never talked about it," I said. "He's not like the rest of us."

"Not a computer geek."

"I'm not a computer geek," I said. "Computer geeks wear pocket protectors."

"You've got five colors of pens, Kidd," she said, pulling on her rain jacket. "I saw them once when I was ransacking your briefcase."

"I'm an artist, for Christ's sakes," I said.

JOHN LIVED IN a little Mississippi River town called Longstreet. He and his wife and LuEllen and I were friends. I'd stop and see them a couple times a year, as I migrated up and down the Mississippi between St. Paul and New Orleans. LuEllen would stop if she was stealing something nearby.

I called him from a Conoco: gas stations with pay phones should get a tax break. He answered on the first ring.

"John, this is Kidd, calling you back," I said.

Rain was hammering on the car, and I could see a discouraged-looking redneck behind the plate glass of the station window.

"You know about Bobby?" John asked. He had a baritone voice, calm and scholarly, with a trace of a Memphis accent.

"I know he's down. Are you a member of the ring?"

"I'm the guy who puts the words together. Do you have a pen?"

"Just a minute." I got out a pen and found a blank page in a pocket sketchbook. "Okay."

"Here's his address."

"You sure you want to give it to me?"

"Yes. Just in case something happens . . . to me. Ready? Robert Fields, 3577 Arikara Street, Jackson, Mississippi 38292. Or it might also have been Robert Jackson, 3577 Arikara Street, Fields, Mississippi 38292, except that there isn't a Fields, Mississippi, as far as I can tell."

"The name I had for him, the rumor I had, was that his name was Bobby DuChamps—French for 'fields.' "

"That's the name I had," he said. "What's an Arikara?"

"An Indian tribe, I think. Did you try to call him?"

"Can't find a phone number."

"Yeah, well—he might not have one of his own," I said. "He didn't need one, since he practically owned the phone company."

"That's what I figured. Listen . . . I checked airlines from St. Paul into Jackson—"

"I'm down by Biloxi," I said, interrupting. "Between Biloxi and Gulfport."

"Really?" His voice brightened. "Could you meet me in Jackson? You could be there in three hours, right up U.S. 49. It'll take me an hour and a half at least. It's raining like hell up here."

"Down here, too."

"But I got bad roads. Kidd, I need some backup. We gotta try to do this before daylight."

I thought about it for a minute. This could be a bad move, but John was an old friend who had helped us through some hard times. I owed him. "All right. Where do you want to hook up?"

"I got a room at the La Quinta Inn, which is just off I-55. It's what, almost ten o'clock now. See you at one?"

"Soon as I can get there," I said.

WHEN I TOLD her, LuEllen frowned, looked out the window at the slanting rain. "It's a bad night for driving fast."

"I gotta go," I said.

"I know." A couple of seconds later, "Shoot. I put some Chanel on. Now it's wasted." She stood on her tiptoes and gave me a soft peck on the lips, her hands on my rib cage. She *did* smell good; and I knew she'd feel pretty good. "You goddamn well be careful."

Some things to think about on my way north: sex and death.

3

THE NIGHT WAS as dark as Elvis velvet, with nothing but the hissing of the tires on the wet pavement and the occasional red taillights turning off toward unseen homes. I listened to the radio part of the way, a classic rock station that disappeared north of Hattiesburg, fading out in the middle of a Tom Petty piece.

As the radio station faded, so did the rain, diminishing to a drizzle. I turned the radio off so I could think, but all I could do was go round and round about Bobby. What had happened to him? What were the implications, if he was dead? Where were his databases, and who had them?

Bobby had backed me up in a number of troubling ventures. People had died, in fact—that they'd most often deserved it didn't change the fact of their death.

Say it: of their killing. Bobby knew most of the details in the destruction of a major aerospace company. He knew why the odd security problems kept popping up in Windows. He knew why an American satellite system didn't always work exactly as designed. He knew how a commie got elected mayor of a town down in the Delta.

He had worked with John. John had been a kind of black radical political operator all through the deep South, especially in the Delta. He didn't talk about it, but he was tough in a way you didn't get by accident; and he had scars you didn't get from playing tennis.

So Bobby knew too much for our good health. He knew stuff that could put a few dozen, or even a few hundred, people in prison. Maybe even me.

Thirty miles south of Jackson, I ran into a thunderstorm—what they call an embedded storm, though I wouldn't know it from an unbedded storm. The rain came down in marble-sized bullets, lightning jumped and skittered across the sky, and I could feel the thunder beating against the car, flexing the skin, like the cover on a sub-woofer.

I hoped John had made it all right. He had a treacherous route into Jackson, mostly back highways through rural hamlets, not a good drive in bright sunlight. I'd met John on one of my special jobs, set up by Bobby, a job that ended with me in a Memphis hospital. The scars have almost faded, but I still have the dreams. . . .

Still, we'd become friends. John had been an

investigator with a law office in Memphis, and, underground, an enforcer of some kind for a black radical political party—and at the same time, an artist,
like me. Instead of paint, John worked in stone and
wood, a sculptor. He'd begun making money at it,
and had started picking up a reputation.

THAT LAST THIRTY miles of bullet-rain took
forty minutes to drive through, and it was nearly two
in the morning when I arrived in Jackson. I pulled
into the La Quinta, stopped under a portico, and
hopped out. Before I could walk around the car, John
came through the door. He was wrapped in a gray
plastic raincoat and was smiling and said, "Goddamnit, I'm glad to see you, Kidd. I was afraid you'd gone
in a ditch." He was a black man, middle forties, with
a square face, short hair, broad shoulders, and smart,
dark eyes.

As we shook hands in the rain, I said, "Picked a
good fuckin' night for it."

"If you don't have to pee . . ."

"I'm fine, but I'd like to get a Coke."

He stuck his hand in his pocket and produced a
can of Diet Coke. "Still cold. Let's go."

AS SOON AS he'd come into town, figuring that I'd
be later, he'd gone around to convenience stores until
he found one that sold a city map. In his room at the

La Quinta, he'd spotted Bobby's house and blocked out a route. "We're a ways from where we need to be," he said. He pointed down a broad street that went under the interstate. "Go that way."

I went that way and asked, "How's Marvel?"

"She's fine. Up to her ass in the politics. Still a fuckin' commie."

"Nice ass, though," I said. Marvel was his wife, but John and I had met her at the same time, and I had commentary privileges.

"True. How 'bout LuEllen?"

"She's with me, down in Biloxi, but we're not in bed. I've, uh, I'd been, uh, seeing this woman back home. She broke it off a couple of weeks ago. I'm kinda bummed."

"You were serious?" He was interested.

"Maybe. Interesting woman—a cop, in fact."

A moment of silence, then, "Bet she had a nice pair of thirty-eights, huh?"

We both had to laugh at the stupidity of it. Then I said, "What about Bobby?"

"I don't know," John said. "He sounded good—I mean, bad, but good for him—last time I talked to him. That was like two weeks ago, one of those phone calls from nowhere."

"No hint of this."

"Nothing. I tried to remember every word of what he said, when I was coming over here, and I can't remember a single unusual thing. He just sounded like . . . Bobby. Hey, turn left at that stoplight."

———

JACKSON, MISSISSIPPI, MAY be a perfectly nice place, assuming that we weren't in the best part of it. The part we were in was run-down and maybe even run-over. Some of the houses that passed through our headlights seemed to be sinking into the ground. Driveways were mostly gravel, with here and there a carport; otherwise the cars, big American cars from the eighties and nineties, were parked in the yards.

The streets got bumpier as we went along, and eventually we got into a spot that was overgrown with kudzu, the stuff curled up and down the phone poles and street signs. Water was ponding along the shoulders of the roads; street signs became hard to locate and, with the kudzu, even harder to read.

"Too bad you can't smoke that shit," John said. "Solve a lot of problems."

At one point, a big black-and-tan dog, probably a Doberman, splashed in the rain through our headlights, looking at us with lion eyes that said, "C'mon, get out of the car, chump, c'mon . . ."

We didn't. Instead, John picked out streets on his map, confirmed it from one street sign to the next, and finally got us onto Arikara Street. "He ought to be in this block, if the numbers are right." The street was bumpy, potholed, with trees hanging over it, and was lined with widely spaced houses with dark exteriors and dark windows. I'd brought a flashlight along with me, and John had it on his lap, but we didn't need it. We came up to a bronze-colored mailbox, the best-looking mailbox I'd seen all night, and in the headlights saw 3577 in reflecting stick-on numerals.

"That's it," he said.

I went on by. We looked for light, for movement, for any kind of weirdness, and didn't see or feel a thing. The house had a carport, but it was empty. Some of the houses had chain-link fences around the yards, but this one was open. A porch hung on the front of the place.

"Take another lap," John said. "Goddamnit. We shoulda worked out an alibi."

I shrugged. "Tell the truth. That we're old computer buddies of his, that we knew he was near death, and that he asked us to check on him if he ever became nonresponsive."

"Yeah." He sighed. "I wish we had something fancier."

"At two-thirty in the morning? We were out looking for Tic Tacs, Officer. . . ."

"Yeah, yeah. I just rather not have them run my ID through their database."

"No shit." The next lap around, I said, "I'm gonna pull in, unless you say no. You say no?"

"Pull in," he said.

I PULLED INTO the driveway, up close to the house, and before I killed the lights, noticed a wheelchair ramp going up to a side door from the carport. The neighborhood was poor, but the lots were large and overgrown. The neighbors to the left could see us, if they were interested, and the people across the street might get a look, but there were no lights in the windows. Working people, probably, who had to get up in the morning.

When I stopped, John climbed out, with me a second behind, and we shut the doors quickly and as quietly as we could, to kill the interior lights. Dark as a tar pit, rain pelting down; the place smelled almost like a northern lake. We squished through the wet side yard to the porch, then walked up to the door. John hesitated, then knocked.

Nothing.

Knocked again, then quietly, to me, "Jeez, I hope there's no alarm. I never even thought of that."

"If there is, we run." I tried the knob. "Shit."

"What?"

"It's open. Don't touch anything." I pushed the door with my knuckles, and immediately smelled the death inside.

"Got a problem," I said.

"I smell it."

The odor wasn't of physical decomposition, but simply of . . . death. An odd odor that dead people gather about them, an odor of dying heat, maybe, or souring gases, not heavy, but light, intangible, unpleasant. Something best not to think about. I was afraid to use the flashlight, because nothing brings the cops faster than a flashlight in a dark house. Instead, I pulled John inside, closed the door, groped around, found a wall switch, and turned on a ceiling light.

The first thing we saw was the wheelchair, and then what looked like a pile of gray laundry in a corner. We both stepped that way and saw the nearly weightless, eggshell skull of a young black man, with a scattering of books around his head. There was no question that he was dead. His face had been wrinkled, maybe from pain, and though you could tell he'd been young, he had a patina of age.

"Ah, shit," I said.

"I would have liked to have met him," John said softly.

I moved closer, saw the gun in the corner, and said, "There's a gun," and then stepped over the body and saw the misshapen skull and the blood. "Somebody killed him."

"Somebody . . ." John stepped over, saw the blood. "Oh, boy."

"Let's check around," I said. I glanced at the wheelchair, noticed the tray with a series of clamps. "John, look at this."

"What?"

"Looks like a laptop setup."

"No laptop."

We both knew that was bad. We did a quick run-through of the house and found a wi-fi router in a back closet, plugged into a cable modem. "No servers," I said. "I wondered about that."

"What?"

"He seemed to have servers, but that would have made him vulnerable. So he has virtual servers. All of his stuff is . . . out there, somewhere. What wasn't on the laptop."

John said, "Let's see if we can find some gloves, so we don't leave fingerprints all over the place."

BOBBY'S HOUSE WAS a mix of old and new. The entire house had wooden floors—board floors as in old southern farmhouses—covered in the dining room by a semi-threadbare oriental carpet that looked as though it came from the turn of the twentieth century. But it wasn't cheap; it fit the room well and looked inherited. A dozen plants were scattered through the half-dozen rooms, including five or six orchids, one blooming with gorgeous white flowers like a spray of silvery moons. An upright piano sat in one corner of the living room, the keyboard cover up, sheet music for Cole Porter's "I Get a Kick Out of You" perched on the music stand. There was all the usual stuff—a big TV, game cartridges, a stereo system with a CD player and maybe a thousand jazz and classical CDs, a modern turntable for vinyl records, and three or four hundred records to go with it. He liked Elvis Presley, I noticed, along with all the big blues masters.

There were photographs. Framed photos of single faces, and groups of people gathered around cars or

standing in front of houses, black people, all, smiling at the camera, dressed in suits and dresses as if
they'd just gotten back from church, maybe a wed-
ding; and the style of the photos, and the contents,
judging from the cars that were visible, went back
to the 1930s, and came forward, perhaps, to the
eighties.

And there were books. Big piles of computer stuff,
but also detective and thriller novels, and general fic-
tion. A copy of Annie Proulx's *That Old Ace in the
Hole* was split open over a chair that faced a wide-
screen television. A comfortable house, a comfortable
home, all come to a pile of laundry in a corner, with a
starved-bony face and a pool of blood.

We found a toolbox in a kitchen drawer, and a box
of vinyl gloves: actually, three boxes of vinyl gloves,
which suggested that Bobby had had allergies, as well
as the problem that had been killing him, whatever it
was.

We spent an hour going through the house, working quickly, trying to cover everything. For practical
purposes, the house was one-story—no basement, and
while there was an attic space, access was through a
ceiling hatch, and Bobby couldn't have gotten to it.
Anything important, we thought, would be on the
main floor. We wanted computer disks, written files,
anything that might involve Bobby's complicated computer relationships.

I spent a half hour going through two file cabinets,
mostly income tax and investment records. Nothing,

as far as I could see, that related to his computer work except for computer purchase records from Dell and IBM. I took those, dropping them in an empty Harry and David fruit-delivery box.

Every time we went in the front room, we curled our faces away from the bundle in the corner—I saw John do it, and I felt myself do it. But there was the curiosity . . . what did the mysterious Bobby really look like? I couldn't touch him, didn't want to move him, but looking down at him once, forcing myself, I decided that he looked a little like photos I'd seen of Somalis on the ragged edge of hunger. He had been nice-looking, but there was not much left of him; and now he looked deflated, sad, unready to be dead. He gave us a sense of silence and gloom.

Under some shoes in the bedroom closet, John spotted a board that looked out of place. When he rattled it and then lifted it, he found a green metal box, and inside that, an expired U.S. passport with the photo of a teenaged Bobby inside, a small amount of inexpensive, old-fashioned women's jewelry—his mother's?—and $16,000 in twenties and fifties.

"Take the money?" I asked John.

"If we don't, the cops might," John said, looking at me over the cash. "I don't need it."

"What if, uh, he has a will, and wants it to go to somebody?"

"We find that out and send it to them," John said. "But I'm afraid that if we don't take it, it's gonna disappear."

We put the money in the Harry and David box.

The biggest find came in the front room, in a built-in book cabinet not far from Bobby's outstretched hand. It was hard to see—it had been designed that way—but the cabinet was deeper from the side than it was from the front. In other words, if you looked at it from the side, it was a full fifteen inches deep. If you looked at it from the front, it was barely deep enough for a full-sized novel. Some of the novels that had been in the shelves had been pulled out and were scattered around the floor by the body.

I turned and said, "Come look at this."

John stepped carefully past the body and I pointed out the depth discrepancy. It took a minute to figure out, but if you pressed on one corner of the back of each shelf, a board simply popped loose. When you removed the board, you found a narrow little space behind the books. It was convenient, simple, and mostly effective.

Inside were seventy DVD disks: Bobby's files. We put them in the Harry and David box. Working around the body, John said, morosely, "That smell—Jesus, Kidd, I feel like it's getting into me."

"Keep working. Don't look."

When we were done, we put our raincoats back on, put the Harry and David box in a garbage bag, and toted it out to the car. The rain was constant, but not cold, and I could hear it gurgling down drainpipes off the tin roof—a sound that was sometimes light and musical, but tonight sounded like Wagner. Before we finally closed the door and wiped the doorknobs, John said, "I hate to leave him like this."

I looked back at the crumpled body on the floor and said, "You know, we really can't. Somebody killed him and the sooner the cops get here, the more likely they are to catch the guy."

"So we call the cops?" John didn't like cops.

"We call somebody," I said. "We've got to think about it. The thing is, we didn't find a computer, and it looks like whoever came in took it. That means that Bobby's main machine is floating around out there."

"You think . . . no." John shook his head at his own thought.

"What?"

"Wishful thinking. I was gonna say, maybe this was neighborhood thieves, and he caught them at it, and they killed him. But then, if it was just a burglary, they would have taken other stuff. There was all kinds of stuff that thieves would take, just sitting around."

"Yeah. But they only took the laptop. That means that they came for it. And were willing to kill for it," I said.

"Shit."

"If we're lucky, he encrypted the sensitive stuff. Every time he wanted to send me something serious,

I'd get the key, and then after I acknowledged it, the file would come in. If he whipped some encryption on it, we're okay."

"But if we're not lucky and he didn't encrypt . . ."

"Then we could be in trouble," I said.

4

WE WERE AN odd couple, wandering around in the middle of the night, in a monsoon. If we'd been noticed at Bobby's house by an insomniac neighbor, and if the cops later said something in the newspaper about looking for a white guy and a black guy seen together in the rain, I didn't want the desk clerk at the La Quinta to have that memory.

Instead of going back to the motel to talk, we drove a loop through Jackson, windshield wipers whacking away, windows steaming up, talking about what to do. We had two problems: getting some kind of justice for Bobby, and finding the laptop. The lives of a lot of us could be on that thing. Events, dates, times, places. Bobby knew way too much—it was as if the legendary J. Edgar Hoover files were out wandering around the country on their own.

"It's gonna be tricky," I said. We drove past an open space with orange security lights inside, and a chain-link fence around the perimeter. We couldn't see much of the buildings, which were huddled low and gray, as if depressed by the rain. "If we call the Jackson police, we're gonna get a homicide guy with a notebook or maybe a desk computer, but most of what he figures out he'll keep in his head. Calling up people on the phones and so on. There won't be any way to track the investigation. If the killer-guy is a sophisticated outsider, which he probably is . . . they're not going to come up with anything."

"How do you know that?"

"Because I've gone into enough places to know the signs. The guy didn't leave much. Besides, I was dating a cop, remember? And I've done some, mmm, preliminary research into the Minneapolis cops' computer system."

"That's cold, Kidd." He was a romantic, and offended.

"Hey, I wasn't dating her to get at the system," I said defensively. I fumbled around for the defroster and turned it on, blowing hot air on the windshield. All the heavy cogitation was steaming things up. "I was dating her because I liked her. It just happens that the system was sitting there."

"All right." He wasn't sure he believed me. "So what do we do?"

"If we call in the FBI and tell them that the dead guy is the Bobby that everybody's been looking for, they'll be all over the case. Then, we might be able to track the investigation—half the people in the ring are inside the FBI system. But what if they find the laptop? The worst thing that could happen to us is to have the laptop land at a computer forensics place, and have it turn out that the files aren't encrypted."

"Even if they are encrypted, the FBI's got those big fuckin' computers. They'll crack it like a walnut."

John's not a computer guy. I said, "No, not really. If Bobby encrypted the files, and kept the keys in his head, they're safe."

"Really?" A little skeptical. "What about the CIA and the NSA and the FBI and those other three-letter agencies?"

"Some of the software that Bobby used—that everybody uses, now—can encrypt stuff so deeply that if the entire universe was made of computers, and they did nothing but try to crack the message, there wouldn't be enough time in the life of the universe to do it."

He thought about that, then laughed. "You're bullshitting me."

"Nope."

"Why would anybody encrypt something *that* deep?"

"Because they can. It's easy. So why not?"

"Okay. But still, the idea of calling in the feds is scary," he said. "I hate messing with those guys. If we only knew what was on the laptop. . . ."

"That's the problem," I agreed.

"Maybe, as a security thing, Bobby kept all the good stuff on the DVDs."

We bumped across a set of railroad tracks. I wasn't sure, but I thought I was lost. I did a U-turn and headed back the way we'd come. I picked up on John's suggestion: "I don't think so. Access is too slow. No computer guy wants to thumb through a stack of DVDs and then wait for ten seconds for something to load when he can get it in a half-second. That's just the way it is. He'd keep the good stuff on the laptop."

"Then maybe he backed up the laptop on the DVDs, so we can figure out what's on it, without finding it."

I shook my head. "There are what, seventy DVDs? That's a huge amount of stuff. You could probably put the Library of Congress on those things. There's so much stuff that we won't even have time to read the indexes, if there are indexes."

"I could take some time off . . ."

John used to work on a law firm's computer system, and he was about as far into computers as a typical high school teacher. He didn't have any notion of what I was talking about, and I struggled around to find an explanation.

"Look," I said finally. "A few weeks ago, I put the *Encyclopaedia Britannica* on my laptop, since I had lots of space. Okay? That's seventy-five thousand articles, thirteen hundred maps, ten thousand photos. That's what the advertisement says. Something like that. It sucked up about 1.2 gigs. That means you could put about, uh . . ."—I did some quick calculation—"something like thirteen *Encyclopaedia Britannica*s on one DVD. And we have seventy DVDs. They might not be full, but if they are, that'll be like paging through what, sixty-seven million articles and eight million pictures, looking for your name or your picture. You don't have enough time left in your life to do it."

"Then what use are they?"

"Bobby didn't look piece by piece. He knew what he had. I'd bet he's dumped whole databases to the DVDs and the index is on the laptop. It's like a hacker's reference library. When he needs something, he can look it up."

WE FORDED A couple of low cross streets and came up to a well-lit intersection. I took a left on a major street, no idea what it was. John had been silent for a few minutes, then said, "So we gotta get the laptop."

"Yup. Or destroy it."

"But we gotta get the guy who killed Bobby, too. That's just as important—to me, anyway. The local cops won't do it. I think we've got to call in the feds."

"Yeah," I said reluctantly. Then, after a few more minutes, "I wish there was some way to get the feds interested in Bobby, without them knowing that he's

Bobby. Some way to get them chasing the killer. Like seriously on the job."

More thinking, then John half-laughed, looked at his watch, and said, "Well, I know one way. If we got the time."

John's a smart guy. When he told me his idea, it made me laugh, as it had made him laugh, the heart-sick sound you make when somebody presents you with an insane proposition that would probably work, and that you're probably gonna do.

After a little more talk, I said, "Ah, boy." I couldn't think of anything nearly as good. I told him so, and added, "Or as fuckin' nuts."

WE FOUND AN all-night convenience store where I bought some cookies and candy and a couple of cans of motor oil and two gallons of spring water from a sleepy clerk. John dumped the spring water out the window as we drove along, poured in the oil, and, after wiping them clean, threw the oil cans out the window into a roadside ditch. We stopped at an edge-of-town gas station, parked so the filler cap was away from the station, filled the tank with gas, and then added gas to the two water jugs until they were three-quarters full.

Then we went back to Bobby's, nervous as cats, cruised the neighborhood, saw only two lights—it was past four in the morning now, and working people would be getting up in the next hour or two.

Everything around Bobby's was quiet, though, so we pulled in and went inside.

Tried to ignore the body, though John said, talking to him, "This is for you, Robert."

We were planning to use clothes-hanger wire if we had to, but Bobby had a long roll of picture-hanging wire that worked just fine. We used the heavy side boards from the bed for the main frame, and the picture-hanging wire to strap a couple of old cotton blankets around the boards.

We'd been working frantically, gloved again, fumbling everything so we had to do everything twice, but we were ready to go by four-thirty. I carried our creation outside and soaked it with the gas, then threw the empty jugs in the backseat of the car.

"I'm going to hell for this," John said to me across the yard, as he wired it to a front-porch upright.

"Think of it as performance sculpture," I said. "Don't light it until I've got the car in the street." I backed the car out of the driveway, got it pointed, pushed open the passenger door, and John struck a match and threw it at the gas-soaked rags.

I can tell you from experience that when you've got a lot of gas, it doesn't just flame up, like paper: it goes with an audible *whump*. The thing was burning like crazy, even with the rain, and John was running and then he was in the car chanting, "Go, go, go," and we were out of there.

We planned to stop a mile or so away and call the fire department, but by the time we got to the pay phone, we could hear sirens and they were getting closer. So we kept going. But I'd looked back from the corner as we'd gone slewing around it, and even in the driving rain, the fire looked like a bad dream out of Revelation, or out of Jackson, Mississippi, in 1930.

John had been right. For bringing in an FBI investigation, nothing worked quite as well as a dead black guy and a great big stinking Fiery Cross.

5

AT TEN O'CLOCK that morning, the bedside alarm went off. I sat up, disoriented for a moment, in a bed at the Days Inn across Interstate 55 from the La Quinta. I'd dropped John just before five, then crossed the highway and rented a room.

When I checked in, I told the clerk that I'd intended to arrive earlier, but I'd gotten stuck in a casino, and then in the rain. He did a desk-clerk's indifferent chuckle-nod-and-shuffle—he could really give a shit what I'd been doing—and told me I had to be out by noon anyway, or they'd have to charge me for another day.

That was fine. I'd just wanted to get on the record, at the same time hoping I didn't smell like gasoline. When I woke up at ten, I slapped the clock to kill the alarm, turned the TV to the Weather Channel, and called LuEllen on my cell phone.

LuEllen answered just as a satellite picture of Hurricane Frances came up on the TV. "Where are you?" she demanded. "Is everything okay?"

"Well, our friend is gone," I said. "We went into his house and found some DVDs."

"I know he's gone." She wasn't shouting, but she was emphatic. "I assume that's him that's been all over CNN and Fox. Was that you? My God, what were you thinking?"

We were not mentioning names or actual incidents. "Hey, hey. Slow down," I said. "I just got up. I'll tell you everything when I see you. The hurricane looks like it's getting closer."

"That's the other thing. They're saying landfall in twenty-four hours, somewhere between New Orleans and Panama City. We're right in the bull's-eye. People are closing up."

Rule of thumb: bad weather always comes at the worst possible time. "What about the casino?"

"They're open until six o'clock tonight," LuEllen said. "I called them, but I haven't been over today— I was too worried about you guys, I was afraid I'd miss your call. Why did you turn off your cell phone?"

"I didn't want it to ring last night, in the middle of things. I forgot to turn it back on." I started clicking around the channels on the television, and stopped when I got to Headline News.

"Jesus, I was afraid you were in jail or something," LuEllen said.

"Listen, this thing up here is a mess—I might have to get more involved. But we're close on the slot-machine research. Get the assignment notes and get over there and start dropping coins. I can be there by two o'clock, I think. You oughta be about finished and we'll throw our shit in the car and get out."

"Where're we going?"

"I don't know. Figure something out. I'll be in the car on the cell phone. You say there's a lot of TV?"

"Can't get away from it. The big guys have been called in." She meant the FBI.

"We were hoping for that," I said.

"What?"

"I'll see you in three or four hours, and explain."

DONE WITH LUELLEN, I called John on his cell phone. "I'm on my way to an Office Depot," he said. "Buying supplies for the city. Just got up, tried to call, but I kept getting your answering service." He was out establishing an alibi. He added, "If you look at TV . . . it worked."

"That's what I hear. I haven't seen it yet—have you called Marvel?"

"Not yet. Should I?"

"Probably. I just talked to LuEllen and she'd about laid an egg. If Marvel sees it before you call . . ."

"I'll call her now. The report is on CNN and Fox."

"CNN's stuck on sports," I said. "I'm heading back—I'll call you at home when I figure something out. I'll be on the cell phone full-time."

"Good luck," he said. "Oh, one other thing. I was thinking about it last night."

"Yeah?"

"You oughta jump back in the sack with LuEllen. You're acting like a kicked puppy and it can be pretty fuckin' tiresome."

I WAS SHAVING when the Bobby story came up, and I stepped back into the main room to watch. The anchorwoman, who was wearing an amazing lilac shade of glitter lipstick, had one minute earlier been laughing excitedly about the lame excuses of a Hollywood celebrity charged with drunken driving, and had now wrenched her features into a semblance of solemnity as she told about the cross-burning. Though she took almost a minute to relate the story, she had nothing but the fact that a cross had been burned and a dead man found. The FBI was investigating. I finished cleaning up and took off.

In the daylight, Jackson didn't look too much better than it had at night, though I'm probably not giving it a fair shake. All I saw were the highway sights, the usual run of discount stores and fast-food joints and quick-lube garages, and that was it for Jackson.

Going south, into the hurricane—all right, into a ten-mile-an-hour breeze—was a lot quicker, even with the rain, than the drive up the night before. I was in my sort-of-new car, an Olds Aurora, the most anonymous V-8 in Christendom, and not a bad car except for the soggy suspension, numb steering, and underpowered engine. I'd had it modified at a tuner shop in Wisconsin, squeezing maybe 300 horses out of it, and the suspension was now reasonable and the custom seats were actually good. A new passenger, riding in a straight line, with his eyes closed, might think he was in a BMW 540i. Cornering, though . . . you can only do so much with front-wheel drive.

I pushed hard, out of the motel by 10:20, staying on the gas, and pulled up to the *Wisteria* at 1:30. Now the coastal highway looked like hurricane season. Pickup trucks full of plywood, and even sedans with plywood roped to their roofs, were rolling up and down the beachfront, and people were boarding windows and moving boats. Big rollers were coming in from the Gulf, kicking up chest-high spray.

I'd had a pack of chocolate-covered doughnuts and a Diet Coke for breakfast, so I was an unhappy camper when I boarded the *Wisteria*. LuEllen was back in the slots, four machines down from a guy who looked like he'd just climbed off an oil rig.

"How're we doing?" I asked.

"Another hour," she said, slamming a quarter in the slot. "Another half hour, with you here."

"I gotta get a sandwich," I said. The oil-rig dude was giving me the hard eye. "Are they still talking about closing at six?"

"They're talking about five, now. The hurricane is picking up speed." She slammed another quarter, the last in her bucket, dug a notebook out of her pocket, and entered a number.

"Just a quick sandwich."

"I'll come with you. Won't make any difference on the time. We're almost done."

"You're gonna bum out your fan club," I muttered.

"I know," she said, with a smile. "He's kinda cute, too, in a razor-fight way."

We went back to the aptly named poop deck, where I got a meatball sandwich and I filled her in. She'd done something to change the look of her hair, or maybe she'd just gone to smaller earrings, little diamonds that sparkled against her dark curls. She was curious about Bobby, since he'd been involved in two or three incidents where she'd nearly gotten her ass killed. I told her how fragile he looked and about the wheelchair.

"So we're dealing with some kind of incredible asshole," she said when I finished.

"Yeah. An incredible asshole with a laptop that's got God-knows-what on it."

"I gotta believe that Bobby was careful." One of the reasons LuEllen hung out with me was that I was careful. She worried when people weren't careful. She was perfectly willing to break into a jewel merchant's house in the middle of Saddle River, New Jersey, at three o'clock in the morning, knowing that place had more alarms than Wells Fargo . . . but she was *careful* about it. "He always seemed careful—you didn't even know his name or where he lived, and you guys have been working together for years."

"I hope he was," I said. "But we can't take the chance. He knows all about Anshiser, about what happened in Longstreet, about the whole deal down in Dallas—and if Microsoft ever finds out about the XP trapdoor, about that whole thing up in Redmond, *they'll* probably hire a couple of killers."

"Fuck Microsoft. I'm more worried about the people in Washington." She wouldn't even say the initials.

THE MEATBALL SANDWICH met the *Wisteria* standard, which wasn't good but at least filled some space. When I finished, we went back to the slots. To avoid the notice of cracker thugs, we'd been carefully taking our time and moving around. Now we just pounded quarters, and nobody noticed. We had our numbers and were out of the casino at 2:30, and out of the motel by three o'clock. I resisted the urge to pee on the carpet before I left, though it would have given the place some character.

Because the hurricane had taken a bit more of a northeasterly track, we headed west on I-10. Until recently I'd had a condo in New Orleans, but the place had been taken over by a group of Ohio retirees, who'd begun messing with the association rules, and I'd sold out. I'd been planning to buy another one, but got distracted and hadn't. Now I would have given my eyeteeth to have the old place back, to be where I was comfortable and had really good gear to use on Bobby's files.

As it was, we were homeless. We took I-12 north of the city, stopped at a CompUSA in Baton Rouge, and bought a heavy-duty external DVD box that I could hook into my laptop. Because LuEllen said she couldn't stand the rain any longer, we got back on I-10 and pushed on into the night. We finally stopped at a motel in Beaumont, Texas, just over the Louisiana border, still under a cloud deck, but no longer in the rain; the weather stations were promising sunshine in the morning.

By the time we stopped, we'd both grown tired of speculating about Bobby, tired of the casino job, and a little tired of each other. We got separate rooms and crashed.

CRASHED FOR FIVE hours, in my case. I don't like short nights, but I'd been running on sugar and caffeine, and found that as I got older, they tended to screw me up. At four in the morning, I was looking at Bobby's DVDs. Looking at them, as they sat in a plastic bag on top of a pile of clothes in my open suitcase. Not doing anything with them. The idea of all that stuff was intimidating. I walked down the hall and got a couple of straight Cokes and another roll of vending-machine chocolate doughnuts—more sugar and caffeine—and went back to the room, fired up the laptop, and finished the casino numbers.

Finishing the casino job was like knitting: it used some time and calmed the nerves. I was checking my work when LuEllen rang. "You up?"

"Since four," I said. "We're done with the casino."

"What's the verdict?"

"They're taking two percent."

"The greedy fucks," she said, aghast. "That's my money."

"Technically, it was Congressman Bob's money."

"It's the principle," she said. Then, "You wanna run across the street for some French toast?"

"Give me ten minutes."

"Well, give me a half hour. I just got up."

I USED THE time to call Congressman Bob in Washington, where it'd be after eight. I called on his direct line and he answered, with his rustiest voice, on the second ring. "Yeah?"

"Congratulations on your reelection to the U.S. Congress," I said.

He took a minute to sort out my voice, then he roared with laughter. "You got 'em."

"They're taking two percent. Two or three million a year, cash money, is going up in smoke and mirrors."

"How sure?"

"Extremely sure. Exactly ninety-eight percent sure that we aren't more than a half-percent off. What I'm not sure of is whether they're doing it all the time. But they're doing it right now, and if you want to do an audit, you better move on it."

"Sincy, Blake, and Coopersmith are sitting in my driveway with the engine running," Bob said. "We been waiting to hear from you."

"You got a hurricane down there."

"Nah. Just a pissant storm. It ain't nothing."

"Okay. Well, you owe me."

"I do," he acknowledged. "You know I'm good for it."

He was. Crooked as a crutch and absolutely good for his word.

WHEN I HUNG up, I clicked on the TV, watched until LuEllen knocked on the door. As I went to answer it, the talking head on CNN came around to the burning-cross story. We both stood and watched it, and learned nothing. FBI said that they were developing leads and working in cooperation with the Jackson police. Yeah. A black reporter interviewed some fleshy guy who was pulling a fiberglass bass boat up a launch ramp, and who acknowledged that he was, in fact, an Imperial Cyclops in the Ku Klux Klan, and who said that the Klan believed in racial separation but not in hurting other people. Right. Eyes rolled nationwide and the talking head talked on.

"Did you look at the Weather Channel?" LuEllen asked, as we went down the hall to the parking lot.

"No. I was just finishing the numbers when you called. It's not coming this way, is it?"

"It wasn't even a hurricane when it came ashore. It's up in Georgia, already, just a big bag of wind."

"All right. What're you gonna do today?"

"What are *you* gonna do?"

"Take a look at the DVDs. If they're totally encrypted, that'll take a couple of hours. See if I can figure out what's going on with the FBI, if I can find a safe way to do it."

"Then I'll probably just look around town, I guess. See if I can find a driving range, hit some golf balls. Find a bookstore, get some magazines."

WE HAD BREAKFAST at a family restaurant, French toast and link sausage and coffee, and then, as long as I still had the car, we went out to a pay phone and I called a friend in Livingston, Montana. He hadn't gotten up, apparently, and was a little grumpy when he answered on the twentieth ring.

"Sorry," I said. "You told me if I ever needed a channel, you had one. You still got it?"

"Yeah, but you'd have to wait until after six o'clock tonight, Eastern time."

"What, it's on somebody's desk?"

"Yup." That didn't seem to bother him. "He's a primo source, though. He gets a daily memo on every hot case in the country . . . criminal case, he's not good on espionage. You wanted criminal, though, right?"

"Yeah, that's great. How much you want?"

"For you? How about a five-hundred-dollar gift certificate on Amazon?"

"I can get it to you this morning," I said.

"Got a pencil?"

He gave me a phone number, a name, and a password, and I was good. We went down the road to another phone and I charged a $500 gift certificate to a Visa card belonging to my old invisible friend, Harry Olson of Eau Claire, Wisconsin, the guy with the cleanest credit record in the United States of America. He kept it clean by not existing and by paying all bills immediately.

LuEllen spent most of the day screwing around. She was a jock, was quietly turning into a golf nut, and had always been a power shopper. I expected her back in the late afternoon with a sunburn and an armful of bags from the local shopping center.

As she was acquiring a burn and assuring the financial stability of Abercrombie & Fitch and the Gap, I was digging through Bobby's DVDs. Since I didn't have an index, I wrote a little four-line Perl script that sorted through the files on each one and eliminated all the encrypted files.

When all the encrypted files were eliminated, there wasn't much left. I then sampled the remnant and found garbage—or if not garbage, then a pile of stuff that was simply useless unless you specifically needed it: databases from government agencies and newspapers, mostly. If, say, you needed sixteen hundred memos from the U.S. Department of the Interior written between August 1999 and January 2002, then I had them. But if you didn't know what memos you wanted, you were wading in garbage.

Six hours in, I'd concluded that the DVDs were probably safe enough. The unencrypted stuff was all public record, as far as I could tell. I would save them to examine more thoroughly, but they didn't feel threatening.

I HAD DONE maybe sixty of the DVDs when Lu-Ellen got back, laden with shopping bags. She dumped the bags on a bed, turned on the TV, checked the remnants of the hurricane on the Weather Channel—it had stalled as a deep low-pressure system over Tifton, Georgia, which had gotten forty-eight inches of rain in twenty-four hours, drowning out the local McDonald's among other worthy civic monuments—and then moved to CNN, where the burning-cross incident had dropped down the play list.

The only new wrinkle was a hard-faced, disdainful rejection of racial murder and cross-burning as not only criminal, but un-American, by the presidential press secretary. He worked up a good head of steam, using words like "miserable excuse for a human being" when talking about the killers. He seemed pretty cheerful a moment later, though, when talking about a breast cancer operation on the presidential dog.

As we watched the dog story, I told LuEllen about the DVDs, and she nodded. "Told you Bobby was careful."

"But damnit, I'd like to find that laptop," I said. "Can't look at the FBI until seven o'clock tonight. From the TV, it doesn't sound like they're doing much."

"TV doesn't know shit," she said. "TV knows press releases."

She said she'd hit six buckets of balls while she was gone, and smelled bad. "I'm gonna take a shower. Back in fifteen minutes."

"I can tell you're getting bored," I said. "But if we get an idea about where the laptop is, I might need you around."

"I'll stick around," she said. "Just to see how it comes out."

I WENT BACK to the final DVDs and on the last one found a single file that was smaller than anything else on the disks, and unencrypted. I opened it and found a high-res photo of John Ashcroft, apparently taken when he was a U.S. senator—there's another well-known senator standing not far away, and they're both in evening clothes and the other guy is holding a drink and Ashcroft is holding what appears to be a bottle of mineral water. There was no notation with the photo, which looked like any standard publicity shot, until I noticed that Ashcroft was apparently standing next to one of those chintzy, overdecorated French Baroque mirrors, the kind that Georgetown hostesses hang in their hallways. That wouldn't mean much either—except that Ashcroft didn't seem to have a reflection.

I was puzzling over that when LuEllen came back. She smelled good. She must have touched on a perfume counter during her shopping expedition. Coco, maybe. She asked, "Anything new?"

"More stuff. Take a look at this Ashcroft photograph."

She looked, her left breast brushing my ear. She was wearing a silk blouse, and it felt kind of good. After a moment, she stood up, frowning, and said, "He doesn't have a reflection."

"Might be the angle of the shot," I said.

"I don't know. His shoulder's right against the mirror."

"Well, maybe it's not really a mirror. Or maybe it's curved and we can't see it."

"Maybe," she said.

"Huh."

I thought for a few head-scratching minutes that it might be a clue to something in Bobby's files. Maybe even a clue to the encryption keys. If it was, it was too subtle for me, and I reluctantly decided that it was a joke. At least, I hoped so. No reflection?

As I finished with the DVDs, LuEllen went to the clothes she'd bought. The motel room door was covered with a large mirror, and she started trying on blouses and slacks. Neither one of us is particularly body-shy and we'd spent enough time rolling around in bed together, on other occasions, when we weren't involved with third and fourth people, that a little skin shouldn't have been a big deal; and I'd only drawn maybe three hundred nudes starring LuEllen.

But that was drawing . . .

She's basically a small woman with small breasts and a small butt. She was also wearing a small brassiere, which she really didn't need, other than as anti-leer protection in convenience stores; but the brassiere sat under her breasts like a couple of daisies, just barely covering her nipples, and her underpants were of the low-cut Jockey variety. And she smelled good.

She changed blouses and then changed slacks and then changed blouses and into some other slacks, and the perfume was going round and round and I kept looking at more meaningless photographs and I could hear the pants coming off and see the shirts being tossed and I finally turned around and she was looking at herself in the mirror, posing in a half-open blouse and the underpants, and I shouted, "Jesus Christ, woman," and threw her on the bed.

We didn't get much more done that afternoon. But if LuEllen had been concerned that her brains were becoming overly tight, she no longer had anything to worry about.

6

GETTING YOUR LIFE back on track after an enthusiastic change of direction isn't always the easiest thing. There's guilt, when you reflect on other relationships, and you're not sure you want to look your partner in the eye. Once you do, you'll be able to see both that what happened was not a mistake, not an incident, not a fantasy or a dream, but actually, you know, *happened* . . . and that there are implications.

I woke up when I felt LuEllen moving around, turned my head, cracked my eyes. I felt her stretch; and the additional weight and warmth in the bed felt pretty good, even though we'd only been in it for two hours, and it wasn't even dark yet. Finally, as I watched out of the corner of my eye, she sat up, stretched, and yawned. She hummed. She fluffed herself up. She purred for a while. She said, "You up?"

I feigned near-sleep. "I guess," I groaned.

"We need to get some chocolate in here." She bounced out of bed and ran around naked, all pink and jiggly. I had the urge to draw her, as I had so many times before, but I knew where that would lead.

"Let's do it again," she said.

"I'm an old man," I groaned.

"Better to wear out than to rust."

"Let me brush my teeth . . . but you go first."

We did all of that, and what seemed to be a little while later, I looked at the clock: two hours had gone somewhere. "Ah . . . shit."

"What?" She was looking at her toes, wiggling them, like little piggies.

"We gotta call Washington." I stretched and yawned. "Like right now."

"So come on in the shower."

"If we get in the shower together, we might not get out of the room in time to make the call," I said.

"Naw, come on . . ."

WE GOT OUT of the room, eventually, down to the car, still a little damp from the shower, to another pay phone. LuEllen had one of those anonymous prepaid phone cards, and I went out to Washington.

Somewhere, in what I hoped was the locked office of a high-ranking FBI bureaucrat, a computer got busy. I've been into the FBI any number of times, and usually you have to work the system. This time, the guy's desktop came up, and his files were right out front. When I popped them, I found one labeled *Jackson*. The file had last been opened two hours earlier.

"Is that too easy?" LuEllen worried. She looked up and down the street: no black helicopters; not even a black-and-white.

"Naw. It's what my guy said it'd be. Besides, I don't care," I said. "We'll be out of here before they could snap a trap even if it is one."

The *Jackson* file contained a series of memos saying that: (a) the feds hadn't found anybody who'd seen the cross-burners; (b) Bobby had been killed at least twelve hours before the cross-burning, according to early forensic tests, but no more than fourteen hours before, because he'd been seen alive then; (c) he'd been suffering from a degenerative nerve disease since early childhood and he'd been in a wheelchair for fifteen years; (d) he made his living writing computer code; (e) he had a caretaker named Thomas Baird who had seen him alive and well at two o'clock on the afternoon he died; and (f) the cross-burning might have been an effort to shift blame for the murder.

This last memo said that the time difference between the killing and the burning seemed to suggest that they were not part of the same act, and the motive for the act may have been computer theft, since an expensive computer was known to be missing. Huh. They had at least one perceptive guy on the job.

There was also a reference to some unwashed intelligence about the local lads of the KKK, most of which was apparently canned Jackson Office file stuff.

"LET'S GO," LUELLEN said.

"Not yet," I said. We were outside a convenience store, and a large man in a Hawaiian shirt, khaki shorts, and flip-flops, carrying a brown shopping bag, was walking toward us. His face was obscured by a pale straw hat and big sunglasses.

"Look at this guy."

"Not yet," I said. "Just a minute."

I stayed online for another five minutes—the guy in the Hawaiian shirt went on by and never looked back—saving everything to my laptop. LuEllen got increasingly nervous the longer we were hooked up. The last document was saved and I unplugged.

"All done."

"We're gone," LuEllen said. She put the car in gear and turned slowly onto the street, her turn signals working. LuEllen would never be caught in a routine traffic stop. She continued up the street for a hundred yards, then pulled into a strip shopping center and parked in front of a store that sold Levolor blinds and Barrister bar stools.

"What are we doing?"

"Watching." We sat there for ten minutes, watching the phone a block away, to see if any cops showed up. None did. She backed out and turned toward the street.

"Probably watching us by satellite," I said.

"Funny man." She leaned over and sniffed me. "You know, we ought to fool around more often. You *really* smell good."

I won't tell you where she'd splashed the Coco when we finally got out of the shower, but hey: when she was right, she was right. I *did* smell pretty good.

BACK AT THE motel, we read the memos again, talked about them, then, as it began to get dark, changed into some running clothes and went for a jog. We did three miles in nineteen minutes, running around the edges of a golf course. When we finished, I felt better than any time since we first walked into the *Wisteria* and started dropping coins in the slot machines.

We ate a quick dinner and then I went back to the DVDs; and a little more sex. And finally, after one of the longest days I'd had in a while, we crawled into bed.

"Would you like me better if I was more boobilicious?" LuEllen asked as I began to drift away.

I mumbled at her.

"What was that? What?"

I pushed myself up from the pillow. "I'm nowhere nearly stupid enough to answer that question," I said. "Go to sleep."

As a news service, CNN is pretty predictable: bullshit, bullshit, bullshit, weather, sports, bullshit, bullshit. The next morning, though, things were more serious. We turned on the tube a few minutes after 7:15, to a professionally cheerful guy just finishing up the sports.

The next thing up was a silent film showing a man in blackface, wearing a stovepipe hat, with an open black umbrella overhead, doing a vaudeville-style softshoe with two other guys, who were similarly dressed.

There was no commentary for a full five seconds, then one of the talking heads, speaking with his Voice of Doom, said, "You are looking at a videotape of a racially charged fraternity show in which one of the participants was National Security Advisor Lyman Bole, the man with the black umbrella. The videotape was sent to a number of news outlets this morning by a man identifying himself only as 'Bobby,' who said that many more such revelations would be coming in the next few weeks. CNN has learned exclusively that while Mr. Bole has yet to comment, the film is genuine, and that the fraternity party took place approximately nineteen years ago at Ohio State University, Bole's alma mater."

"Oh my God," LuEllen said, goggling at the TV.

I was already rolling across the bed. I picked up

my cell phone and dialed John. He came on, sounding sleepy, and I asked, "Have you seen it?"

"What?"

I told him, not using the name Bobby, and he said, softly, "Oh, no. The guy's working the machine, whoever he is."

"Yeah. And I'll tell you what—I'm coming up empty on the DVDs. There's not a thing about who might have the laptop. I'll tell you what else: the big guys don't know, either."

"You got in, uh . . ."

"Yeah. And they don't know."

After a long moment of silence, he said, "I've been thinking . . ."

"You're gonna retire to Guam."

"No, I'm serious. Our friend was crazy about his security. There are only three ways somebody could have gotten to him. One: the asshole knew who our friend was, and where he lived, because our friend knew him and trusted him. Two: the asshole tracked him somehow, by computer. Three: it was purely local and purely random, done for money or something we don't know about—something that doesn't have anything to do with anything."

He was using the "our friend" circumlocution because we'd shared an earlier difficulty involving Bobby and had learned about the government's ability to intercept and sort meaningful phone conversations from billions of words of garbage.

"That last one's out," I said.

"It is now. That leaves the other two. But who knew our friend better than we did? That leaves the computer. If they tracked him by computer . . ."

"I know one guy who knew him better than we did," I said. "I was looking at some information from the big guys. There's a memo that says he had a caretaker. The caretaker lives in Jackson. I've got his name."

More silence, and I heard a woman's voice—Marvel, John's wife—in the background saying, "It's on right now," and then John said, "I'm looking at the tape. We've got to talk to the guy in Jackson. Personally."

"Hate to go back there," I said.

"No choice—unless you can figure out how the asshole tracked him over the computer."

"I *can't* figure it out," I said. "I tried a couple of times, really carefully, and I'm pretty good at it. Our friend called me up and told me to knock it off. I tripped some alarms I never saw. I think he was amused—he seemed amused. I bet everybody on the ring, except you, went looking for him at one time or another."

"So either the guy who found him is a lot better than you ring guys are, or it's somebody who knew him."

"That would be it—and I don't think it's somebody who's better than us. That's not vanity, it's just that there are a limited number of ways that you can track somebody online, and there's no way to know whether you're stepping into a trap unless you step in it. In other words, if somebody was tracking him, even if it's like . . . the really big guys . . . they'd still set off his alarms."

"Maybe some technological thing not having to do with computers?"

"And somehow it falls into the hands of a fruitcake who uses it to cut up government bigshots? John . . ."

"I know, I know. Can you get up here?"

"If we had to," I said.

"Come on up, bag out here. You and I can go down to Jackson and talk to this friend."

"Ah, man."

"No choice." Then he laughed. "I'm looking at this blackface thing. They are gonna stick this movie so far up the guy's ass he's gonna have videotape coming out of his nose."

"Hang on." I turned to LuEllen, who was sitting on the end of the bed, watching the TV, and told her what John had suggested.

She shrugged. "Always happy to see those guys."

I put the phone back to my ear. "We'll be up," I said. "Call you on the way."

WE PACKED UP in a half hour and I carried the luggage down to the car. A quick check of the e-mail turned up nothing. As LuEllen was shoving the last of her stuff into a bag, she said, "Before you zip up your briefcase, why don't you try the cards?"

"Cards won't help us," I said.

"Just try them," she said. "For me. So I won't worry."

"Or you'll worry more," I said.

"Just try them."

There's a word for what LuEllen can be, in Yiddish or Hebrew-Russian-English or whatever: the word's *nudnik*. The best definition I've ever heard came from an Israeli professor of archaeology: "It's a person who is like a woodpecker sitting on your head, all the time pecking you."

SO I GOT the cards out, my tarot cards, a Rider-Waite deck. I'm not exactly a scientist—I was trained as an engineer—but I've studied the philosophy of science, and I'm a true believer. The tarot, as a predictive system, is the same sort of superstitious nonsense as astrology. The deck *is* useful as a gaming device, though, and that's how I use it.

Like this: when we are forced to deal with complicated problems, when some of the facets of the problem are unknown or unreachable, we deal with them in terms of past experience. That's almost inescapable. But approaches that are useful with some problems don't work with others. The tarot deck, when used as a gaming system, pushes you outside past experience and encourages you to think of new ways to deal with it.

Say, for example, you were involved in a complicated business transaction and that the group you were dealing with, the opposition, consisted of six members, five men and a woman. You begin doing tarot spreads and see a number of indications of female influence.

This does *not* mean that the deck correctly predicts female influence in the transaction, but suggests that you should sit back and think about the woman on the other side, who might otherwise seem to be just another functionary. Why is she there? What specific influences does she have? Is there some way to approach her that would help with your deal?

This has nothing to do with the supernatural—it's simply a human way, and a fairly subtle way, to game a problem.

LuEllen doesn't believe that. She believes that I'm tapped into the Other Side. At one time she'd hassle me for a daily reading, until finally she asked me to do a spread on how long she'd live. I did a spread, and came up with ninety-four years.

"That's not bad," she'd said.

"Yeah, but this card"—I'd tapped the Tower, I believe—"suggests that the last fifty years will be in the high security unit at the Valley State Prison in California."

"Kidd," she'd sputtered, "you, you gotta, what are you talking . . ."

"Made you look," I said. She didn't bother me so much after that.

———

I CARRY A deck with me, in an old wooden box, wrapped in a piece of silk, just like the gypsies tell you to do. Because LuEllen showed signs of slipping into a nudnik state, I did two quick tarot spreads on the motel room telephone table.

Like most tarot spreads, the results were complicated. What should have been a clear outcome in both spreads, the final resolution card, was, in both cases, self-contradictory.

"The Hanged Man," LuEllen said, tapping the card with an index finger. She knows the cards well enough to pick out the major arcana. "The Hanged Man comes up twice, as the final resolution, and you're saying that you don't know what it means?"

"It's not a very useful outcome for gaming," I said.

"You're not lying to me?" She looked at me suspiciously. "It doesn't mean we're going to die together in an automobile accident on the way to Jackson?"

"No." I pulled the cards together, wrapped them in the silk cloth, and put them back in the box. "The Hanged Man indicates a kind of suspended animation, a suspense between two states—a waiting state. Transition, maybe. Okay, so Bobby's dead and everything is in transition. Well, duh. We already know that."

"It doesn't even *hint* at what's going to happen?"

"LuEllen, the cards *do not predict anything*."

"Yeah." She crossed her arms, looked at me with exasperation. "You always say that, then it turns out that they always do."

"There have been some coincidences, but that's all they were."

"Coincidences, my ass. Let's go. You can tell me more about this Hanged Man on the way to Longstreet."

LONGSTREET IS ON the Mississippi River northwest of Jackson. There isn't much there, but there is one critical thing: a bridge. That by itself gives the town a regional importance. Bridges are uncommon on the lower Mississippi. People can go their entire lives never seeing towns that might be only a mile away, across the river, but fifty miles away by road.

Longstreet was a tough place to get to from Beaumont. The trip took most of the day, even cooking along in the Olds. LuEllen's a good driver, and she'd rather drive than ride, so she spent most of her time behind the wheel. I plugged in the laptop and continued to dig through the DVDs.

"The pattern is, he encrypted everything but inconsequential stuff," I said. "If the same pattern holds with the laptop, then we're good."

"That cheers me up. But even if he does have some stuff, it'd hardly be on me, do you think?" She was paranoid about personal security. She'd led a long life as a thief, including some fairly outrageous episodes, and had never done time, never been arrested, never been fingerprinted.

"Not unless . . ."

"What?"

"Bobby knew where we were sometimes. Exactly where, and exactly when. There's a tiny chance that he had us photographed, just out of curiosity."

"You think?"

"No. I don't think so," I said after a moment. "For one thing, he knew who I was, exactly, and he could get a picture of me online. That show at the Westfeld Gallery last winter had an online catalog along with the regular one. You could get my picture there. Still can. So I think we're good, or you're good, but man—I'd like to get that laptop. John's worried, too. His friends, you know . . . Bobby may have some details on them, too."

"Political stuff."

"Yeah." We rode along for a minute. "You know, you sometimes get these charismatic assholes, the racist preachers and bigot politicians who are too smart to join the Klan or the Nazis. They can do a lot of damage, especially in local elections, school boards, and so on. Sometimes you think, *If there was only some way to make them go away.* I've always wondered if John's people, and maybe Bobby, didn't make some of these guys go away. For good."

"You mean, kill them?"

"That's a harsh word, kill."

"Ah, jeez."

———

WE ALSO HAD time in the car to consider our individual guilt as involved the previous night's sexual episodes; and there was some. LuEllen had been seeing a Mexican guy, a modern-dance teacher, at the university in Duluth. She was drawn to the dark-eyed tribe . . . but she said she considered the attachment to be purely temporary. She might consider all attachments purely temporary, even me; she was a lot like a cat.

I was in a different situation. Even though Marcy had broken it off, I was sure I'd precipitated it, and then I'd jumped straight into the sack with an old flame.

I said all of this to LuEllen, who immediately brightened up. Women, in my experience, are the social engineers of the human race, and love to analyze and dissect relationships. Even their own. All that began a conversation that meandered through our relationship and all the people we'd known since we first got together, and why we couldn't seem to stay together.

LuEllen argued against guilt. She said we were old enough friends, and had had on-again, off-again sex for so long that it no longer counted as infidelity. It was more like a hug, she said. What she'd done was the emotional equivalent of first aid.

"It didn't feel like a hug," I said. "You were barking like a dog. Anytime somebody's barking like a dog, you can be pretty sure it's not a hug."

"I was *not* barking like a dog," she said. "You know what you're doing? You say stuff like that to be funny, and to take the importance out of things. But this is pretty important, since you really liked the woman . . . not that I ever knew what you saw in her, her being a cop and all. But you knew *six months ago* that she wanted a kid, and you knew her time was running out, and you were stringing her along in your continuing quest to get the milk without buying the cow."

"That's a disgusting phrase; I bet it's from Wisconsin."

"You're doing it again, making light," she said.

"I was not stringing her along," I insisted, though the phrase touched a guilty chord. "She never even brought the subject up. It's just when I saw her around kids . . ."

"You were stringing her along," LuEllen said with satisfaction. "That's my last word on that. Well. Maybe not my last word . . ."

Nudnik.

7

LONGSTREET IS SO green that it hurts your eyes to look at it. Green, humid, and hot, a Delta town, a jungle, smelling of blacktop and spilled peach soda, melting bubble gum and dead carp, curdling exhaust from old cars; not as bad a combination as it might sound.

The town is laid out along a high point on the Mississippi—not too high, maybe forty feet above mean high water where Main Street parallels the river. The oldest part of town, closest to the river, is mostly red and yellow brick, with pastel colors popping up in residential areas farther from the river, along the narrow tree-lined tar streets.

"Maybe I'll move here someday," LuEllen said as we came over the last hill above the town.

"And every single person would know every single thing you did, every day," I said.

"I'd call myself Daisy, and plant poppies in my backyard garden, and then invite the village women to come over and quilt, and drink my special tea," she said. "When I died, everybody would say I was a witch."

"I already say that," I said. "Did you ever sleep with that Frank, the liquor dealer with the Porsche?"

She was prim. "No histories; that's always been the agreement," she said.

"That's not history. I introduced you to the guy."

"Try to concentrate on what we're doing here."

WHEN I CONCENTRATE on Longstreet, on the picture in my head, I see flop-eared yellow dogs snoozing on a summer sidewalk, pickup trucks and bumper stickers ("when it's pried from my cold dead fingers") and the bridge. The bridge is a white-concrete span, the concrete glowing with the colors of the sky and the Mississippi, as the river turns through a sweeping bend to the east. Across the water, you can see the yellow sand beaches along the water, and every night, wild turkeys come out to dance along the sand.

We came in from the Longstreet side of the river, so we didn't actually cross the bridge. We dropped down from the high ground, stopped at an E-Z Way convenience store and got a Diet Coke and a box of

Popsicles from the strange fat man who worked behind the counter, and threaded our way through
town to John's place, a tan rambler on the black side
of town.

John and Marvel had kids bumping around the
house. The kids stood with their mouths open when
Mom, laughing, jumped on me and gave me a kiss,
and LuEllen gave John a big hug. Black people didn't
kiss and hug white people in Longstreet, not in the
kids' experience, anyway. I found it pleasant enough.
Marvel was beautiful, a woman with tilted black eyes
and a perfect oval face, a woman who naturally moved
like a dancer.

The kids were shy—they knew us a bit, from earlier visits—but loosened up when I produced the
Popsicles. Marvel handed them out and told them
to go outside so they wouldn't drip on the furniture.
In the resulting silence, after they went, slamming
through the screen door, Marvel said, "You guys are
looking great," and John said, skipping the niceties,
"You can stick a fork in Bole. He's all done."

"They fired him?"

"He's gonna quit tonight," John said. He had his
hands in his pockets, almost apologetically. "He tried
to say that it was all college high spirits, they had a
couple of black guys in whiteface, but the media pack
is howling after him, and the only thing you can actually see is that film loop. And we—you and me—
probably are the ones that made it impossible for him
to defend himself."

"How?" LuEllen asked, looking from me to John.

"That burning cross," John said. "We got the FBI into Jackson, all right, but then the Administration, the press secretary, made that big deal about how racism is indefensible in the New South and blah-blah-blah . . . and then the next day this comes along. Bole is toast. He's gonna talk to the President tonight."

"So he did it to himself," LuEllen said. "He's the one who did the blackface."

"That's what I say," said Marvel.

John, the radical, said, "He was a college kid when he did it and it was a joke. And he doesn't have anything to do with race. He had to do with missiles. There are a thousand guys we'd be better off without, before him."

"So you get who you can," Marvel said.

"Fuckin' commie," John said, shaking his head. "It's not right and it's not fair and we've got to start worrying about that."

"You're getting old and conservative," Marvel said. "Your hair is gonna turn white and woolly and you'll go on one of those religious shows and start talking about Jesus."

"Not fair," John said. He did sound a little like a preacher; and he had a point.

WHILE LUELLEN AND Marvel went off and caught up with each other, I showed John the FBI files on Thomas Baird, Bobby's caretaker. John read them carefully, then made calls to two different people in Jackson. One of them knew Baird—knew who he was, anyway—but didn't know anything of substance. He volunteered to ask around, but John declined the offer.

"I think we should go down and see him," John said. "Tonight. Right now." He looked at his watch. "If we go now, he'll probably still be awake when we get there."

THERE WAS MORE talk, and I took the time to do a few laps of the town park. At seven o'clock, we stopped at the E-Z Way for cheap premium gas and headed for Jackson, leaving LuEllen and Marvel with the kids. We talked about Bobby a bit, then about a sculpture series that John was working on.

John said that he had talked to a local woman, a quilter, about learning to quilt. "There's something I can't quite get with sculpture," he said. "I need something that's more . . . narrative, I guess. If I did it in 3-D, I'd need a sculpture garden."

"So why don't you learn to paint? Once you can see what you want to do, the techniques aren't that hard."

"Bullshit. I know about techniques, I've watched yours change. How long did it take before you got control? I remember that piece you did, that *Sturgeon Rip Number 1*. You couldn't of done that when I first knew you."

We talk like that, can't help ourselves. We'd get intent on our work, and start laughing and chattering along, and then the whole Bobby topic would come up, and we'd go all glum again. Even with that, the time went quickly. Before we'd finished talking about the art stuff, we were nosing into Jackson. One good thing: we were under a cloud deck, but we hadn't caught up with the rain.

THOMAS BAIRD LIVED in the left half of a duplex that might have been built as part of a low-income housing project: low-rent modern design, crappy materials, a lot of bright contrasting painted-plywood panels. Sidewalks already beginning to crumble. A light showed in the front-room window, and John said, "I'll go. I'll wave you in."

We didn't argue about it: the neighborhood was black and so was John. As he was getting out of the car, I said, "Don't touch anything with your fingertips. If you do, wipe it."

I went around the block. When I came by the first time, he ignored me: he was talking to somebody behind a door. When I came by the second time, he was standing on the porch, and he waved me into a puddle that marked a parking strip.

ON THE PORCH, John said, "He's got our names."

"What?"

"I told him my name was John and he asked me if I knew a Mr. Kidd."

"Oh, Jesus." I put my hands to my forehead: this was not good. An outsider knew who we were. What else did he know?

"Come on in," John said. He pulled open the door and we stepped inside, John in the lead. A black guy, probably forty years old, was standing in the middle of a small, tidy living room. There was no television, but there *were* a dozen or so old-fashioned mahogany-cased radios, RCAs and Motorolas and other names I didn't recognize, that must have come from the thirties and forties. They were all polished and neatly kept, and one showed glowing lights behind a wide glass face. Radios with *tubes*, for Christ's sake. The place smelled of furniture polish.

John was saying, "Mr. Baird, this is Kidd."

Baird looked at me doubtfully, then said to John, "He's a white man."

John looked at me carefully. "No shit? I just thought he was passing."

Baird looked at me for a moment—my hair's not quite blond—and then laughed, scratched his ass, and said, "You boys want some beer? It's been a bad day."

He got three bottles of Budweiser and a bag of nacho-cheese chips from the kitchen, passed them around, and dropped into a tattered but comfortable-looking green chair. John and I settled onto a sagging couch, facing him; the beer tasted good after the long ride. An overweight black-and-white cat came out of the kitchen, hopped up on the arm of Baird's chair, stretched out, and looked at us.

"Bobby told me that if anything bad ever happened to him, that you two might come snooping around. I was supposed to tell you whatever I could and he told me not to mention you to anybody else. Like the police."

"I hope to God . . ." John began.

"So I didn't. I didn't even remember that you was supposed to come snooping until you got on my door and said you was John," he said. "So what can I do for you? You know anything about this mess?"

"You don't have Bobby's laptop, by any chance?" I asked.

"No. The FBIs said that the computer equipment was gone. You boys are computer experts, right?"

"I don't know a disk drive from a joystick, but Kidd is pretty familiar with them," John said.

Baird nodded and focused on me. "Okay. Well, Bobby had one IBM laptop and about a hundred DVDs hidden away somewhere, but I don't know where."

"A hundred?" I asked. "You know that the number was a hundred?"

Baird's forehead wrinkled. "No, I don't know the real number. He had a whole shitload of them, though."

"You know what was on them?"

"He called them his archives. He had his active

things on the computer and his archives on the disks."

"So there was stuff on the computer that wasn't on the disks," I said.

"Yeah, and vice versa. As I understood it. The FBIs went all through his house yesterday and today, they took every scrap of paper. They found a safe-deposit-box key and had to get me to okay that they open it—I'm Bobby's executor for his will—but all they found in the box was old pictures and his ma-ma's diaries from when she moved down here from Nashville, and two old gold chains."

"So what, uh, is gonna happen to the house?" John asked.

"I sell it. After funeral expenses and bills, the money goes to the United Negro College Fund. He told me I could keep the money from the yard sale, the furniture and all, and said I could keep any cash I find, but he was just jokin'. The FBIs said there weren't no cash, but that's all right with me. I'm just sad to see him go. He was the smartest man I ever met."

"He might've been the smartest man, period," I said. "Do you have any idea of what might have happened?"

He started shaking his head halfway through the question. "If the FBIs are right about the time he was killed, then I saw him two hours before that and he was happy as a clam."

"Bobby had good security," I said. "People have

been looking for him for a long time. The question is, how did they find him now? Did he change anything recently? Get any phone calls or talk to anyone in person?"

Again, he started shaking his head early. "He didn't get around much, anymore. I'd take him around to the stores when he wanted to go, but he got tired real easy. He had his computers and his movies and his music. He played the piano, some blues and some fancy stuff. He was a good piano player one time, but he was starting to lose the coordination in his left hand, and it made him sad. I saw him crying about it, once. He didn't go out much. He never talked to anyone, 'cept maybe a neighbor or on the computer. 'Course, I wasn't there to see if he used the phone."

"Goddamnit," I said to John.

John said to Baird, "If you have a few minutes, let's go back through the last month or so . . ."

John talked him through the past two months. Two weeks in, Baird remembered one anomaly in Bobby's behavior, a tiny thing. Bobby had been interested in helping smart, underprivileged black schoolkids get involved with computers. I knew for sure of one case—the case that had brought John, LuEllen, and me to Longstreet for the first time, when John had met Marvel. There had been other instances that I'd heard about, as rumor, anyway, from friends on the 'net.

The latest case, Baird said, came when Bobby heard of a kid in New Orleans, a hot little code writer who had actually broken into her grade school to get machine time, because she didn't have a machine of her own. Bobby had talked to her online a few times, Baird said, and then had sent her a laptop.

Or, Baird said, what Bobby had actually done was send Baird to the local CompUSA to buy a laptop with cash. He then put some additional software on it and had Baird FedEx it to the girl. Baird paid cash at FedEx. Bobby always had Baird front for him when physical packages had to be sent somewhere, so there'd be no deliveries—no invoices—that would tie to him.

"When you FedEx'ed it, whose return address did you put on it?" I asked.

Baird looked at me for a moment, then said, "Mine. The computer was worth two thousand dollars, and if it got lost . . . the insurance, you know."

"You didn't see anybody around, there was no chance you were followed? Nobody came to talk to you?"

Baird said, "Nobody talked to me. I didn't see nobody. But I . . . wasn't looking. You think somebody followed me?"

"How often did you go to Bobby's?"

"Every day. I mean, I was his caregiver. I did the shopping and cut the grass."

We went forward day by day, and a week or maybe

ten days after he sent the laptop—Baird didn't have a good grip on the relative time, but didn't think it was too long—we tumbled over another anomaly.

"White boy came by selling Bibles and it turned out he liked old radios, too," Baird said. "I been collecting these for years. I didn't want no Bibles, but he asked if he could look at the radios and I let him in. That was pretty unusual."

"Did he seem to know about the radios? Really know about them?"

"He knew a bit. Not so much about the value as how they worked. 'Course, the value changes all over the place. I was up in Memphis last year and found out that I have a radio—this one, it's a 1938 Stewart-Warner tombstone"—he pointed at a tabletop radio with a burnished red-colored wooden case—"that baby's worth six hundred dollars now. In Memphis, anyway. Down here, it's probably fifty bucks at a garage sale. But he knew how the radios worked, okay. We talked for a while, looked at them for an hour, and then he left."

"You ever leave him alone in here?" I asked.

"Well . . ." He scratched his ear, then twisted it, thinking. "I went out to get the mail, talked to the mailman for a couple of minutes."

"The mailbox is that communal center box," John said.

"That's right, just over there." He looked at John and then at me, and after a few seconds of silence he said, sadly, "The guy stole Bobby's name out of the house, while I was out talking to Carl, didn't he?"

"If you were out there for a few minutes, he might have looked around. Or if you left your keys lying around, and he was ready to do it, he might have made a copy and come back some other time, when you were gone," I said.

"He was just looking at the radios," Baird said. He wiped the corners of his eyes with his index fingers. "We popped the back off a couple of them, so he could look at the tuning layout."

"There's no way to tell, really," John said, trying to be kind. "Maybe he was really selling Bibles."

"Just a minute," Baird said, and heaved himself out of the chair. To John, he said, "Watch the white man while I'm gone."

He went out the front door, and as soon as he was out, I stepped around the rest of the lower floor, as an intruder might have; John tagged along, the black-and-white cat watching us without an apparent concern in the world. Ten seconds after we started looking, we found a little parlor off the kitchen that had been turned into a home office with a two-drawer metal file cabinet. I pulled open a drawer, and the first file carried a tag in black felt-tip pen that said *Taxes and Job*.

Inside the file we found a sheath of tax bills and workman's comp statements from the state. Two of them listed Robert Fields as Baird's employer, and included Bobby's address. "Goddamnit," I said.

I pushed the drawer shut and we went back to the living room. I said, "I don't think we should tell him."

"He might already know," he said. "About that cash we took out of Bobby's . . ."

"I was thinking the same thing."

Baird came back a minute later, shaking his head mournfully. "Neighbor was still up. Too hot to sleep. She says she never had a Bible salesman come by, white or black, either one."

"Okay," I said. "You wouldn't still have the FedEx receipt for the package you sent, would you?"

"I do have that," he said. He went back to the parlor office, looked in another file, and found the receipt. The package had been sent to a Rachel Willowby in New Orleans.

"You never heard anything more from her? No thank you?"

"No, but I think her and Bobby were chatting on the computer. One of those chatterbox places."

We talked for a couple more minutes, then I went out to the car and got the sack with Bobby's cash in it, brought it back in, and gave it to John. "This'll seem a little funny," John told Baird. "But this is the last of Bobby's cash supply, as far as we know. Bobby wanted you to have it for . . . expenses, and transition and so on."

"Bobby did?" He was suspicious, but not too—you tend not to be too suspicious when you need the money and somebody's putting a brick of cash in your hand. "Where'd you get it, then?"

"Bobby kept some of his resources . . . outside," John said. "Just in case. Anyway, he said to give it to you, and for you to do whatever you need to."

"Better stick it somewhere out of sight," I said. "You don't want the feds to see it."

He went to put it out of sight, and in the twenty seconds that he was gone, I wiped both John's and my own beer bottle on my shirt. "Touch anything else?" I asked quietly.

"I'm trying to keep my hands in fists," he said. "I don't think it's necessary."

"Better safe," I said.

When Baird returned, I asked him not to tell the feds about the Bible salesman or the laptop he'd sent to the little girl. "Listen, it's this way. That laptop could kill Bobby's friends, if we don't find it first."

"But what about catchin' the guy who did Bobby?" he asked.

"We want him as bad as you do," John said. "One way or the other, he'll get taken care of. I promise you. If we can't figure it out ourselves, we'll give everything we have to the feds and let them try."

I nodded, and Baird said, "Okay."

THE LAPTOP DELIVERY was the key.

Fifteen minutes after we finished with Baird, we

were at a pay phone, and I was online with a friend
who was a specialist in the National Crime Information Center, which is one of the more interesting
branches of the FBI. He looked at Baird's NCIC file,
found that Baird had been convicted of misdemeanor
theft in 1968 and a car-theft felony in 1970, served
three months in a county jail, and had no record
since. He also found that the last inquiry on Baird's
file had come ten days earlier, from the Slidell, Louisiana, police department. Slidell was somewhere outside New Orleans.

Then I went out on my own to accounts at the
big-three credit services, and found recent checks on
Baird from a credit-counseling firm in New Orleans.

"Bobby was mouse-trapped," I told John, when
we were headed back toward Longstreet. "I don't
know by who, but it wasn't the feds. Whoever it was
did a pretty interesting job. Most people who've gone
looking for the guy have been techies who tried to
track him down online. This guy must of heard about
Bobby's kids."

Over the years, I told John, I'd heard online ru-
mors that Bobby had helped out more kids than the
one we knew about in Longstreet. Some inner-city
kid would get a new computer in the mail from an
anonymous donor, along with certain kinds of software, or a kid in Tennessee would come up with an
unexpected laptop, or maybe expensive software like
AutoCAD or Mathematica. Bobby had become an
urban legend among the people who made up the

computer world; the stories were like those about a kid who hangs around the playground and one day Michael Jordan comes along for a few minutes of one-on-one.

"So somebody set up a fake kid, puts the fake where Bobby will hear about it, eventually gets a package, and tracks it back to Baird," John said.

"And before he goes to Baird, he checks him on the NCIC and the credit services, and probably a few other ways, and finds out that whoever Baird is, he isn't Bobby. Doesn't have the background, doesn't have the education. Too old, for one thing. So then he tracks him, somehow. He's probably a hacker at some level, so maybe he looks at Baird's phone bills."

We both thought about it for a while, then John said, "If there were all these people looking for him over all those years, why didn't somebody do this sooner?"

"Different kind of mentality at work," I said. "This was really subtle. He floats a rumor, just a whisper out there, about this kid . . . puts it where Bobby will see it, but he can't even really know that Bobby *will* see it. Then he lets Bobby do the investigation and make the approach."

"And he's so good that Bobby can't see through the bullshit."

I shook my head. "You know what? I bet there is a kid. I bet somebody went looking for a kid to use as bait. That the kid is real."

"So what now?"

"New Orleans," I said. "Talk to the kid. If there is a kid."

"And if she knows . . ."

"She had to talk to somebody about the package and somebody had to see the return address. If she's real, she knows the killer."

8

LYMAN BOLE, THE President's national security advisor, resigned that evening after conferring with the President. We listened to an all-news radio station as we whistled back through the dark to the river, and the general opinion seemed to be that Bole's public life was over. So here's a lesson for all you frat boys: At this point in the life of the Republic, you better pick your indiscretions carefully.

Back in Longstreet, we talked about New Orleans. I told LuEllen that there seemed to be no point in her coming along, but she insisted on it. She was bored, she said, and didn't have any work shaping up. And she liked New Orleans—maybe we could spend some time looking for a new condo up on the lake. If she didn't live where she did, she said, she might live there.

"Where do you live?" John asked.

"Up north," she said, and smiled.

John thought he should go, because the computer girl was almost certainly black, and his being black might give him an edge in talking with her. Marvel didn't like the idea of John going.

"Kidd could probably talk to her better, geek to geek."

"I'm not a geek," I said.

"You're a cutie, but you have geeklike thoughts," Marvel said. She reached out and pinched one of my cheeks and shook it. She went back to John. "You know what the cops are like down there. You can get picked up for walking around black. You don't want to get picked up."

"I won't," he said, with a little heat. "I'm tired of never going anywhere. And if we both go, I can talk to her black to black and Kidd can talk to her geek to geek."

"Sounds like a fuckin' dance," said LuEllen. "Dancin' geek to geek."

They all laughed, and I said, "I'm getting pretty tired of this geek shit."

AFTER SOME MORE talk, we decided to head down to New Orleans the next day, and at least take a look around. LuEllen went off to the bathroom before we headed out to our motel, and John went to kiss the kids good night. They'd been asleep for hours, but Marvel believed that they subliminally knew when their father had tucked them in—and Marvel caught me alone in the kitchen.

"I've never said anything to anybody about this, Kidd, but when John was a young man he got into serious trouble," she said. "He'd still be in prison if they'd caught him, but they didn't—but they've got his fingerprints and his real name there with the FBI. If they catch him and get his fingerprints . . ."

"Okay," I said.

"You take care of him," she said, profoundly serious. "I'm putting it on you."

WE WERE OUT of Longstreet at eight o'clock the next morning, still yawning and sleepy, and rolled into New Orleans in the middle of a steamy afternoon, with rain clouds building in the west. The car thermometer said it was 92 degrees on the freeway, and in the blacktop of an E-Z Way convenience store, where we stopped for water and Cokes, it felt closer to 100. The air was absolutely still, and completely saturated.

In the same convenience store, I caught a few minutes of Fox News and what looked like a photograph of a man wearing desert camo and an American helmet pointing a pistol at the head of an Arab man in Middle Eastern robes. The Arab seemed to be reacting in shock, as though he'd just been shot—a photo something like the famous Viet Cong execution photo from the sixties. The sound was down, so I didn't know what they were talking about.

A skinny white kid was standing there, probably a skater because, even in the heat, he was wearing a black wool watch cap pulled all the way over his head, and I asked, "What's going on?"

"Shot that dude in the head, man," he said. Then, "Guns are bad." I left not knowing whether he meant that guns are evil or that guns are desirable—getting old, I guess.

WE DECIDED TO set up a base—a bolt-hole if we needed one—at the Baton Noir Motel in Metairie, a nice place with a good dining room and a friendly attitude toward multiracial convocations. I'd spent a month there before buying my New Orleans condo, and a couple of weeks while I sold the place.

After checking in, I went to a map program in my laptop and we pulled up the kid's address and a map. As I was doing that, LuEllen clicked on the TV and a few minutes later, while I was writing down directions to the girl's house, she said, "Hey! Hey! Look at this! Look at this!"

She was watching the same story I'd seen in the convenience store. The anchorwoman was saying, ". . . denies that any such execution took place and that the photo may be a composite. The person called Bobby says that the officer in the photograph is Captain Delton Polysemy of the U.S. Army's Special

Forces then stationed in Yemen. Fox News has learned that there is a Captain Polysemy, but his current assignment and whereabouts are not known. Presidential Press Secretary Anton Lazar said that the President is aware of the photograph but had not seen it, and said that further comment would have to come from the Department of Defense. Lazar said that the U.S. government does not support summary executions, but repeated that there is no evidence that any such execution had taken place and that the photograph may be a composite. . . ."

"AH, MAN," JOHN said. "He's gonna have every fuckin' federal agent in the country chasing him."

"But they still don't know it's not Bobby," LuEllen said.

"We might have to tell them," I said. "They've got some ideas about Bobby, and people who might know about him. If this shit keeps up, they'll start knocking down doors under some Homeland Security pretense. A lot of good guys could go down."

"Maybe you," LuEllen said, looking at me.

"I think I'm okay," I said, but I was a lot more worried than that. I'd been working for a long time, and there were dozens of people who had ideas of what I'd been doing with my time, in addition to the painting. "We really gotta go see this Rachel Willowby."

"Wait, wait, wait," LuEllen said. "You said, tip them

off on Bobby being dead. We gotta think about that. That might be an idea. If they believe he's dead, they'll look somewhere else. Problem solved. Mostly."

"Maybe—but we don't have to do it right now," I said. "Let's think about it."

IF YOU GET off the main roads of Louisiana, back in the marshy ground, you find the worst poverty in America—worse than some of the South Dakota Indian reservations, which is saying a lot. Rachel Willowby's address came down to a crumbling concrete-block-stucco triplex, painted a harsh limey green, a dusty place with sick-looking thorn bushes in front of the windows as burglary deterrents. The neighborhood was marked by oil-stained driveways and crumbly carports full of junk and junkers, old and fading gang symbols on the sides of stores and service shops. Black kids with tough, calculating eyes looked out of their cars at us as we drove through. They put us down as cops. "No car," John said, as we drove past the Willowby place. "Her folks may be working."

"If she's got folks," LuEllen said from the back-seat. "The place looks deserted. And if she had to get a laptop from Bobby, there can't be much money around—you can get a used one for almost noth-ing."

"But it'd have to be a priority," John said. "Might not be a priority with her folks."

"We're stalling," I said. "What do we do?"

"What we do is, we go in. Right now. It's our best shot," John said. "We know she goes to school, but she should be home by now, and there's no car."

"All three of us?" I asked.

John said, "Really, the best combination would be me and LuEllen, 'cause I'm black and could be a cop and LuEllen could be a social worker—but you're the one who knows the computer shit, so you gotta come."

"Man, I love this. I could do this for a living," I muttered. I made a U-turn, drove back past a kid in a striped shirt and shorts, who had a bicycle helmet on his head, and who shook a finger at us and then laughed.

"That kid worries me," LuEllen said, looking back at the kid in the street. "Why's he walking around in this sun with a helmet on? Why doesn't he have a bicycle?"

WE ALL WENT together to the Willowby apartment, a little cluster, a scrum, three sweating, cranky people in clothes that suddenly looked too good, knocked on the door, and got nothing. We were standing there, listening for anything inside, and LuEllen said, "Now what?"

"Try again later," I said, and stepped back. We were headed reluctantly back to the car when a woman pushed open a door on an adjoining apartment, sweeping dust out on the sidewalk. She fussed at it and then called, "You looking for somebody?" She wasn't actually sweeping anything—the broom was an excuse to see what we were doing.

John stepped toward her and put out his best official vibration. He was wearing slacks and a yellow short-sleeved shirt, and looked like he might just have taken off a sport coat in the heat. He said, "We're looking for Rachel Willowby."

"She in trouble again?" The woman's head was cocked away from us.

"No. Not exactly. But we would like to talk with her. Have you seen her?"

"Playing hooky again," the woman speculated. Her eyes hit me, then went to LuEllen, and finally back to John. "Takes three of you, now."

"I'm sorry, ma'am, but we're really not allowed to talk about it," John said. "Do you know where she might be?"

Another long pause, but John's official stare got on top of her. "She's home. Probably hidin' under the bed."

"Where's her mother?"

"Her mother took off. Two months ago. I wouldn't tell you about the girl, 'cept I don't know what she eats, and she ain't gonna be let live there much longer. It's been rented. She sneaks in now."

"Thank you." John walked straight back to the door and knocked on it, then tried the knob. The door was locked, but was so loose in its frame that he put a shoe against it, pushed, and it popped open. He called, "Rachel? We know you're home." A moment later, "There you are." He stepped inside, out of sight, then stepped back to the door, looked at the woman, and said, "Thank you," and to us, "Come on in."

WE ALL TROOPED inside and found ourselves looking at a skinny little girl in shorts and a tube top. She wore big unfashionable plastic-rimmed glasses and had a ferociously unhappy look on her face. The house was unlit, with most of the blinds pulled, so she was working in semidarkness. The place smelled of onions and sweat. I could see one piece of furniture in the front two rooms, and that was a kitchen table. A laptop sat on the table, with a wire leading to a telephone. The laptop screen showed three open windows; a digital counter blinked in the lower right corner. She said, "That ol' bitch gonna get her snoopy nose cut off, one of these days."

John shook his head and said, "We need to talk."

"I'm sick." A sick look slipped onto her face. "I really am."

Fuck it: she was a hacker. I said, "We're not from the schools. We're not from the cops. I'm a hack and I want to know what you have to do with blowing Bobby out of the system."

That stopped her. She looked at me, forgot the others. "Where'd he go?"

"We don't know," I lied. "We're part of his backup

group. He's not at his house anymore, and something you did caused the trouble."

"Not me," she said shrilly. She stepped protectively toward her laptop, eyes wide. "I hardly even know the man."

"He sent you the laptop," I said. "You're the only person who could've given anything away."

"I did not."

"You did something. You might not even know it." I bent over the laptop, looking at the screen. "What're you doing here, running a dictionary? What're you trying to get into?"

She flinched, put a protective hand out toward her screen. "I didn't give shit to nobody." She was loud, defiant, and still pretty small; I loomed over her.

"Then somebody came over and got an address from you. Got it off the FedEx package. Who was that?"

Her tongue curled over her bottom lip and she glanced at LuEllen and John and saw nothing but more adults, all ganged up on her. So she just said it. "That was Jimmy James Carp. He said he was gonna get me a laptop from Bobby and he did."

"Where does he live?"

She shrugged, and relaxed a notch: she felt the blame shifting. "I don't know. He used to be a teacher up to Adams and then he moved to Washington, D.C., and I only saw him when he said he came back to visit his momma. He told me to call him if I got the computer. I called him when I got it and he came over."

"Came over right away?"

"Next day."

"White man or black man?" John asked.

"White man. Really white."

"You know his phone number?"

"I got it on my machine. You gonna do something to Jimmy James?"

"Talk to him. We're trying to find Bobby."

She went to the machine and her fingers danced across it. She was a hack, all right; the best way to tell is to watch the hands. Hacks are so deep into it that they essentially *will* a computer to act, their thoughts appearing on the screen as if by magic, the fingers working by reflex and so quickly it's like watching a spider's spinners as it weaves a web. In a few seconds, she'd closed down her online connection so we wouldn't see it, dumped whatever program she was using, called up the Address Book from the Windows accessories program, and located Carp's number.

As she did it, I said, "If you call this Carp guy and tell him we're coming over, he's gonna hide out, and we're not gonna find out what happened to Bobby. The only reason he got you the computer was so he could find Bobby. Carp might pretend, but he's no friend of yours."

"I know," she said grudgingly. She poked one of the laptop keys and the address program vanished. She looked back up at me; her face was thin, hungry. "He's a creep. I wondered why he helped me. He didn't even know me when he worked at Adams and then I see him and he's all, 'Hey, Rachel, how are you doin'?' I thought he wanted to fuck me or something and then he goes on about computing, you know?"

"He's a hack?"

"He knows some shit," she admitted.

"Jimmy James is a strange name," LuEllen ventured. "Is that his real name?"

"That's what everybody called him," she said. "I think it's real."

"I'LL TELL YOU what," I said. "If you don't call Carp and tell him that we've been looking for him, then I'll give you three phone numbers."

"To what?" She was interested. Good phone numbers, to hacks, are like little diamonds.

"Won't tell you. And I won't give them to you until after we talk to Carp. But if you're any good on that laptop, you've been looking for them."

She considered that for a moment and then said, "What do you know about Wal-Mart?"

"What do you need?"

"I'd like to get good access into their computer system. Just to see how it works."

"What do you have now?"

"Can't get further than the front end."

She had a friend who worked at a Wal-Mart somewhere, I thought. "One of the ways hacks get caught is when they try to use a computer system to deliver inventory to people who'll steal it. Inventory systems are pretty carefully protected from beginners."

"I just want to look at the system," she said sullenly.

"I don't know about Wal-Mart, but I can suggest a piece of social engineering that'll get you in."

"Like what?"

"If I tell you, you're on your own," I said. "And you can't call Carp."

"Let's have it," she said. "And I'll want those three numbers, too."

"When I know you can't hurt us. Do you have a chat name?"

"Yes. You can get me anytime." I got her AIM name and told her I'd call back.

"So tell me how to get into Wal-Mart."

I told her. John was watching while we talked, and finally he asked, "Where's your mother?"

"She took off with Leon—her boyfriend. She told me to go over to my aunt's, but my aunt said she didn't know nothin' about it, so I come back here and I been waitin' ever since."

"You don't know where they went?"

"Said it was to Hollywood, to dance, but she's dreamin.' She's gonna go out there and whore around, just like here. Nobody's gonna pay her to dance. Or Leon neither."

"The lady next door said they're gonna rent the apartment to somebody else," John said.

"I'll figure that out when I get there," Rachel said, but she was worried.

John shook his head, looked at the girl, then at me, then said, "Shit."

BACK IN THE car, with all the windows down and the air conditioner running full blast, John said, "This isn't gonna work. I gotta do something about the kid."

"Like what?"

"Take her with me. We can leave the number with her aunt, for when her mom gets back."

"I don't think her mom is coming back," LuEllen told him. "But taking her with you . . . John, you ought to talk to Marvel, first."

John finally went back with some money, pushed his way into the house, and left it with her.

"She can get something to eat, anyway," he said, miserably, when he got back. "I only had a hundred bucks. How in the fuck could somebody ditch a kid like that?"

"She's probably on her way to CompUSA," I said. "Computer memory is better than food, at that age."

We turned a corner, and all three of us looked back: nothing good could happen to that kid, not as things were.

WITH CARP'S NAME and phone number, I suggested to John that we access a local analog database and see if we could come up with an address.

"Which database?" John asked. He was hot, unhappy, and mopped his forehead with a paper towel he'd taken out of the Willowby kitchen. "You got a number?"

"It's an old, old, *old* geek joke," LuEllen said, sounding deeply bored. "He means, we look in the phone book."

"You can kiss *my* analog," John said to me. He looked out the window. "How can it be so hot here? I thought Longstreet was hot."

"It's not the heat," I began, earnestly.

"Shut up," LuEllen said.

We took a while finding a phone book, but finally got one at a shopping center. While LuEllen went off and got three cinnamon rolls, I found one Carp in the White Pages—a Melissa Carp, in Slidell, which was on the opposite shore of Lake Pontchartrain. The phone number was right.

"We're on a roll," John said. "Let's go right now." On the way over, still looking out the window, he said, "That fuckin' kid."

WE HEADED UP to Slidell on I-10, not one of the nation's scenic roads. The Carp place was a mobile home in a mobile-home neighborhood on the east side of town, or maybe out of town, to the east. From the street, nothing was visible except a chin-high concrete-block wall, over which we could see the tops of the homes and willowy-looking trees clogged with Spanish moss.

"These places are a problem," LuEllen said, as we cruised by. "I know people who live in places like this. Everything is close together and the streets are more like lanes, and you can't get in and out fast, and everybody sees you coming and going."

"That's encouraging," John said.

"And they're pretty segregated," LuEllen said. "The ones I've been in, anyway. If this is a white park, you're gonna be noticeable, John."

"Even better."

IN THE END, we drove through just at dusk, looking for the right place. All the streets were named after trees, like Cherry, Chestnut, Olive, and Peach. As LuEllen had suggested, the lots were small, and cut at odd angles to each other, some neatly kept, some not. We went past a couple who were barbequing on a small grill, then wandered past a double lot with an aboveground pool to one side of the home; we saw a few young kids here and there, and one older kid blading along the main drag, hands locked behind his back, earphones cutting him off from the world. Other than that, the streets were mostly empty, probably because it was still so hot.

The streets were marked, at least, and we found

Quince Street at the southeast corner of the neighborhood, a loop that ran just inside the concrete-block wall. The Carp place was a once-forest-green mobile home, now sun-faded, with a white roof, closed-curtained windows, and a rickety carport at the far end. A dusty red Toyota Corolla squatted in the carport. Light could be seen through a back window, but the front of the place was dark.

"What do you want to do?" LuEllen asked.

"How about if we drive around for two minutes, figure out these roads, then you take the car while John and I brace the guy? We look enough like cops."

"I wonder who Melissa Carp is? Mother? Wife? Ex-wife? Sister?"

WE DROVE AROUND until we were oriented, then LuEllen dropped us off a hundred feet down the street from Carp's. Most of the homes around us showed lights, or the bluish-white glow of TVs. I could hear somebody playing an old Cream recording called "Strange Brew" somewhere down the block; other than that, it was all the hum of air conditioners.

"If I was a cop, walking up to doors like this would scare the shit out of me," John muttered as we walked up a flagstone walk to Carp's front door. I knocked, and the door rattled in its frame, and we felt a change from inside, as though something not quite audible had been going on, and now had stopped. Maybe, I thought, somebody had stopped typing.

Then footsteps. A curtain moved. Whoever looked out—the window was dark, and he was invisible—could see only John, because I'd moved to the other side of the door, away from the window. Then more footsteps inside, and the inner door rattled, and finally a man looked out.

He was younger than we were, probably in his late twenties or early thirties, large, with a fatty, football-shaped face, a long, fleshy nose, and a thatch of brown hair. He hadn't shaved, and a wispy beard showed on his jowls and under his full lips. He had small eyes, and he blinked at us and then asked, "Who're you?"

"Are you James Carp?" John asked.

His forehead wrinkled. "Uh, that's my brother."

"Is he here?" John asked.

He was about to lie to us. I could see it in his face. "He's uh, back in the . . . he's in the back."

"We really need to talk to him," John said. John sort of wedged himself in the doorway. "It's really pretty important."

"I'll, uh, go and get him," the man said.

He pushed the door mostly shut, looked at us one more time, and John said, "That's you, isn't it, Jimmy James?"

CARP BROKE FOR the back of the mobile home and John and I went after him. We crunched into each other trying to get through the door, and then, once inside, in the dark, I hit the front edge of the folding table and almost went down—a near fall that might have saved my life, because as I was twisting off to the side, Carp, in the back, fired three quick shots at us with a pistol.

I continued down, hearing the gunfire and seeing the muzzle flashes, and heard John crash out through the door and I thought, *He's hit*, and I scrambled that way and fed myself through the door like a snake.

I thought Carp might be coming after us, and I reached up and pulled the door shut and looked for a place to run. John was on his knees, getting to his feet as I rolled out, and now he was looking down the length of the trailer and calling, "Hey!" and I looked that way.

There was a back door, somewhere out of sight, or he'd gone out a window: Carp was there, the laptop under his arm, a power cord trailing away. He was climbing into the Corolla and when I rolled to my feet he pointed the pistol at us, and we both dodged back, toward the back of the trailer, and he started the car with his computer hand and rolled out and down the street, and a second later was gone in the twilight.

JOHN LOOKED AT me. "You okay?"

"I'm okay, you hit?"

"No, no."

Then LuEllen arrived and we climbed in the car and she took off, fast for the first hundred feet, then slowing, slowing, and then she asked, "Was that a gun?"

"That was a gun," I said. I felt like I could start shaking. "That was Carp. He's somewhere out ahead of us in that Corolla."

"Wasn't very loud," she said. "Maybe a .22."

"Even a .22'll shoot your ass off," John said. Then, "Maybe not your whole ass."

Two minutes later, we were back on the street, heading toward I-10. We were coming up to a gas station and I saw a "Telephone" sign. "Pull over, there," I said. We'd only been out of the place for three or four minutes.

I got on the phone, dialed 911, and when the emergency center came up, I shouted, "There's been a shooting at 300 Quince Street in the Langtry mobile home park. There's a guy shot. He's hurt real bad. I gotta go, I gotta go."

The woman at the other end was calling, "Wait, wait," when I hung up.

Most 911 centers will show a phone number and location when you call. We got out of there as quickly as we could, losing ourselves in traffic.

"What was that all about?" John asked.

"I'm hoping they'll send a cop car or two." Then we heard the first siren, and we all shut up to watch a squad car zip by, going in the other direction. "I'm hoping it'll keep Carp on the run. I hope he thinks he shot a cop."

"I just hope nobody got our plates in there," Lu-Ellen said.

"I didn't see anybody close enough to do that . . . or curious enough," I said.

"I thought that motherfucker had shot you, Kidd," John said. "You went down like a dropped rock."

"No damage," I said.

"I HATE SURPRISES," LuEllen said. And she did—whenever she was working, she was a meticulous planner. Our planning on Carp had not been the most meticulous.

"Lost the laptop," John said. "But we sure as shit got some answers: Carp did it, and he's got it."

We heard another siren and then another cop went by.

"Keep running, Jimmy James," I said. "The hounds are on your ass."

9

AFTER THE FIASCO at Carp's, we retreated to the motel to think it over. If this had been a thriller novel, we would have tried trolling the back roads, looking for Carp, and might even have found him. But this wasn't a novel, and since we weren't cops, and didn't know the town, we had no resources for tracking him. Even if we located him, he had a gun and we didn't. Nor did we have a way to get one quickly, if we wanted one.

"If we find him again, we need to surprise him, disarm him, and grab the laptop," John said. "If we'd known for sure what he looked like, we could've grabbed him at the trailer before he had a chance to get the gun."

"We should have researched him before we tried

to grab him," LuEllen said. "At least, we should have found a picture of him."

"Yeah. We blew it," John said. To me: "What do you want to do?"

"Go out on the 'net and do what we should have done before—research him," I said.

"When he shot at you guys, I could barely hear the shots," LuEllen said. "He was inside. There wasn't anybody else around, and with everybody using air-conditioning, it's possible nobody else heard the shots. If nobody called the cops and pinpointed Carp's place, we might be able to get back inside."

"That'd be a last resort," I said.

"It might be full of stuff that would tell us where he's going—if the cop sirens chased Carp away, and nobody heard the shots."

I looked at John and he nodded.

"THE OTHER THING," LuEllen said. "I hate to keep harping on it, but I can't see any downside to telling somebody that Bobby is dead. If we don't, they'll start going after people they think might be associated with him. Might know something. There's no way to tell where that would stop. The thing is, Carp is fucking with politicians. You know how they hate that."

John shrugged. "I don't see a huge problem with telling somebody. Except, who'd believe us?"

"There's one person I can think of." I looked at LuEllen. "Rosalind Welsh."

LuEllen thought for a moment, then nodded. "Yeah. She'd do."

"Who's she?" John asked.

We'd only met Welsh once, I told him, during a spot of trouble that led to a car getting melted in a Maryland shopping center garage while LuEllen and I stole a van from a housewife, and black helicopters—well, sort of a greenish-black . . .

"Just green," LuEllen said.

. . . green helicopters landed in the parking lot and people ran around like ants and waved their arms until the fire trucks came.

"She works for the National Security Agency," LuEllen said to John. "She's a security expert, not a computer freak. She's too heavy by fifteen pounds. She thinks Kidd's name is Bill Clinton."

"Hmm," John said. "Sounds perfect."

We decided to make the call that night—I had all of Rosalind Welsh's phone numbers, unless she'd moved or died, and I was sure she'd be happy to hear from me. First though, we needed to find a Radio Shack.

If there weren't such things as Radio Shack stores, I probably would have become a humble shepherd, instead of the hardened criminal and painter that I am. But there *are* Radio Shack stores, and after the discouraging session with John and LuEllen, I looked at my watch, and figured I had about twenty minutes to get to one.

Fortunately, there are as many Radio Shacks in the New Orleans area as there are blues singers: I ran in

the door of my favorite store five minutes before closing, gathered up most of what I needed—a screw-on
N-type female chassis mount connector, a little roll
of 12-gauge copper wire, some solder, a pigtail with
an N-type male connector at one end, and the cheapest wire cutters, tape measure, and soldering iron I
could find—and carried it to the counter.

The clerk recognized me as a one-time regular. He
looked over my purchases, rang it up, and asked
cheerfully, "Gonna do some war-driving?"

"Huh?" I said as I paid him.

"Ah, you know," he said. He was too tall, too
skinny, and had spent twelve seconds getting dressed
for work that morning. Maybe less. "Or maybe you
don't need a Lucent gold card."

"What's that about?" I asked.

"About ninety dollars," he said.

I took two fifties out of my billfold and stood
there. He disappeared into the back for a minute,
then came back with a Lucent card in the kind of Zip-
loc bag usually used to hold marijuana and cocaine . . .
and maybe peanuts and raspberries and other legal
stuff, for all I know. He handed me the card and I
handed him the money and said, "Keep the change,"
and he put it in his shirt pocket.

"If you go about nine blocks that way, there's an
all-night supermarket that sells Dinty Moore beef
stew," he said for the extra ten dollars. "I recommend
the can. It's just about perfect for a waveguide. And the
area around Tulane is your happy hunting ground."

"You are a prince among men," I said. "Have a nice day."

Did I mention the service at Radio Shack?

I STOPPED AT the supermarket, got the can of Dinty Moore and a can opener, drove back to the motel, and built the antenna. The worst part was trying to flush the cold beef stew down the toilet: it just didn't want to go. John stood there, grimacing at the bowl, flushing it over and over, saying, "Man, that's nasty. It looks like somebody was *really* sick." A bright orange ring-around-the-bowl was still there the next morning.

After cleaning the beef-stew can, I went online to an antenna site with a calculator, did some figuring, and with the soldering iron put together a nice little wi-fi antenna. Wi-fi stands for "wireless fidelity" and works as a high-frequency wireless local network—it's cheap, and it allows several people, in several different places around the house, office, or classroom to use the same Internet connection. It'll probably be obsolete by tomorrow, but today, it was spreading around the country like a rash. Usually, the range is limited to just about the area of a big house. With an antenna, though . . .

Normally, I wouldn't ride on somebody else's Internet connection, simply because it wasn't necessary. Connections are a dime a dozen, if you're legal. Most Starbucks have a wi-fi connection. But the Carp

problem made me nervous, and if I rode on somebody else's network connection, there'd be no way to
backtrack our inquiries. And it would be faster than
doing it from the motel: working over a telephone
hookup was like having water drip on your forehead.

The kid at the Radio Shack store had recommended
the Tulane area as a happy hunting ground, but I had
a different idea. I'd found that lots of warehouses use
wi-fi because warehouses are constantly involved in
inventory movements, and those movements are often
uploaded via the Internet to central control offices.
Few of them have any kind of protection.

LuEllen and I took I-10 out toward Kenner and
New Orleans International, LuEllen driving while I
watched the laptop, and eventually we found a truck
stop parking lot next to what looked like a warehouse, where we got a strong signal from a wi-fi network.

And it was a fast one, maybe a T-1 line. In the next
hour, I pulled every bit of information I could out of
the National Crime Information Center, out of credit
agencies and insurance companies, and from three
different credit card companies. When I was done, I
still didn't have a photograph of Jimmy James Carp,
but I had a different kind of picture, and it was one
that scared us.

"THE GUY MIGHT be working for the Senate Intelligence Committee," LuEllen blurted to John, when

we got back to the Baton Noir. John was stretched on his bed, watching CNN. "He might be a spy or something."

He sat up, dropped his feet to the floor. *"What?"*

"The last job I can find for him, the last one that paid Social Security taxes, was the U.S. government, and the reference number traces back to the Senate Intelligence Committee," I said.

"The *government* killed Bobby?"

"I don't know—the Social Security payments stopped a month ago, but if he's fucking around with the intelligence community, that might not mean anything," I said. "On the other hand, that didn't look like a government operation out at the trailer park. If the feds knew what was on that computer, they'd have it locked in a vault somewhere."

"It feels bad, though," LuEllen said.

"Tell you something," John said, pointing at the TV. "He's done it again. Bobby. Carp. There's a story out there, coming out now, about how some Homeland Security department might have sprayed a virus into San Francisco to see how it would spread. It was supposed to be a test in case of a smallpox attack, they wanted to see what would happen, and they used a virus called, uh, Newport? That's not right, but something like that. Anyway, a lot of people got sick and four people may have died . . . the shit is hitting the fan, and CNN says the leak involves a lot of classified government computer files and the sourcing resembles the Bobby releases of the past couple of days."

"Norwalk? Norwalk virus?" LuEllen asked.

He snapped his fingers. "That's it."

"Weren't there a whole bunch of cruise ships a while back, where they had epidemics?"

"Exactly!" John said. "That's the one. They're saying—they say it's only speculation—that those could have been a more controlled test, before they dumped it into San Francisco."

"Ah, man. That means there must be a bunch of stuff that's not encrypted—or he found a key."

"We've gotta find the fucker," John said.

LuEllen said, "He's probably not twenty miles from here."

"Might as well be in Chicago," I said. "I got his credit card numbers, if he uses them . . ."

"Everybody's gonna be looking for him," John said.

"Everybody's gonna be looking for Bobby, unless we tell them he's dead. Or for one of Bobby's friends, if we decide to tell them," I said. "We're the only ones looking for Jimmy James Carp."

WE TALKED ABOUT it as we watched CNN, and then LuEllen said, "Hey, we found out about Melissa. Melissa Carp."

"Yeah?" John said.

"She was his mother. She's dead. She was killed in an automobile accident a month ago."

"Maybe flipped him out," John said.

And we talked about other trips we'd been on together, we talked about Longstreet, we talked a little more about Rachel Willowby, and what would happen to her. "If she thought Jimmy James Carp wanted to talk to her because he wanted to fuck her . . . then there *are* people who are talking to her because they want to fuck her," John said. "She's about ten-to-one for winding up on the corner."

Something to mull over. Even later, after watching more about the Norwalk virus story, and more talk, we decided to tell the NSA that Bobby had been murdered.

LATE THAT NIGHT, I went back out—way back out—up I-10 into Baton Rouge. I found a pay phone in a bar parking lot and, using LuEllen's anonymous calling card, called long distance to Glen Burnie, Maryland. The phone rang seven times before Rosalind Welsh picked it up. She sounded as though she'd been asleep, and I realized that it was after two in the morning, Eastern time. "Hello?"

"Rosalind. Bill Clinton here. Remember me? Hope I didn't wake you up, but I guess I must have." At that moment, honest to God, a rat walked past the pay phone on its way to the bar, as confident and casual as a cat heading home. "Jesus," I said.

"Who?" Welsh was struggling up out of the sleep. "Jesus?" I heard a man's voice say, "Who is it?"

"Did you get remarried?" I asked cheerfully.

"What do you want?" she snapped. "This is the man with the mask?"

"Who is it?" the man asked, and I heard her say, "Never mind; it's for me."

"You remember me, now," I said. "You're awake."

"I'm awake." But not happy.

"You remember that guy Bobby who caused you all the trouble? And you went looking for and got your ass kicked? And is causing all this trouble with these pictures and the Norwalk virus thing, and all of that?"

Long pause. "Yes. Where is he?"

"He's dead," I said. "He's been dead for a couple of days."

"What?"

"Did you see the news stories about the black man killed in Jackson, Mississippi, and the Fiery Cross that was burned on his front porch?"

"Yes. Of course."

"That was Bobby. He was murdered. Somebody killed him for his laptop, which has all that stuff on it that you're seeing on TV. We think maybe—maybe—it was you, that you're running some kind of an operation against the government. Was it you guys, Rosalind?"

"You're crazy," she shrilled. "We don't do that."

"What is it?" the man shouted in the background. "Let me talk to him."

"You're talking to Bill Clinton, here, Rosy—I *know* what you do," I said. "Now, I would suggest, for your

own health, that you stop chasing us innocent computer folks around the country, and find out who
killed Bobby. If you don't, we'll start fucking with
you again. Remember the last time we did that? How
your Keyhole satellites went nuts and all the GS-80s
started pooping in their Italian pants? You don't want
that again."

"Listen, Bill," she said earnestly. "Do you have any
proof . . . ?"

"Nothing you would believe," I said. "But if you
check out the dead black man in Jackson, it won't take
you long to figure out who he was, all on your own.
The FBI is already involved; all you have to do is give
them a hint."

"Bobby DuChamps?" she asked. That surprised me.
They'd actually gotten a name.

"Almost," I said. "His name was Robert Fields.
Get it? And listen, Rosalind, really: have a nice day."

I hung up feeling that I'd been mean to her, but
sometimes, with security people—she was NSA internal security—it's the only thing that works. Hate will
wake you up, if not set you free.

"YOU DO IT?" John asked, when I got back to the
motel. He and LuEllen were watching the end of a
movie called XXX, about a boy and his GTO.

"All done. Can't tell what will happen next, but
maybe some of the feds will . . . what?" I looked at
LuEllen.

"Reorient themselves," she suggested.

"That's good," I said. "Reorient themselves."

JOHN WAS IN one room, LuEllen and I in another. We were beat. We'd been flying, driving, hacking, and getting shot at for twenty hours and needed some sleep. We arranged to meet at eight the next morning, and LuEllen and I said good night to John and crawled into bed.

Just before we went to sleep, LuEllen said, "Think about Carp's trailer. Ten o'clock in the morning is the best time to hit an open target like that. Think about it in your sleep."

I did that.

THERE'S NO BETTER source for burglary supplies than your local Target store. You can get cheap, disposable entry tools, plastic gloves, Motorola walkie-talkies, backpacks, and everything you need to change your appearance. Like khaki shorts.

Everybody knows what a burglar looks like—an ethnic minority, probably, lurking in the bushes until the coast is clear. After dark, on a moonless night. Wearing a ski mask. Which is why most professional house-breakers go in at ten o'clock in the morning or two o'clock in the afternoon, during the workday, when school is in session and the house is probably empty. And they always knock first.

We synched the walkie-talkie channels on the way over to Carp's, and I changed into the shorts, tore the price tags off a pair of wraparound sunglasses and put them on, along with a Callaway golf hat.

We first made a pass outside the park, but could see no activity over the wall near Carp's. Then we went in and cruised down his street. There was a door on the back end of the Carp mobile home, the one we hadn't seen the night before, that Carp had gone through, and it was hanging open an inch or two.

The front door, where John and I had spilled out onto the lawn, was closed, as we'd left it. Just around the corner, and about four houses up, an old guy was mowing his tiny lawn with a tiny electric lawn mower. He glanced at us as we went past and LuEllen said to John, "When we pull into the place, go straight ahead and get out on another street, so you won't drive past that guy again."

John nodded. "All right."

LuEllen looked at me. "Ready to try it?"

"I didn't see anything that said no."

John would be waiting outside the park. If we called and said, "Dave, come on," he'd come in through the park, taking his time. If we said, "Hey, Dave, hurry it up," he'd come down the outside street, and we'd jump the wall.

IN OUR SHORTS and golf shirts and over-the-shoulder pack, LuEllen and I were an unremarkable, almost invisible, couple knocking on Jimmy James Carp's door, knocking just loud enough to attract somebody inside. There was no answer and I tried the door. It opened and we waved at John. As he left, we stepped inside as though we'd been invited.

The place was dark, with curtains and shades on all the windows. I hit the lights and found that we were in the kitchen. The place was a mess, with dirty dishes stacked around a sink. An overflowing garbage bag sat on the floor between a small dinette table and the line of cupboards on the opposite wall. The garbage bag was jammed with pizza boxes, corn-curl sacks, instant dinner cartons, and microwave popcorn bags, and that's what the place smelled like: like every kind of stale cheese you can think of.

The next room along was the living room, with the furniture arranged to focus on a large-screen TV. Most of the furniture had a patina of dust, and the room was littered with paper: the *New York Times*, the *LA Times*, tabloids, popular science magazines, a facedown copy of *Penthouse*. An all-in-one stereo sat on a corner table, with a couple dozen CDs. On the wall, somewhat askew, was a full-color framed copy of the Praying Hands.

There were two bedrooms along a single hallway in the back: the first was a woman's room, not much neater than the rest of the place, and even dustier. The second bedroom belonged to Carp. A dozen computer books and manuals were scattered on the floor around the bed, all but two on IBM hardware.

One of the others dealt with encryption, and the last one was an *O'Reilly's Guide* to the C++ language.

I moved the pack to the back door, closed and locked the door, and we started tearing through the room. We didn't take long: we'd done this before. In two minutes, I had a ream of paper—old bills, new bills, bank statements, notes, employment records—a dozen floppy disks, and a half-dozen recordable CDs. I was loading it into our backpack when LuEllen, who'd moved back out to the front room, said, "Hey."

I poked my head out of the bedroom. "What?"

"Laptop," she said.

"What?" I went out, and sure enough, a Toshiba notebook sat under the edge of the couch. The power supply was still plugged into the wall. It looked exactly like somebody had been lying on the couch with the laptop on his stomach, while watching TV, had shut down the laptop and then pushed it under the couch so it wouldn't be stepped on. I know that because I'd done it about a thousand times. We pulled the plug and took it.

"Bobby's?" LuEllen asked. "Is that too much to expect?"

"Yeah, that's too much," I said, as we put it with the pack. "Baird said Bobby's was an IBM. And this one doesn't have a built-in optical drive. It's a travel machine like my Vaio. Bobby's was probably a lot heavier, with a bunch of built-in stuff. He didn't travel."

We'd been inside for five minutes at that point and

my internal egg timer was telling me to get the fuck out. Same with LuEllen. "Unless you've got something special to look at . . ."

"Let's go," I said. That's when we heard a car's tire crunching on the gravel outside.

LuEllen touched my arm and moved to a window. She could see out through a crack in the blind, and she hissed at me, "Two guys," and then, "Coming to the door."

I couldn't see out, but I glanced at LuEllen's face: she seemed pleased. She liked this shit, because it cranked her up, and she lived for the crank.

She pointed to the bedroom, and we tiptoed to the back door, hardly daring to breathe. The thing is, houses give off vibrations—footfalls, weight shifts, voices. Mobile homes, which are more lightly built than regular houses, are the worst. At the back, Lu-Ellen put her hand on the doorknob, and we waited. The idea is to open your door at the same time the other person is entering the other one; the noise and vibrations cancel each other out.

But they didn't come in. They knocked, loudly. We heard them talking, and then one of them crunched around to the back, and a second later, knocked on the door where we were standing. The knob rattled—LuEllen lifted her hand when she realized what was happening—and then the guy crunched back around the house.

I moved to the window and peeked out. Two guys: one black, one white, both wearing short-sleeved dress shirts and khaki slacks. They looked like hot, out-of-shape office workers, both too fleshy and with careful, thirty-dollar haircuts. The white guy, blond, pink-faced, chubby, had a tidy spade-shaped soul patch, the kind worn to demonstrate cool; he was probably taking saxophone lessons somewhere. The black guy was wearing a pink cotton shirt, and he looked terrific.

They were talking, nervously, I thought, then they looked up and down the street, as if checking for somebody they might interrogate. Then they got in the car, bumped back onto the road, and left. I read their license number to LuEllen, who wrote it on her arm with a ballpoint pen. Then she put the Motorola to her mouth and said, "Dave, come on."

We went out the back door and walked sideways across the narrow lawn, then up the street, carrying the backpack. John came up behind us, slowed, and we got in. The old guy had finished mowing his lawn and was sitting in a lawn chair drinking beer out of a brown bottle. He never turned his head as we went by.

"Goddamnit," I said.

"Nothing?" John asked.

"Two guys came by and knocked on the door. We got their tags," LuEllen said.

"Ah, shit. I didn't know. I was outside."

"Ford Taurus. Could have been a rental."

"Cops?"

"I don't think so," I said. "They were indoors

people. Office workers. Maybe we'll find out from the tags."

"Damn," John said. "We waste our time and almost get caught at it."

"No, no—we got a laptop," I said. "We found a laptop."

"What?"

He checked my face to see if I was joking. "Jimmy James left it behind when he ran last night. It's not Bobby's, but it might tell us a lot about Jimmy James."

I STILL HAD the stew-can antenna. Before we started messing with Carp's laptop, we went back to the truck stop and warehouse, went online, checked with a few friends for entry routes, and then went into the Louisiana auto registration database. The two guys' license tag went back to Hertz. Hertz was an old friend. I was in the Hertz database two minutes later and pulled out the name William Heffron of McLean, Virginia. He was using a credit card issued to the U.S. government.

"McLean," LuEllen said. "Weren't we there when . . ."

"Yeah. It's about a foot and a half from Washington."

10

WE SPENT THE afternoon at the Baton Noir. A small but pleasant swimming pool hung off a second-floor deck, and LuEllen put on a modest black bikini and went out to sun herself before the gathering insurance salesmen and lawyerly deal-makers. John began reading through the paper we'd taken out of Carp's, and I did the laptop.

Among the paper John found dozens of bills, mostly unpaid, indicating that Carp owed upward of $30,000 to various credit card companies. Most of the bills had been sent to an address in Washington, D.C.

He also found Carp's online service account numbers and e-mail addresses, and increasingly unpleasant letters both to and from a lawyer concerning his mother's estate. In the latest of those letters, Carp accused the attorney of looting his mother's bank accounts. John's impression was that when the lawyer was finished, Carp got the aging mobile home and a few thousand dollars—but he also got the impression that there wasn't much more than that anyway.

"But he's really pissed," John said. "If I were that attorney, I'd be watching for guys in clock towers."

"He's desperate for money," I said. "His mother's estate must have seemed like a dream come true, and it turns out to be a mirage."

I GOT STARTED on Carp's laptop by working my way around the password security. I plugged my laptop into his via a USB cable, ran a program that took control of his hard drive from my laptop, deleted his password file, and I was in. It ain't rocket science.

One thing I found immediately was that Carp had dozens of documents from the Senate Intelligence Committee: CIA briefings on Cuba, Venezuela, Korea, Nigeria, Zimbabwe, and a half-dozen Middle Eastern countries, including some negative assessments of the leaders of Israel, Syria, Saudi Arabia, and Egypt. None of it was encrypted.

In another file, I found letters to Senator Frank Krause of Nebraska, the head of the committee. There was no indication of whether any had actually been sent, and several showed signs of incomplete editing. All of them were written to object to Carp's firing, which had happened three months earlier. The other side of the correspondence wasn't on the computer, and John couldn't find it among the papers, so it was hard to know exactly why he'd been fired. Judging from Carp's side of the issue, it may have involved his political views, which were unstated. There was a draft of a note to someone else, another staffer, complaining about the unfairness of his firing, which referred to "crazy feminist politics."

The letters suggested that his employment involved office computer support—he kept the committee's computers running, helped with basic software issues and security problems. In an e-mail file, I found a couple hundred complaints and questions typical of an office system: questions about ethernet connections, lost e-mail, distribution lists, password changes, equipment upgrades.

LuEllen came back, carrying a Coke, looking for her suntan cream. The pool was getting crowded, and she was moving from display to exhibition mode.

As she was about to leave again, I hit the mother lode: a file of photographs and short films, two of which we'd already seen on television—the military execution and the blackface film. Nothing about the Norwalk virus.

"This is the Bobby file," LuEllen said. "This is it."

We paged through the photos, looking at the captions. John, who'd spent most of his life in politics of a kind, was fascinated. "You could do an unbelievable amount of damage with these things," he said. He wasn't enthusiastic, he was awed. "Some of the biggest assholes in the Congress would go down . . . if this stuff is real."

"What are they doing in Carp's computer?" Lu-Ellen asked.

"Must've transferred it from Bobby's," I said. "A backup, or something, before he started messing with the other files."

"Okay," John said, still looking over my shoulder. "Oh my God, look at this. This guy's a cabinet guy, he's what? HUD? HEW? Something like that."

We talked about the effect of the photos for a while. LuEllen thought they'd be revolutionary, but John shook his head. "You read those books about people finding the body of Christ and it ends Christianity, or somebody finds out that the President likes to screw little boys, and that leads to an atomic war. It doesn't work that way," he said. "Nothing is simple. Stuff like this ruins careers, it might change the way things work for a while, but the world goes on."

"You're an optimist, John," LuEllen said. "I'm going back to the pool. There are a whole bunch of guys from Texas up there."

"That's a blessing," John said. "Wouldn't want to miss that."

I went back to the computer and John finished with the paper. A half hour later, sitting in a dwindling pile of scraps, he said, "Ah, man." He was holding a slip of paper, shook his head and passed it to me. It was a phone bill for cable repair service, made to Robert Fields. Bobby's address was right there. "Took it out of Baird's file," I said.

"Gotta be," John said.

LuEllen HAD COME back, glowing with the sun, took her bikini-ed self into the bathroom to clean up and dress, and when she came back out, turned on the TV. A little while later, changing from *Oprah* to CNN, she said, "Look at this."

The Norwalk virus story was exploding: the President, in person, was promising a full investigation. If the so-called test had actually taken place, he said, the persons responsible would be prosecuted. He added that the government had no evidence of such a test and suggested that this "supposed revelation" might be a new kind of terrorist attack intended to discredit the American military and shake up financial markets.

"Getting ugly," John said.

I went back to the laptop. In a file called *Carly*, I found thirteen letters to a woman. The earliest ones were friendly technical advice on printing photographs from a new digital camera. They gradually became more personal, and he began trying to cajole her into a date. That apparently didn't work. In a file called *Linda*, there were six letters to another woman, with the same tone. There were other files named *Shannon* and *Barb* that were a bit more businesslike, but still had that feeling of attention that would make most women nervous.

Another file contained unremarkable glamour shots of supermodels, along with a major selection of hardcore porn. Half of it seemed to be young Japanese schoolgirls in plaid skirts; or out of plaid skirts. Given the resolution of the photos, it appeared that most of it had been downloaded from the 'net.

In a file called *Contacts*, I found addresses and phone numbers for Thomas Baird and Rachel Willowby. In his Microsoft address book, there were several hundred e-mail addresses, and in a PalmPilot sync file, there were thirty or forty home addresses and phone numbers for people I'd never heard of.

Then I stumbled over a file called DDC *Working Group—Bobby*, and inside, a list of names, e-mail addresses, and a half-dozen phone numbers and a few memos. One of the memos referred to a Deep Data Correlation working group, which explained the "DDC." I showed it to John and LuEllen.

"What the heck would that be?"

"I don't know, but we better find out, if we can," I said. To John: "Anything else?"

"Most of it can be tossed," he said, patting the pile of paper on the bed. "It's just bullshit."

"So toss it," I said. "I'm gonna call one of these numbers, and then get online, see if there's anything new from the guys on the ring."

———

BACK TO THE truck stop. From a phone inside, I called the first of the phone numbers for the Deep Data Correlation working group. After the usual long-distance clicking, I got a computer tone, and hung up. Called another number, got another tone. All right: computer access, but no way to get in, not yet.

Then I checked my blind addresses and got an alarm from the address I'd given to Rachel Willowby. It said, "Jimmy James Carp is parked outside—4:17 P.M."

I looked at my watch: a few minutes past 4:30, so the note had just come in. I fired the car up, took it back to the motel in a hurry. John and LuEllen were flipping cards at a wastebasket when I came in.

"We gotta go get her," John said, when I told them about the note.

"If there's trouble . . ." I remembered what Marvel had said about his fingerprint status. "And he's got a gun."

"Gotta go anyway," he said. He was already headed toward the door.

"Made a mistake not bringing a gun with us," Lu-Ellen said, a step behind him. "Every asshole in Louisiana has a gun in his car except us. And when you need one, like the NRA says, you need one."

"I'm not sure the NRA would want *me* to have one," John said.

"Let's figure this out on the way over," I said. "There's gotta be something we can do. Besides trying to tackle him in the street."

———

WE WORKED THROUGH a series of harebrained plans as we drove into New Orleans, but there wasn't time, and there just isn't much you can do when the other guy has a gun and you don't.

"One big thing is that none of us can get hung up with the cops," LuEllen said. "We can't just jump him in the street and then haul him away. That's kidnapping and it looks like kidnapping and somebody's gonna get the license plate number and then we're toast."

"Track him, get him inside, wherever he's staying . . ."

"But what about the kid?" John asked. "There's only one reason he's after the kid, and that's to find out who tracked him to the trailer."

"Two reasons," I said. "The other one is, to shut her up. She can connect him to Bobby."

"Ah, Jesus. And since he already killed Bobby . . ."

"You better drive faster, Kidd," LuEllen said.

"We still gotta figure out the gun."

"Catch him in the open, and he might be afraid to use it," I said.

"Gotta get to the girl, though," John said. "That's the number-one thing."

WE WENT STRAIGHT into Rachel Willowby's. Didn't see a Corolla, nothing but the usual beat-up full-sized Chevys and Oldsmobiles; one guy far down the street was washing off the floor mats of his car, but he was the only person we could see moving around outside.

At the Willowby place, John was out on the street before the car stopped rolling, heading for her door. I was out and called, "Take it easy, take it easy." LuEllen was trailing, hurrying to catch me, and I was hurrying to catch up with John, but he was a dozen steps ahead of me and I didn't want to run, because running attracts the eye.

Then he was at the door, and instead of knocking, pushed it, and then was inside and the shouting started, "Hey, hey, hey . . ." and then I was in, blinking in the sudden darkness of the interior. John was halfway across the small front room, Rachel Willowby was sitting at the kitchen table in front of her laptop, and Carp stood beside the table.

He had the gun.

". . . are you motherfuckers?" Carp was shouting.

"Friends of Rachel's," John was saying over the top of Carp's question. "We're friends of Rachel's and she says she's in trouble."

"Is this a friend of Rachel's?" Carp asked, waving the gun barrel at me. "Where in the hell did he come from? And who's that?" He looked past me, and I half turned. LuEllen peeked around the door frame and said, "We called 911, they're on the way."

Carp glanced toward the back door on the other side of the kitchen, and his tongue flicked out. "You guys are from the working group. Tell Krause to stay the fuck away from me or I will bomb them. I will fuckin' blow them up."

"Who? What group? What are you talking about?" John asked. He stepped toward Carp, but he looked at me. He needed a couple more steps.

"Krause," Carp said.

"What?" John asked. Another short shuffle step.

CARP SHOT HIM.

The gun was a .22, but even a .22 sounds like a cannon when it's fired in a small concrete cubicle, and the muzzle flash lit us up and John staggered and went down and Carp was already across the kitchen and banging out the door. I went as far as the door and saw him running toward the back of the lot, aiming for a space between two duplexes. He'd parked one street over, I thought. He was running awkwardly and I knew I could catch him and took two quick steps and was snagged by LuEllen's voice: *"Kidd!"*

I stopped, then went back.

"John's hit. We've gotta move."

Rachel was frozen next to her laptop. John was on his feet, his left hand clapped over his right triceps, and looked at her and said, "I'm a pretty nice guy who lives up north of here on the Mississippi and I've got two kids and a nice wife. If you want to come with me, you can stay with us until we find your mom. But you gotta decide right now."

She looked at him for a long three seconds, then turned and pulled the power cord on her laptop. "I'm coming. I gotta get my bag."

JOHN WAS HIT in the middle of his triceps, and though he didn't think the bone was broken, he thought the bullet might have grooved it. The slug was still inside his arm, and he was shaky as he was walking out to the car: trembling now from postfight adrenaline and shock. We were operating in full daylight yet, but I could hear traffic passing and a plane overhead and music from somewhere, and we didn't seem to be attracting much attention. I've heard a theory that you can shoot a gun once anywhere and get away with it; it's twice or three times that causes a problem. Maybe that's right: in any case, we got John into the backseat of the car without any trouble.

LuEllen slid in beside him, on the wound side, and Rachel, carrying a plastic Wal-Mart shopping bag full of clothes, got in the front passenger seat.

I had no idea where Carp had gone. Never saw a Corolla. And at that point, didn't much care.

LuELLEN LOOKED AT the bullet hole and said, "There's no pulsing blood, but he's bleeding. What do you want to do?"

"Get back to Longstreet," John said. "I can handle it if I can get back home."

"That's six hours, man."

"Doesn't hurt that much yet. Put a pressure bandage on it back at the motel."

"I've got some Vicodin at the motel," LuEllen said, looking at me. "We could get back to Longstreet, if he doesn't bleed to death."

"Is he gonna bleed to death?" I asked. Rachel was now kneeling on the front seat, looking wide-eyed at John over the seat back.

"I don't think so," LuEllen said. "Not if we keep some pressure on it. He may be down a pint when we get there."

SO THAT'S WHAT we did: checked out of the Baton Noir, a pressure bandage, made out of a fresh towel, tight against the wound. Couldn't speed: had to stay right on the limit. On the way north, when we were clear of New Orleans, John placed a long-distance call to Memphis and asked to talk with Andy. He had to wait for a moment, and then said, "Hey, man, this is John. I been bit. Uh-huh. Went in right in the triceps, not too bad, there's no artery bleeding, but it didn't come through." He explained the bandages, and where we were. "We're about five hours out from Longstreet, coming up from New Orleans. I'd appreciate it if you could have George come down and take a look. Uh-huh. Uh-huh. That'd be good. Some shit this chick gave me, um, Vicodin, and it doesn't hurt much. Uh-huh. I'll see you then."

We didn't talk much. I was focused on driving, and John was trying to sleep. We caught snatches of news from various talk-radio stations and it was all about the Norwalk attack; that and the upcoming high school football season. At one point, John said, "Jesus, this is boring," and then, "Carp said we should tell Krause to stay away from him. That'd have to be the senator. Head of the committee."

"Carp said that?" LuEllen asked. "I didn't hear that."

Rachel said, "He asked me if a Mr. Krause had called, or somebody from the government, and I thought he meant you because he said it was a white man and a black man together."

"What'd you tell him?"

"I told him that a white man and a black man came and said they was Bobby's friends, and they were looking for Bobby."

John exhaled and said, "Not good."

"He was gonna kill me, man," Rachel said. "He said he'd shoot me right in the eyeball, and he would have. He's a crazy man. And he *does* want to fuck me."

ONCE IN LONGSTREET, we paused at the local Super 8 just long enough for LuEllen to check in. LuEllen didn't want to see any new faces—she'd already seen too many that day, and there wasn't any point to her coming along. After she had a room,

John and I and Rachel continued to John's place. A new Chevrolet was parked in the driveway, and Marvel was pacing around in the yard. When she saw me coming, she ran up to the car window and looked in the back and saw John and jerked open the door and cried, "How bad? George is here, how bad?"

MARVEL WAS ANGRY and unhappy and scared, and also worried about Rachel, never quite understanding from me what was going on with the girl. George, as it turned out, was a doctor, a big squared-headed, square-chested guy who might have been a tight end in another life, and he was prepared to operate right in the house. He frowned when he first saw me, a white guy, but never asked a question.

John was the calmest of us all, and took some time to explain to Marvel the exact situation with Rachel. As he did that, George was checking his blood pressure: checked it once, checked it again, then nodded. "Good blood pressure," he said to Marvel.

When that was done, John told Marvel to go away—"Go anywhere, I just don't want you fussin' around"—and we went into the kitchen, where George had spread a sterile sheet on the kitchen table.

After washing John's arm with an antiseptic, George gave him a blocking shot, pulled on some sterile plastic gloves and a mask, and went to work on the arm. He didn't have any X rays, but he seemed familiar with gunshot wounds, and located the .22

slug with a probe. He had to work it awhile, with a variety of small tools that would have looked at home on a dentist's tray. In twenty minutes he'd winkled the slug out into his glove.

"Gonna hurt like heck in the morning," he told John. "I'll give you some stuff to take, some painkillers and antiseptics, but it's still gonna be sore."

There was more to it than that—especially on Marvel's side, because she was royally pissed—and sometime after two o'clock, I went down to the Super 8 and fell into bed next to LuEllen.

THE NEXT MORNING, first thing, without bothering with security, I went out on the Super 8 phone line and checked my mailboxes.

There was nothing from the ring, but there was a letter from Bobby.

Kidd:

I've been gone for a while now. I assume that I'm dead, though maybe I'm just too sick to stop this from going out. Here is the important thing: a good friend of mine, who calls himself Lemon, has a selected set of my working documents, and will continue my operation now that I am gone. He does not know you or of you (unless you have a connection that I don't know about) but will take you as a client. To sign on with him you need to identify yourself as 118normalgorgeousredhead

at lemon@ebonetree.net and provide him with a
dump address. I leave that to you, if you want
a new hookup. He's not a bad guy and has sub-
stantial resources. Anyway, good luck and good-
bye; it's been interesting working with you.

—Bobby

That gave me a chill: a voice from beyond, more or less.

LuEllen got the same chill. "Dead people should stay dead. You shouldn't be talking to people after you're dead."

"He might not be completely dead."

"What?"

"He's like Janis Joplin or Frank Sinatra. I heard 'Me and Bobby McGee' on the radio the night I drove up to Jackson. Janis is dead, but I never knew her personally, and I keep hearing her song, so to me, it's the same as if she was still alive. Her song keeps going."

"Yeah, but this . . . I mean, the guy's talking to you, personally."

GEORGE, THE DOCTOR, had gone home. No longer worried about another person seeing her face, LuEllen came with me to John's. Marvel ushered the kids out into the yard, where they wouldn't hear it, and said—shouted—something like this at us:

"I don't know what the three of you could have

been thinking of. What the fuck could you have been thinking of? You already got shot at once. You already got your asses shot at in the trailer. Why did you think he wouldn't shoot you again? You knew the crazy motherfucker had a gun, because he already shot at you. Why didn't you call the cops? Fuck this laptop. What was going on in your stupid heads? Is there anything in there at all? Look at this silly motherfucker sitting at the kitchen table with a big bandage on him and that shit-eating grin on his face like some watermelon-eatin' coon in a goddamned travelin' show. Oh, Lord, why does Thy servant have to put up with this shit? Why is that . . ."

You get the idea.

JOHN WAS OKAY. He was going to be okay, though George was right: he hurt like hell. And Rachel was okay. She and Marvel had come to an understanding, and she sat at the kitchen table with John, pounding down the Cream of Wheat, enjoying the Marvel show. After we got Marvel calmed down— calmed down wasn't exactly the idea, but quieted down, anyway—I went back to the motel and continued mining Carp's laptop, going online to look for names, places, dates. LuEllen went visiting, out to see a farmer friend who lived across the river. She came back in the early afternoon and told me that the Norwalk attack was getting more and more play, and that there was virtually nothing else on television.

"It's like the days after nine-eleven," she said. "It's really brutal."

I KEPT WORKING, since I couldn't think of anything else to do.

Two-thirds of the names in the PalmPilot sync list were identifiable through Google: I'd stick the name in and the information would pop up. Most of the names were associated with the Intelligence Committee and belonged to minor political onions in the Washington stew. Others belonged to computer people, and only a few seemed to be personal.

The personal names were the hardest to get information on. Of the dozen names in the file, I struck out on four of them, and while I found the other eight, I couldn't determine any particular connection between Carp and the person named, except in the case of his dentist.

The *DDC Working Group—Bobby* remained a mystery.

"WE'RE COMING TO a blank wall," I said. We were back at John's, the three of us together. Marvel was down at city hall, perpetrating some commie plot. Rachel had gone with her, and the two kids were taking a nap.

"Could we hack into CNN and when he attacks, figure out where it's coming from?" John asked.

I shook my head. "Not unless we had the phone line, right when he was on it. We'd have to monitor thousands of calls."

"You can't tell just from his address."

"Naw. He can just grab a wi-fi system like we did and ship it from some one-time e-mail address. I'm sure that's what he's doing, or the feds would have grabbed him by now. He's like Bobby—he's coming out of nowhere."

LuEllen asked the key question: "What do you think about him?"

I said, "He might be nuts. He probably killed Bobby, he lost his job and he has no money and he's way deep in debt, he doesn't seem to have any friends, women don't like him, his mother just died, he feels like he's been ripped off by this lawyer."

"Anything in there about his dog?" John asked.

AFTER MORE TALK, I decided to get in touch with Lemon, Bobby's successor. Among other things, I needed to tell him that Bobby was dead, in case he didn't know for sure, and to set up a routine we could use to communicate with each other. I also wanted to check again on the FBI investigation.

That evening LuEllen and I drove down to Greenville and located another warehouse with a friendly wi-fi. I called into the FBI first, went straight to the guy's folder, and found some snappy memos back and forth from Jackson, the essence of which was that

they were getting nowhere. I signed off and went
looking for Lemon.

> *Lemon from 118normalgorgeousredhead:*
>
> *I am a friend of Bobby's and a member of the
> ring. Went to Bobby's house with another member
> of ring, found Bobby murdered and his laptop
> gone. His true name was Robert Fields of Jack-
> son, Mississippi; see news stories on cross-burning
> in Jackson. We have informed National Security
> Agency of his identity in effort to close attacks on
> hack community. We have Bobby's backup DVDs
> but they are encrypted. The current holder of the
> laptop is launching attacks signed Bobby. Appar-
> ently not all files are encrypted; we are trying to
> recover it. We are searching for a man named
> James Carp, a former employee of U.S. Senate
> Intelligence Committee who we believe now holds
> the laptop and is launching the attacks. Any help
> appreciated. We believe it necessary to find Carp
> before government agents. Believe agents already
> searching for him.*
>
> *—Estragon*

I dumped it with a return address, and then went
looking in another direction. We had all of his credit
card numbers from the bills we'd found at his place.
Credit card databases are basic stuff, and I checked
the ones I had for card activity: as far as I could tell,
he hadn't used a credit card for a month.

LuEllen had the inspiration: "Check his mom's cards."

I did, and immediately found a Shell card that was getting activity. It had been used the afternoon of the shooting—once, an hour later, near Slidell. Had he gone back to his mother's place, or was he just heading east on I-10? No way to know from just that. But the next use of the card was at a pump in Meridian, Mississippi, way north on I-59. Then, the next morning—just about the time Marvel had been screaming at us about John—he'd used it to charge gas and food in Chattanooga, Tennessee.

"Going north," I said. "Going fast."

"Headed for Washington."

"Maybe."

A HALF-HOUR HAD passed by the time we finished with the credit cards, and I went back to my dump site. We found a note from Lemon:

Estragon:

YOU MUST RECOVER THE LAPTOP. When I was online with Bobby, he rapidly accessed multiple encrypted laptop files, I believe with encryption codes kept on the laptop itself. I don't know how codes were kept, but maybe disguised as another encrypted file. While Carp may not be able to use them, any encryption center would break them out almost immediately, if that is how

*they are disguised. GET THE LAPTOP. I will
search for Carp and advise at this address. Much
Carp information online. He maintains current
address at 1448 Clay Street, Apt. 523, Washington, D.C.*

I went back with the three e-mail addresses we had
for Carp, suggested that Lemon monitor them, but
not give away his presence:

*We maybe try to find Carp for face-to-face using
e-mail, if nothing else works.*

He was back in a second:

*Will do that, will begin research now. You go to
Washington?*

I went back:

*Think so. Will advise. Will check here every six
hours.*

He said,

Who did burning cross?

I said,

We did—wanted FBI investigation, so we could

monitor. Monitoring now, they find nothing, but should start working on Bobby angle.

He said,

Okay. Will get back in six hours.

"ARE WE GOING to Washington?" LuEllen asked.

"Tell you in a minute. I'm gonna run a little check on this Lemon stuff."

I went back out, looked in a couple of databases, and came up with a phone bill—a big phone bill—for Carp at the Clay Street address in Washington. "There it is," I said.

"So . . ."

"Everything goes there. Carp's headed that way, Lemon says he has a current apartment there, and so does AT&T, and there's this working-group thing. I think that's where it'll happen." I turned and put my arm around her shoulder. "But it's getting a little strange for a simple burglary wench," I said.

"I'll hang on for a while longer. Guy's starting to piss me off."

BACK IN LONGSTREET, we lost John, which we'd expected. Marvel, arms crossed, said, "I'm putting my foot down. If John gets killed, I'll have to find work to support the kids. To do that, I'll have to go out of town and the whole Longstreet project goes down the drain. So I'm telling him, *No*."

John looked abashed, the guy who didn't want to appear to be under his wife's thumb, but who knew she was right. I couldn't see any reason for him to come with us. "It's all gonna be computer stuff at this point. If we need help carrying a body, we'll give you a ring."

"Do that," he said. But I think he wanted to come.

WE LEFT FOR Washington the next morning, driving. We were driving because that's about the only anonymous way to travel around the U.S. Everything else will wind up in a database.

Even by car, anonymity is tough: if you pay for motels or gas with credit cards, if you speed and get a ticket, if you use your cell phone, you're gonna be on a computer, fixed at an exact spot at an exact time. I'd noticed, once—you can see for yourself—that when you pull up to the parking-garage exit booth at Minneapolis–St. Paul International Airport, to pay your money, they'll give you a receipt with your license tag number printed on it. This is four seconds after you pulled up, so your tag is being automatically read somewhere along the line.

Both LuEllen and I had a couple of alter egos who had their own credit cards, all carefully paid, and we used hers in the only motel we needed while heading north. Building an alter ego is almost like identity theft, but backwards. You build a nonexistent life, rather than steal someone else's. It's fun, if you're careful.

The trip was pleasant enough, nine hundred miles or so with the inevitable side trips to look for decent food and places to run. We did it in one long and one reasonably short day, riding up I-40 to I-81 through the heart of the summer, along the Appalachians and up the Shenandoah, then over to Washington on I-66.

The first night, in a mom-and-pop hotel, I went online and found a note from Lemon:

Find six calls last night and this morning from Carp's Washington apartment.

I went back:

On the way. Need anything new.

WE WOUND UP in a Holiday Inn in Arlington, checking in separately, for separate rooms, although we'd only use one or the other. It's better to have a bolt-hole and not need one, than to need one and not have it.

LuEllen checked in first, dropped her bags, then walked back out to the parking garage and gave me her room number. I checked in, put a bag in my room, stuck a sport coat in a closet, rumpled up the bed, hung a "Do Not Disturb" ticket on the door, then toted the rest of my stuff up to LuEllen's. There was one big bed, and the room was decorated with colors that you forgot when you weren't looking at them. Like almost everything now, it smelled of cleaning fluids.

"So," LuEllen said. She pulled back a curtain and looked out: cars and tarmac. The sun was still well above the horizon. "What's first? Carp's?"

"That seems reasonable. Take a look at it, anyway. Watch the news for a while."

WE'D MISSED THE initial newsbreak, being stuck in the car, but Senator David Johnson of Illinois was being accused of covering up a drunk-driving incident involving his oldest daughter. According to what CNN referred to as "the source known as Bobby," Debra Johnson's car had struck a middle-aged bicyclist in downtown Normal, Illinois. The man had suffered a broken wrist and bruises and scrapes, and his bike had been destroyed.

Debra Johnson had paid a ticket for careless driving, but the initial ticket had been for Driving While Intoxicated, issued to her after she had failed a Breathalyzer test. She'd been transported to a local hospital after the accident, complaining of head pain, and had never been taken to police headquarters.

The bicyclist had settled for twenty thousand dollars for pain and suffering. Initial reports said that the money had come from Johnson's campaign fund, which is illegal.

Johnson hadn't yet made a statement, but the vultures were circling. A photograph accompanied the news release—a picture of a drunk-looking young woman standing in a city street, between a cop car and a Saturn, looking at the camera, her eyes bright red with the reflected flash.

"Goddamnit," I said. "He's gotta let up."

"Pouring blood in the water," LuEllen said.

From the Johnson story, CNN went directly to the Norwalk virus–San Francisco story, which the talking head said was "consistent in style with other releases from the Bobby source."

California was planning to sue the federal government for a trillion dollars for damage done by the Norwalk virus experiment, CNN said. The money would be used to provide educational programs on the virus and to close the state's budget gap. A San Francisco law firm had signed up seventy thousand people on its website for a class-action suit claiming that the virus did irreparable damage to the victims' health, destroyed their businesses, drove away tourists, caused building foundations to fail, encouraged cats and dogs to interbreed, and allowed Russian thistle to invade the ecosystem. They also wanted a trillion dollars.

A more serious study by UC Berkeley suggested that four people had died in San Francisco of complications arising from an initial Norwalk virus infection. Weeping members of all four families were shown, the cameras lingering lovingly on the tears rolling down overweight cheeks. The victims had all been good providers.

The government was now denying that the experiment took place, but nobody believed it anymore. There was too much money at stake.

In rounding up the Bobby stories, the anchorman said that the special forces officer accused of executing an Arab prisoner had been flown into Washington and was being questioned by members of the Army's criminal investigation division.

THEN A SECOND guy, a media specialist, went off in another direction: "The one question that everybody is asking is, 'Who is this Bobby, where does he get this stuff, and what does he want?'" To help him with this conundrum, he interviewed two congressmen who were newly enough elected to be fairly clean, two media advisors—public relations guys, we supposed—and the mayor of San Francisco.

After cutting through the bullshit, the answer was that they had no idea of who Bobby was, where he got the stuff, or what he wanted. One of the PR guys guessed that Bobby was a hacker who was getting his information from government databases, said Bobby probably wasn't acting alone, and referred to Bobby's group as "Al-Code-a."

"That's bad," I said.

"Carp's gonna have as a short life span as Bobby," LuEllen said. "If we don't get him soon, somebody else will."

CARP'S APARTMENT WAS in the District, two miles due north of the White House, on Clay Street between Fourteenth and Fifteenth, and a half-block east of Meridian Hill Park. The building was a crappy brown-brick five-story wreck; we cruised it once, and on the back side found that half the tenants had their wash hung out on the balconies. The whole area was run-down, with the kind of street life that suggests you might want to look over your shoulder every once in a while: idle guys, walking around with their hands in their pockets, surrounded by an air of hip-hop cool; clusters of skaters; a drug entrepreneur whose eyes skidded right past me; women in government secretarial dress who walked as if they had a cold wind at their back, shoulders hunched, heads down. Alleys, with people in them; trash on the streets and sidewalks; and some graffiti.

Up the hill from the apartment was Meridian Park, with a fountain that dropped in a pretty series of steps down a long hill toward the south. Down the hill was Fourteenth Street, with some ordinary strip-shopping-center businesses—nail places, a pizza parlor, a diner, a branch bank, like that. There was enough automobile traffic that nobody gave us a second look as we made the pass at Carp's place. The curbs were packed with cars, mostly old and beat-up. No sign of a Corolla.

From his bills, we knew Carp's apartment was on the fifth floor, which, from the outside, appeared to be the top one. As we got to the bottom of the hill, at Fourteenth, an aging Ford Explorer started backing out of a parking spot across the street. I barged through oncoming traffic and grabbed the spot.

We were now two hundred feet from the apartment entrance, parked in front of a place called either Lost and Damaged Freight or Major Brand Overstocks, or both; I never figured it out. We sat and watched for a while, then started working on a *New York Times* crossword puzzle, hung up on an eight-letter word across the middle of the puzzle, the clue being, "Old grape's reason for being?"

"Raison d'être?" LuEllen suggested. She took the words right out of my mouth.

"Eleven letters," I said, counting them on my fingers. "Unless I'm spelling it wrong."

"Look it up. Gotta be 'raison' something-or-other. The question mark in the clue means it's a pun."

"Ah, man." But I got out the laptop and called up the Merriam-Webster. Eleven letters.

We were in the car for two hours, off and on, watching the sun go down, still working on the puzzle, hung up on the old grape. There was nothing going on in my brain that would answer that question, but I was still working on it when the streetlights came on.

"Better think about what we're gonna do," I said.

"Shush," LuEllen said. "Look at these guys."

Two guys were walking up the street toward Carp's apartment. They were hard to make out in the fading light, but one was black, one white.

"The guys from Carp's place, the mobile home?" I whispered, even though there was nobody around.

"I think so. They look right. They're built right," she said. "They must be tracking him, just like we are." The two stood on the low stoop for a minute, looking at the street, then up at the face of the apartment. One was dressed in khaki slacks, a T-shirt, and a sport coat, the other in slacks and a golf shirt. They were not from the neighborhood.

"Cops of some kind?" I suggested, as they disappeared inside the building.

"Probably not exactly cops," LuEllen said. "They're not carrying guns, unless they're those little ankle things. They don't have all that shit clipped to their belts that cops have. No beepers, no cell phones, no cuffs, nothing to conceal it with."

"So we know Carp's place is hot. Somebody's inside, probably the feds."

"Probably. All they'd need is one guy inside, in the hallway or on the stairs on the way up, and we'd be toast."

My eye was pulled to another too-fast movement in the direction of Meridian Park. "Uh-oh. Look at this, look at this," I said. A bulky figure was jogging down the sidewalk. "That's fuckin' Carp," I said.

"This guy's a blond, a blond." Floppy blond hair fell around the jogger's rounded shoulders.

"I don't care, that's Carp," I said. "Let's go."

"Let's go where?" She caught my arm.

"Up the hill. See what happens. See what we can see."

"I don't know," she said, with a tone of urgency, but I was out of the car, and heard her car door slam behind me as I crossed Fourteenth and headed into Clay Street, toward the apartment.

Up ahead, most of a block away, Carp dodged a car and ran up the steps into the building. I was moving that way and LuEllen called, "Kidd, slow down, slow down."

I slowed. Slow is always best. "He didn't have the laptop," I said. "It's either in his apartment or it's in his car. If we can find the car, a red Corolla, it's gotta be close."

"But if it's in the apartment, then somebody else is in on the deal. Maybe he's still working with these guys. Maybe they were in New Orleans to meet him, and we chased him away before they could meet."

She had my arm again, restraining me, just a bit of back pressure above the elbow. But I was moving along and we'd started up the hill when we heard the shots.

This was not a .22. This was three or four shots from something a lot bigger. We stopped, then LuEllen said, "Turn around, turn around," and we turned around so we were facing back downhill. A black guy was sitting on a stoop at an apartment across the street, reading a newspaper, and when he heard the shots, stood up quickly and stepped inside his door.

"Keep walking, keep walking," LuEllen said. We were walking downhill, looking over our shoulders, stumbling on the uneven sidewalk. Then the white guy we'd seen go inside the apartment, the white guy from the trailer, we thought, smashed through Carp's apartment door, fell down the stoop, tried to get up, and fell down again, into the street, hurt bad.

Carp was through the door, on top of him with the gun. He fired a single shot into the white guy's head, and the white guy went down like a pancake, flat on his face.

"Ah, Jesus," I said, and LuEllen was chanting, "No, no, no," and her fingernails dug into my forearm.

Carp ran up the hill toward the park, stuffing the gun in his pocket as he went.

Above us, on the second floor of Carp's building, a woman threw open a window and began screaming, "Nine-one-one, nine-one-one, nine-one-one," and I wondered why she didn't call it herself, until it occurred to me that she didn't have a phone. An old white man came out on the steps and pointed a shaky finger at the vanishing Carp. "There he goes. There he goes," but there was nobody to look, and nobody to chase him.

"Don't run," LuEllen said. Her fingernails were digging into me now. Carp was gone. "Do not run. Just walk away. Just walk."

"Who were those guys?" I wondered.

"I don't know, but I bet Carp thought he knew. I bet he thought they were you and John."

"You think?"

"A white guy and a black guy, coming on to him just like you came on to him in the trailer and at Rachel's."

"But he knows John's shot."

"He doesn't *know* it. He knows he fired the pistol, but he was running before John went down." We could hear sirens now, and LuEllen pushed me down to the corner. "The cops. Keep walking. They'll want witnesses, and people saw us."

WE CROSSED FOURTEENTH, got into my car, and carefully drove away, going north. A few blocks up, I turned over to Fifteenth and followed it down past Meridian Park. We could look down the hill toward Carp's, where two white District squad cars were jamming up the street. No sign of an ambulance, although there were more sirens in the air.

LuEllen said, "If we keep doing this, I might have to go out for some Hamburger Helper."

"Naw. C'mon, goddamnit." Hamburger Helper was her euphemism for cocaine. She'd had her nose into the stuff since I'd known her, and I'd given up trying to wean her off of it. But I hate that shit. If American civilization falls, it'll happen because of the drug monkey on our backs.

"Might need to," she said.

"Then why don't you go home," I said. "Better to have you out of it than sticking that shit up your nose."

"Really?"

"It's gonna kill you," I said, avoiding the question. I really wanted her to stick around.

She was silent for a while, and then, a mile out of the motel, her voice morose, shaky, she said, "Raisinet."

"What?" I was still irritated.

"Eight letters. Old grape's reason for being."

11

FEAR AND TREMBLING and a sickness unto death. We held everything together until the execution began to sink in. LuEllen started with, "That motherfucker. That motherfucker. He just killed the guy. The guy was laying in the street, and he just shot him, the motherfucker. . . ."

I kept saying, "I don't know, I don't know."

"He was helpless. Did you see that? He was face-down in the street. I mean, Carp already shot him, he was hurt and Carp just walks up and blows him away. Bam."

With this stunned, incoherent rambling, we drove out of the District back to the hotel, where we sat around looking at CNN and every once in a while breaking out with another *motherfucker*.

That evening, still in shock, we went looking for another wi-fi connection. We didn't have to go far: the Washington area is what you call a target-rich environment. We found a new brick office building not far from the hotel in Rosslyn, got a strong signal, parked in the street beside it, hooked up, went out to the FBI, and popped the Jackson file.

The feds were looking at a guy named Stanley Clanton, who'd been kicked out of the local KKK for being crazy. He'd told friends around the time that Bobby was murdered that he'd been out "rolling a tire," which was apparently nut-group slang for assault on a black man.

"She didn't tell them," LuEllen said, flabbergasted. "Welsh didn't tell them that he's Bobby. They're chasing some fuckin' cracker."

"Ah, man," I said. "If they get on this guy, I'm gonna have to tell somebody that we did the cross."

LuEllen shrugged. She was leaning over into my half of the seat, her face next to mine, looking at the tiny screen. "Why? He might not have killed Bobby, but he sounds like the kind of asshole who's just looking for the opportunity."

"LuEllen, for Christ's sake, I'm not letting some guy I don't know go to prison for something I did, and he didn't."

"Whatever," she said. She was glum, bitter, still reacting to the killing.

———

DURING THE TRIP north from Mississippi, I'd
laboriously gone through the list in the *DDC Working Group—Bobby* file, searching the names on the
Internet, and eventually nailed most of them down.
The names belonged to government employees, a few
of whom were identified in their credit reports as
working for the Justice Department. Three were
members of the Senate staff. The computer numbers
went into a Justice Department system somewhere in
northern Virginia. When I called them, I got a log-in
screen, and nothing more: no way to pry up the
edges.

Eventually, I wrote a memo, and e-mailed it to the
staffers on the Deep Data Correlation working group
list in Carp's laptop:

> *Senator Krause's senior staff will begin next week
> to compile a daily log of the senator's activities
> and positions which may be of interest to key per-
> sons working with the senator and the DDCWG.
> This will be a continuing commentary, somewhat
> like the web-logs now popular on the Internet. The
> log will allow space for questions to the senator,
> and internal arguments concerning positions on
> the issues of the day. If you would like key-person
> access to the log, please supply us with a user name
> and a password that would allow you to access the
> system. You may reply to . . .*

I had to stop and go into my own notebook, and

look up the address of one of the sterile dump sites I keep for this kind of one-time messaging.

As I was typing it in, LuEllen asked, "What good is that gonna do?"

"Everybody likes a chance to talk to the boss," I said. "But nobody wants to remember more passwords than they have to—everybody's already got too many. At least a couple of these guys are going to send me the same name and password they use to sign on to the committee system."

"Yeah?"

"Never fails," I said. I pushed the button that sent the memo. "But we won't hear back until tomorrow."

"So let's go get a decent dinner. Can we do that? I mean, I'm so screwed up."

"Yeah."

"Something French. With snails in it. Or diseased goose liver. Or Italian. I could do Italian, but I'm pretty fuckin' tired of pan-fried catfish."

Before we left, I checked for William Heffron of MacLean, Virginia, one of the guys who'd visited Bobby's trailer. I found his home address and phone number, but no employer listing. Going back through one of the credit agencies, I found *U.S. Department of Justice, 1989–1996,* and then *U.S. Government, 1996 to present.* That usually wasn't enough for a credit agency. They wanted specifics, and since they had settled without them, I assumed that Heffron was an intelligence operative of some kind.

"He's dead," LuEllen said.

"I know. We'll probably find out more about him tomorrow."

I closed down the notebook, and we went looking for a restaurant.

I'M PROBABLY TOTALLY and utterly wrong about this, if totally and utterly don't mean the same thing, but I've always gotten the impression that half of the people in Washington are sleeping with someone they shouldn't be sleeping with, in either the sexual sense or the political sense, or both. As a result, the city and the surrounding suburbs have these great little restaurants with tables where you can't be seen. Exactly the opposite, say, of LA.

We wound up right across the Potomac at Birdie—singular—a French cafe in Georgetown, a half-block off M Street, where LuEllen ate some things that nobody should ever eat. I stayed with rock doves, which I'm pretty sure are pigeons, but looked, on the plate, the size of sparrows with drumsticks like kitchen matches. They also had dainty, feathery little uncooked plant leaves across their roasted breasts. I lifted the leaves off and looked around, and LuEllen said, "No, don't throw them on the floor, give them to me."

We had a bottle of wine with the dinner, and because we couldn't be seen or heard, talked about the Carp pursuit.

"The thing that's interesting is that the FBI is chasing Bobby's killer, but they still think it's a racial killing," LuEllen said. She was wearing black, as she always did when she got into a decent restaurant east of Ohio, and small diamond earrings. "But we know a high-up security person knows that Bobby was Bobby, so they ought to be all over it, but they're not."

I poked a fork at her. "And somebody else, not the FBI, is chasing Carp, and now they might have a couple of dead bodies," I said. "Did they know that Carp killed Bobby? Did they know he's the guy dumping the stuff under Bobby's name? Or is this some kind of operation? Is it the NSA, which it might be, because Rosalind Welsh apparently isn't talking to the FBI? But one of the guys looking for Carp used to be with the Justice Department, and the FBI is a branch of the Justice Department. What the hell does that mean?"

"Whoever it is, we've got government people killing each other."

"No. We've got Carp killing government people. Like you said, those guys didn't even look like they were armed. They did the same thing we did, stumbling into him. I really don't think the government goes around killing people . . . except like in wars, and so on."

"I don't have your faith," LuEllen said. "I know there are cops who've killed people who pissed them off."

"Sure. But they did it on their own. And maybe somebody higher up didn't look into it as deeply as they should, but basically it's not policy. If the killing's found out, there's a trial."

"So? So we've got an outlaw group."

"Maybe," I said. "I'll tell you one thing—if the FBI doesn't figure out that Robert Fields was Bobby, and if Welsh doesn't tell them, then *we'll* have to. Carp ain't walking away from this thing."

"We don't even know that Carp's the guy who killed Bobby. Maybe it was these two guys," LuEllen suggested.

"Oh, bullshit." I swallowed most of a wing. "These guys were a couple of schmucks. And we know Carp is nuts. When we were in the trailer, the first time we ever saw him, he jumped up and fired a gun at John and me without ever asking who we were or where we were from. Nuts."

"Okay, he's nuts," she said. "There are a couple things we've got to know, though, that we don't know yet—the biggest one is, is Carp working for someone? If he's working for someone, then he may have already given the computer away. Or given up copies. And we may run into more trouble than we think, if we ever find him."

"Yeah . . . maybe we'll figure out something tomorrow."

"Hope he doesn't pop something else on the news," LuEllen said. "He's already got a feeding frenzy. What more does he want?"

———

WE SPENT A little time fooling around that evening, in sort of a sad way, and in the quiet after the sex, LuEllen told me why she was thinking of quitting her life.

"No big deal, it was just a TV show. I was down in Texas and they showed this thing about women in prison. They were all doing long terms for murder and . . . well, murder, mostly—and I started thinking that I could end up like them. Just one fuck-up. One alarm that I don't see, or maybe a booby trap or I get hurt, somehow. I'd be in there. It wasn't the jail so much that looked bad, it was the women. They all looked really messed up. Hurt. They looked sad . . . the saddest people you can imagine. I'd hang myself before I got that way."

There wasn't much to say. She was right, it could happen. To either of us.

She went on: "The saddest thing was the day their kids could come visit, and how happy they were to see their kids. Some of the kids didn't even seem to remember their moms that well. And sometimes the women thought their kids might be coming and then they wouldn't show up and they'd just sit in a corner and cry. And I thought, I don't even have anybody who'd come to see me if I was inside."

I said, "LuEllen, you know—"

"You couldn't come," she said. "I wouldn't let you see me that way, even if you wanted to. But I was thinking, if I got caught, nobody would even know who I was. Know my name. Nobody but a couple of people I went to junior high school with. Nobody would even know." She sat up suddenly. "My life has been okay so far. I didn't have a lot of choices. It was this or maybe be a practical nurse like my mom, running pans of shit around a nursing home."

"You're too smart for that."

"In this country, smart isn't enough. You've got to be taught right, from the start. You've got to get that education, or have money from your parents, you just . . ." She flopped back on the bed. "I don't know. But I've gotta find something else to do. I still get the rush, I still get high on it, when I'm inside somewhere, but I gotta get out of this before it's too late."

That made for a great night's sleep. That and recurring dreams that featured an overweight man facedown in the street. . . .

THE NEXT DAY was a Saturday. We both woke early, twitched around a little, trying to get that last little patch of sleep, and I finally gave up and found the remote and clicked on the TV. The *Menu* screen came up with the day, date, and time. I hadn't been paying attention, and when they registered with me, I said, "Saturday. Damnit. If nobody gets our e-mail, we won't get any passwords back."

"I bet political people check their e-mail every five

minutes," LuEllen said. She sat up and stretched. "Let's get breakfast and then go see."

While she cleaned up, I clicked around to the local channels, looking for news. I found it, but there was nothing about the shooting the night before. We went out, ate French toast—she was overly cheerful, and maybe a little embarrassed about the talk the night before, revealing herself like that—and then we got online at our big wi-fi building.

LuEllen was right about political people. They check their e-mail. Seventeen replies had come in to the dump site. I transferred them to Carp's machine, then called into the first number of the DCC working group. I got the log-in screen and started running names. Darryl Finch, the sixth guy on the list, had given us *Dfinch/Bluebird9* in our solicitation for the senator's log. That didn't work, but *Dfinch/bluebird5* punched us right through.

Dfinch/bluebird5 got me into a personnel computer. Lots of details on the staffers, but no files on James Carp or Bobby. Then, browsing through a file on a Linda Soukanov, I spotted a letter that supported a complaint from a coworker against Carp. Soukanov was with the working group. She said that she had witnessed Carp paying "unwelcome attention" to a coworker in the next cubicle. The coworker was identified as a Michelle Strom, with the Bobby project.

"Excellent," I said.

"Got something?" LuEllen was bored.

"Maybe . . . give me a minute."

I pulled the file on Michelle Strom and found a complaint that said that Carp had touched her in an elevator, "pressing his front against my back," and that he'd one other time touched her breast under the pretext of looking at her identification photograph. She said she wouldn't have reported the incidents because she wasn't sure that he had intentionally touched her, but she'd heard reports now from other women. . . .

I looked at my senator-log sign-up list. Nothing from Linda Soukanov, but Michelle Strom was there: *Mickey/DasMausl.* God help me.

I signed out of *Dfinch* and tried *Mickey/DasMausl* and failed, spent five minutes going through possible combinations and got in on *Mickey/Mauser.* All things come to hackers who are patient.

Most things, anyway. I got into Michelle Strom's space, and found that I could push memos or reports into the system, but nothing could be retrieved without another code. From the way the front-end was set up, I suspected the link would shut me down rather than let me experiment—and would tell the system people that somebody was trying to crack the system after getting in with Strom's password.

"Stone wall," I said.

I got in on four more name/password combinations, but the security was better than I'd hoped. I could get administrative stuff, but I couldn't get any operations files. Before I shut down, I entered *William Heffron* into a general search engine and immediately popped a half-dozen reports from Washington TV-news websites. I pulled the first one and read to LuEllen:

"Two Virginia men were shot to death at a Meridian Park apartment building Friday night by an assailant who shot one man on the building's stairway and another as he fled to the sidewalk outside the building, District police said Saturday.

"Terrance Small of Alexandria and William Heffron of McLean, both government employees with a Justice Department data processing center, were apparently on their way to visit a friend when they were shot. Police speculated that the men had inadvertently stumbled into a drug transaction at the Marlybone Apartments on Clay Ave.

"Police say each of the men was shot once in the head at extremely close range, execution-style, in addition to suffering wounds to the body. Neither of the men had criminal records, police said. Terry Banks, a supervisor at the Justice Department's Division of Data Integration, said, 'This is a terrible tragedy. These were fine men; everybody liked them. I just don't understand how these things can happen. The people in this division will be devastated.'"

There was more, but that was the substance of it.

"A drug deal? The government's not even talking to the cops when their own people get murdered," LuEllen said. "They're as nuts as Carp is."

"Maybe they really don't know," I said. "Maybe they don't know what Heffron and Small were doing there, that Carp has an apartment there." I went back into the search engine, looking for Carp, and got only fish-related sites. "Nothing at all on Jimmy or James Carp."

LuEllen shook her head, the corners of her mouth turned down. I'm a skeptic when it comes to government; she's a couple steps further along that road than I am.

"SO NOW WHAT?" LuEllen twisted around in her seat, looking out for passersby. "We've been here a long time."

"If you had to get better entry equipment, instead of the Target stuff, could you get it close by?"

"In Philly," she said. "You met the guy."

"I thought he was just guns." He'd once armed me for a confrontation in West Virginia. Another thing I try not to dream about.

"We can order stuff," she said.

"He creeps me out."

"'Cause he's a creep," she said. "But he can get the stuff and he's trustworthy. We're going in somewhere?"

I rubbed my face, thinking about it. "Michelle Strom is interesting," I said. "I'd like to look around her apartment. Let me . . ."

I went back into the personnel computer using the

Dfinch name, and pulled Strom's file. She was single, thirty-three, with a B.A. in history and Russian, and an M.A. in Russian. She had some kind of supervisory capacity, though I couldn't tell exactly how many people she supervised. There were two good photos of her, apparently used for her ID card. I copied down her home address, and her home, office, and cell phone numbers.

"So . . ."

"If we could get in and out, without her knowing, it would probably be worth it."

"Would we need time inside?"

"Mmm . . . yeah," I said. "Eight, ten, not more than fifteen minutes."

"That's half a lifetime . . . so tell me why, in twenty-five words or less."

This was a joke with us—if you couldn't explain why you were breaking into a place in twenty-five words or less, you hadn't thought it through. I said, "Everybody takes work home, nowadays, even secret work. We can't break into Strom's office, we can't get her online, so we hit her apartment. How many words was that?"

"Less than twenty-five," she said. "If nowadays is one word."

LuELLEN MADE A call and we ran up to Philly. We were going to see a guy named Drexel, gun dealer to the trade, so to speak. I'd met him twice, on other trips to the Washington area. On those trips, he'd been living in an accountant-looking suburban house. This time, he was way west of the city, in a truck-garden exurb, in a house a third smaller than his earlier one.

He met us at the door, smiled, and said, "Package got here fifteen minutes ago."

"Nice house," LuEllen said, looking around as he let us in. The place was furnished in Early Twenty-first Century Discount Scandinavian. "Why'd you move?"

"Soon as my daughter got out of school, she and my wife left," he said. He was tall and thin, wore rimless glasses, and looked like the farmer in the Grant Wood painting *American Gothic.* He'd always been pleasant enough, though creepy, and too prissy for a man who dealt in illegal firearms. An underground gun dealer should, at a minimum, have an eye patch. He led us through the basement door, picking up a laptop as he went. "I guess they spent a few years not liking me."

"Jeez," LuEllen said, as though that were unthinkable. She glanced at me, the glance telling me *don't say it.*

We followed him down the basement steps. His old house had had a basement workshop, too, and this one was much like the other: neatly kept, everything in rigid, soldierly order, and very dry. There were a lot of wires in the ceiling, and I suspected the place had excellent security. "Yes, well—I wish they'd told me earlier, so we wouldn't have had to put up with each other all those years. I didn't like them much, either."

"So you sold the house," LuEllen said.

"Had to. Wife got the money, but at least I've got no strings attached. No alimony. I'm happy." He went to a workbench, flicked on an overhead light, pulled open a drawer, and took out a plastic carrying case. "These little babies are hard to find. I think they might have started out with the CIA—but wherever they started out, the police try to keep track of them."

"This one's clean?" LuEllen asked, as she popped open the case.

"Taken from a locksmith who died . . . natural causes, a heart attack."

Inside the case was a box about the size of a pack of cigarettes, but painted flat black. A probe stuck out the top of the box, with a hairlike plastic bristle sticking out of that; on the bottom of the box was a USB port. The plastic carrying case also contained a USB data key and a short USB cable.

"There are five extra fibers," Drexel told LuEllen. "If you mess them all up, I don't know how you'd replace them. They're supposed to be pretty sturdy, though."

"They're okay," LuEllen said. "I've used one once, but I rented it. Always wanted one of my own. How much?"

"Seven thousand."

She bobbed her head. "I've got the cash in the car. But let's plug it in first."

DREXEL TURNED ON his laptop, explaining to me that the USB data key simply held the software for any Windows-based laptop, and that he'd loaded it into his laptop when he was buying the device from his supplier. He brought the program up, and with a USB cable, plugged the black box into the laptop.

"There's a Yale lock on the storeroom door, if you want."

"Thanks." LuEllen carried the laptop and the black box over to the door and slipped the fiber optic into the lock.

The bristle, which was about the thickness of a broom straw, was a piece of fiber optic that acted like a tiny camera lens, and had been developed for heart and vascular surgery.

When you pushed the fiber-optic probe into a normal lock, you could actually see, on the laptop screen, the pins and the key cuts inside the lock. If you knew your locks—LuEllen wasn't a specialist, but she knew enough—you could cut yourself a key. The software made it unnecessary to actually see the interior of the lock, as it would specify a key blank and spacing for almost any lock in use in the U.S. or Europe, but, Drexel said, most people liked to see the inside, too. "Gives them confidence that the numbers are right."

We were watching as LuEllen probed the lock, and you could see the guts of the lock right on the laptop screen. She watched, grunted, and shut it all down. "I'll get the cash," she said. She handed Drexel the box and headed up the stairs.

AS SHE WENT, Drexel reached up to turn off the light over the workbench, but as he did it, I put a finger to my lips and he paused. When LuEllen was walking away from the top of the stairs, I asked, "Would you have a small gun? Something handy, not too noisy? But threatening-looking?"

"It's best not to threaten people with a gun," Drexel said solemnly. "If you get to the point of taking it out, it's best to pull the trigger. And at that point, you probably shouldn't worry too much about the noise. The difference in noise between a .380 and a .357 isn't that critical, if you're shooting it off in a motel with people all around. It'll be noticeable either way, so you might as well have something that'll do the job."

"So what do you have?"

He looked pleased: guns had always been his first love, and he enjoyed dealing them. "That really depends on what you're going to use it for."

"Look, I really don't want to get too deep into this, and I'd like to get it done before my friend gets back."

"You're not . . ." His eyebrows went up.

I didn't understand the question for a second, then said, "Jesus Christ, *no*, I'm not gonna shoot *her*. We're dealing with a guy who's a little nuts, but if I take a gun, LuEllen might argue."

He nodded. "Good. I'm glad it's not her. She's always been a good customer and I would hate to lose her. Okay, you're not an enthusiast, you need it for close-up protection, nothing fancy. I have just the thing. Seven hundred dollars."

WE WERE CLIMBING the stairs when LuEllen came back, the pistol pulling down my pants pocket. It was a Smith & Wesson hammerless revolver—hammerless so it wouldn't snag on your clothes when you pulled it out in a hurry—loaded with six rounds of .38 special. Guns are for killing. People can make a sport out of shooting, a pastime, a hobby, but all of those things are a perversion of a gun's intention. Guns are for killing and handguns are for killing people; I wasn't comforted by its presence.

And I told LuEllen about it as soon as we cleared Drexel's.

"Didn't ask me about it," she said.

"I didn't think about it until we were down there in the basement," I said. I took the gun out of my pocket and pushed it under the seat. "I didn't want you to veto it."

"At this point, I wouldn't have," she said. "Not after we saw the execution. But it bums me out . . . but why'd you tell me now?"

"If we get caught inside, and we have a gun . . ."

"Yeah."

In most states, armed illegal entry will get you a few additional years. Not that we'd get caught.

12

MICHELLE STROM LIVED in an Arlington apartment, like half of the other DDC employees. The apartment was in a complex fifteen minutes from our hotel. From the street, it was a tidy, well-kept collection of six-story yellow-brick buildings, with a swimming pool deck and parking garage. There were a bunch of trendy chain stores—Crate & Barrel, Pottery Barn, Williams-Sonoma, Barnes & Noble—as part of the same complex of buildings, and a lot of pedestrian traffic around it all.

"Well-off singles, mostly," LuEllen said. "Won't be any trouble getting in the door. Hope the corridor outside Strom's place isn't too busy."

We began by figuring out which part of the building she was in, and then calling her. No answer.

Then I sat in the car, on the street, where I could

see one of the entry doors. LuEllen, carrying a cloth
tote with the laptop and probe inside, sat on a retain-
ing wall a few yards down from the entrance, as though
waiting for a car to pick her up. When I saw a man inside, walking toward the door, I gave her a beep with
the car horn. She bounced to her feet, hurried up the
steps with her key ring in her hand. By that time, the
guy was coming through the door, and she caught it,
smiled at him, and went through.

I sat in the car, not a care in the world, for five
minutes. Then she reappeared, looking positively
perky—she loved doing this. I don't know how in the
hell she thought she'd be able to quit. She walked to
the car, hopped in, said, "Routine Schlage," and we
were out of there.

The software gave us the blank number and we
stole three blanks from a suburban Home Depot.
We also got a tiny triangular file, which we paid for.
LuEllen took three hours to make three keys, looking
at the software designs and working very carefully.
When she was done, we drove back to the apartment
and tried them on the outer door. All three worked,
but outside locks are notoriously loose. We probably
wouldn't have that kind of luck with Strom's lock.

"Single, early thirties, Saturday night. What are
the chances?" LuEllen asked.

"I don't know. We can call."

"Better off if we could watch her, isolate her, then
you go in while I make sure she's out of the way."

"In a perfect world," I said. "But we're short on time."

She thought about it for a minute. "We call her, and if she's in, we go away. Maybe until Monday. If there's no answer, you go in. I do my waiting-impatiently act in the downstairs hallway, and if she comes in, I call you on your cell, and you get out."

"If she still looks like her ID photos. And that assumes she's not somewhere else in the building, and that she won't come in the end doors instead of the main door."

"It assumes she'll take an elevator instead of walking up the steps," LuEllen said. "Nothing we can do about it if she's at the next-door neighbor's. She'll walk in on your ass and you'll have to chop her head off and make it look like Carp did it."

"Got it. I'll draw the sign of the Carp on the walls."

"In her blood."

"Naturally."

We tended toward heartiness when we suspected we were about to do something stupid, of which there had been a couple of instances in the past.

We went back to the apartment complex, walked arm in arm past all the commercial stuff, window-shopping, looking up at where LuEllen thought Strom's apartment was. The window was dark. We called from the Barnes & Noble. No answer. Called her cell phone, and she picked it up on the third ring. "Sharon?" I asked.

"I'm afraid you've got the wrong number," she said. Strom was a natural soprano, and sounded like a nice woman—a polite one, anyway. I could hear other voices in the background, and said, "I'm sorry, is this . . . ?" I gave a number close to hers.

"No, you're very close, but you've got two of the numbers turned around. Okay?"

"Okay," I said. "I hope I didn't disturb you." Another voice, and a clank—dishes—and we both hung up.

I looked at LuEllen. "She's in a restaurant."

"Could be five minutes from here," LuEllen said. "Probably is."

"No better time," I said. "Let's go."

I HAD THE keys in my pocket, my laptop under my arm. We went through the front door, and up. LuEllen pointed me at Strom's and I tried the first key. The door popped open. "I'm a genius," LuEllen said. "I'll be downstairs."

I stepped inside the apartment and called out, "Hello?"

No response. I pushed the door shut with my foot, tripped a light switch, and called, a bit louder, "Hello? Anybody home?"

No answer. I moved quickly, one fast lap of what turned out to be a two-bedroom apartment, looking for the lights on a burglar alarm key pad. No pad. The place smelled of plants and the acrid odor of plant food. I found, in the kitchen, six African violets, all freshly watered, sitting on a draining board across the sink.

Then I headed into the second bedroom, which had a cozy office setup, including a desktop Dell and a good office chair. A black-leather satchel, the kind prosperous women executives use as briefcases, sat next to the chair. I brought the machine up, then checked the satchel. Inside was the usual collection of office junk—pens, pencils, Kleenex, an airlines sleep mask, a telephone connection cord for a laptop but no laptop, a spare pair of regular glasses and a pair of prescription sunglasses, a hundred or so business cards, and, tucked away in a pen slot, a gray USB memory key. Terrific.

I stuck the key into my laptop's USB slot, dumped a half megabyte of something into my hard drive, and put the key back into the satchel. No time to see what it was. I'd been inside the apartment for three or four minutes and was already feeling the pressure.

I sat at her machine, hooked it into my laptop, and started dumping her document files to the laptop's hard drive. Most of the files had unpromising names like *Budget* and *Letters*, and I didn't have a lot of confidence that I was breaking out her computer passwords. While I waited for the files to clear, I checked her desk drawers, the bottom of the keyboard, the underside of the desk, and minutely examined the satchel for any anomalous number-letter combinations that might be passwords. I found nothing.

Probably was around somewhere, I thought. High-security places tell their employees to come up with passwords of random numbers, letters, and symbols, so that they can't be cracked by hackers doing research. The problem is, nobody can remember the high-security numbers, so they get written down.

A better policy would be to tell the password holder to think of a person or place that's significant to him, subtract a letter or two, and add a significant number or two. Say, your father's middle name backwards, with your mother's birthday attached. That way, you'd have a password that you could work out, would never come up in a hacker's dictionary, and wouldn't be written down so it couldn't be stolen. As it is, most high-security passwords look like the registration code on the back of a Windows software box.

And I couldn't find one. I found an address book, flipped through it, looked in a checkbook, scanned a small Rolodex, flipped through the pages of a wall calendar featuring English kitchen gardens. Still nothing. The document files cleared, and I went into her computer, looking for other files, finding not much.

The cell phone rang. A single ring—LuEllen's signal that I'd been inside for ten minutes. Now we were pushing it. Too many things happen when you stay inside too long. People notice lights, decide to stop by for a visit. People come home.

Getting nowhere. Shut down the computer. Gave up.

———

I CALLED LuELLEN on the way out, and when I got downstairs, she was already walking across the parking lot to the car. I got in, and she said, "What?"

"I don't know. Maybe nothing."

"Bummer."

"Well, I dumped a lot of stuff to the computer, but most of it looked personal."

"She's a Russian major, she's gotta have a good memory—maybe she just memorizes her codes."

"Maybe. But a lot of those places change passwords every month, or every week."

I GOT HER passwords, all right, and because of Lu-Ellen, a lot faster than I might have.

At the hotel, I started by looking at the stuff I'd dumped from the USB memory key. When I opened it, I found a novel, chapters 1 through 17.

"Ah, Christ, she's writing a novel," I said. I scanned a page. "She writes okay."

"What's it about?" LuEllen was a reader.

"Some mystery thing," I said. "She's got this bounty-hunter chick or something. I don't know. Not gonna tell us anything about the working group."

I quit the novel files and started through the stuff I'd stripped from her desktop. First up was Strom's personal budget, and it was a little surprising. She was well-off, for a thirty-three-year-old mid-level bureaucrat. Digging in a little, I found that she'd had an inheritance from her grandfather, nearly half a million dollars, all nicely invested with Fidelity. The next file up was what looked like a series of letters, but I couldn't be sure, since they were written in Russian.

I closed that out and rubbed the back of my neck. "I'm gonna go stand in a shower for a few minutes. I've been spending too much time in front of a screen."

"We oughta go out and run," LuEllen said. She stood up and stretched. "I'm getting tight myself."

"So let's find a place," I said. "I'll do the shower later. Let me pee and wash my face."

"Sit down for a minute, I'll do your shoulders." I sat. She did my neck and shoulders, and as she started on my shoulders, looked at the laptop and asked, "Which one is the novel?"

I reached out and clicked on it, Word came up, and the novel ran down the screen. LuEllen was running her knuckles up and down the sides of my spine and I'd just said, "Jeez, that feels good," when she stopped, leaned forward, and scrolled down the novel.

"What?"

"This isn't right," she said. "How do I get the next chapter up?"

I selected *CH2* from the list. She read for a moment, then said, "She didn't write this. This is a Janet Evanovich novel. I read it a couple of years ago."

"Really?"

"Yeah." She reached out and touched the screen, which she did occasionally, and which always left an oily fingerprint. "Novels come on computer files now?"

"I know you can get some for PalmPilots . . . e-books. I didn't know you could get them in Word format. Maybe the group steals them."

She went back to rubbing my shoulders and said, "I couldn't read a book that way. Maybe kids can. You know, people who had their first computer when they were babies."

"Not a friendly way to read a book," I said. "Great for reference stuff, though." A thought struck me and I said, "Hang on a minute. Let me look at something." I spent a couple of minutes combining the files into one large new file, then ran a search for the numeral 1. There was a single hit, but not relevant.

I got another nonrelevant hit with 2, but with 3, I got a hit on *39@1czt8*p** and on *ll5f4!35lp0*.

"She's buried her passwords in the novel," I said. Finding them felt like my fifth-grade Christmas, and I laughed out loud. "Pretty goddamn smart. Instantly accessible and completely portable with the data key, and totally invisible."

"Wonder if she talked to Evanovich about it?" Lu-Ellen asked. But she was pleased with herself; I know she was pleased because she gave me a noogie.

———

WE DROVE BACK to our wi-fi spot, signed in on Strom's account, then took the next step, pushing into the files. I had two passwords to choose from.

"No way to tell?" LuEllen asked. We were set up right on the street, in a dark spot.

"Not that I see."

"Do a scissors-paper-rock. You're the first code, I'm the second one."

We did a scissors-paper-rock, three rounds, and then she won. We put in the second code, and the remote computer cracked open like an egg.

"Shazam," I said.

EVERYBODY PROBABLY HAS a few moments in his life when he feels like he's fallen down Alice's rabbit hole. That's what I felt like when I got into *DDC Working Group—Bobby.*

To begin with, DDC was the official name, with no Bobby—but Bobby was all over the place. The DDC, it seemed, was an actual experimental arm for a package of anti-terrorism techniques being developed by the military and the various intelligence organizations. One of their tests was to find Bobby, using a whole array of Web-scanning devices and surveillance.

I pulled a file labeled *South* and found an elaborate argument that Bobby was probably living in Louisiana, because analysis of the DuChamps name suggested a Cajun French background, and other analyses had already established that he probably lived in the Gulf states.

The *South* file noted a counterargument that suggested that Bobby was active in racial affairs, was probably black and therefore not Cajun at all.

"They were moving closer, but they had no idea of who he really was," I said. "Not yet. Look, they were even analyzing phone-use patterns."

"And they never got the word that Bobby was dead. Nobody told them."

MOVING ON.

"Look at this. They're talking about getting rid of money," I said. I was astonished. "Jesus Christ, they're running models, already. They're talking about a few *years*."

"They can't."

"Sure they could. They're laying it out. Everybody carries a smart card from the bank, backed by the government. It has your ID right on the card, along with a little liquid crystal display to tell you what your balance is." I tapped the screen, a photo of a working prototype of the card. "Use it for everything, but see, they *require* you use it for all transactions over twenty dollars. So you have a card and pocket change, and that's it. No more illegal purchases. You couldn't even buy your dope with pocket change, because anytime somebody showed up with a thousand bucks in twenties, they'd have to explain where it came from."

"It'd totally fuck me," LuEllen said.

"Depending on what you stole," I said. "Jewelry, stamps, high-value stuff . . . take them across the border, sell them in Mexico."

"For what? What would I bring back? Sombreros?"

"That's a point. You might have to move down there permanently."

WE DUG INTO a directory called *Biometric*. They were running 3-D cameras set up at FedEx Field that would examine faces and gaits, compare them to faces and gaits of known criminals and terrorists, and alert the monitoring authority in real time. They were using the faces and gaits of a selected sample of their own people, who would go to the stadium during games to see if the cameras could pick them up.

"You walk past a convenience store camera and a bell rings somewhere," LuEllen said.

"More or less."

The success rate was down at the 30 percent level, but was inching up; they were going for a 150-meter recognition distance. When the success rate moved past the 50 percent mark, the plan was to place the cameras in airports, shopping centers, car rental agencies, and in selected "observation points"—for that, you could read "across the street from the neighborhood mosque."

"Eventually, you could track anyone," I said. "All you'd have to do is be interested in what the person was doing. Take a few observational tapes, get your recognition formula together, and there you are. A guy couldn't walk around town without the cops knowing who you were and where you were, every minute of the day."

"Like *1984*."

"Exactly like that. The camera in the front room."

THEY WERE TESTING programs that would intercept phone messages—the implication was all phone messages—and would analyze conversations for words and phrases that might indicate illegal activity.

"Like how would they do that?"

"You'd say, 'Why don't we get the rest of the Al Qaeda sleeper cell together and spend some time building dirty bombs and talking in Arabic about chemical, biological, and nuclear warfare with which to blow up these infidel dogs.' The computer would then automatically record the message, figure out from the vocabulary that something was going on, and alert a live monitor."

"Wouldn't a terrorist talk in code?"

"I don't know, a lot of them are kinda stupid. Even if it didn't work on terrorists, if they got this set up, it sure would let them fuck with everybody else."

———

THE GROUP WAS also looking at real-time language translation with a heavy emphasis on Chinese and Central Asian languages, and was talking about a new generation of databases that could handle amounts of data several orders of magnitude greater than anything we yet had.

The giant databases would also be tied to the money-card program, because the databases would be used to analyze virtually everybody's purchases—all of them—looking for "suspicious" activity.

The group was also talking about a highly developed computer model that would, in some sense, predict likely futures, so that the government could begin taking early action to avoid whatever outcome it wanted to avoid.

The idea was to intercept futures that led, say, to revolution in Saudi Arabia. The problem was, if it worked, there was no way that it would not be used to prevent the opposition party, the party out of power, from winning an election. That would happen almost at once—probably as soon as the program was running. I mean, it was just too good not to use.

THE FINAL DIRECTORY was called *Background* and showed what could be done by operational units, spies, working with good database search programs. Rent a porno movie? They'd know it. Move a chunk of your portfolio from Intel to Boeing because you're a government worker with an inside source on new military contracts? They'd know that and link the pieces within seconds of the transaction. Kid gets C's in school? Case of the clap in the Army? Prescription for Xanax or Viagra? Go on vacation three times in a row with the same woman, not your wife, in the next seat on the airplane?

They were already running the program on fifty-odd subjects. Some of the names rang bells, but only vaguely, until LuEllen said, "This guy's a senator. From Wisconsin."

"Holy shit," I said. I scanned down the list. "I think they're all senators. Or congressmen. Look, here's Bob. Congressman Bob. Jesus—look at the stuff. This looks like the stuff that Carp's putting out there. The Bobby file. What the hell are they doing with this stuff?"

We'd been slumped over the screen and LuEllen suddenly sat up and looked around. "Kidd, unplug the goddamn thing. Let's get out of here. C'mon, let's get going."

Her nervousness affected me, too. I pulled the plug on the wi-fi and we drove away, slowly, as always. LuEllen said, after a while, "You know what's so weird about all of this? One thing, anyway?"

"What?"

"That you could get into their files. They're this bunch of rocket scientists down in the basement talking about databases the size of the moon—they're talking about building the Death Star—and some broken-ass hacker gets into their system and it all pops out."

"Thanks. I wasn't completely sure my ass was broken," I said.

"You know what I mean. They can't even secure themselves."

"We might be coming to a time when nobody is secure. When nothing is secret. You sit up in your chair and behave yourself, or your little secret is on CNN."

"I'm moving to fuckin' Argentina," she said, disgusted.

"They'd have it in Burundi," I said. "Once the technology is demonstrated, it'll get used. Pakistan and North Korea have the bomb and they can't even feed their people."

We drove around for a while, thinking our own thoughts, occasionally looking out the back window, and then LuEllen said, "I'm glad people don't live forever. I don't think I want to be here when all this gets worked through the system and gets established. It's like . . ."

"A nightmare," I said.

BACK AT THE hotel, I started opening files that I'd simply snatched, without reading, from the DDC database. Usually when I was doing laptop stuff, LuEllen was restless and moving around, watching TV, shopping, playing golf, whatever; now she was glued to my elbow.

The working group was a secret inside the intelligence community. The Senate committee, as the intelligence oversight group, knew about it, without apparently knowing all of the details. The senators apparently got everything about the biometric research, about the money card proposals and the telephone intercept analysis, and the future map, but may not have known about the *Background* files.

Not that an experiment was taking place, at any rate. And some of the items in the *Background* section made me think.

"You know what? Bobby was inside this project. He was in their system. Look, they're talking about the senator's daughter's DWI case, and about the Bole-blackface tape."

"Maybe that's why they were so worried about him."

"No, no—but that's why Carp went after him so hard. He suspected Bobby was in there, or maybe the operation hinted what a guy like Bobby might have. But I bet that's what got the ball rolling."

WE FOUND MORE about Carp, too. Carp had sent a memo around repeating a rumor that Bobby had sent computers to poor black kids and suggesting that the name of a poor black kid be dragged through sites Bobby was known to inhabit. He even had a

name, a young computer freak he'd known in New
Orleans.

The idea was summarily rejected—a notation on a
separate file called Carp a "technician" who seemed
"obsessed" by Bobby, even though it was possible
that Bobby didn't actually exist, but was some kind of
elaborate hacker construct. The memo suggested that
Carp's "access to group personnel" be limited, which
might have been a reference to the sexual harassment
problem.

Then there had been a recent exchange of memos,
begun after the Bobby attacks started, suggesting
that they "keep all bases covered" by contacting Carp
to see if he had had any contact with Bobby. Heffron
and Small, the two guys we'd seen at the trailer, and
who had gone into Carp's apartment building the
night before, had been delegated the job. There was a
note from Small suggesting that somebody else be
sent, because neither he nor Heffron knew Carp by
sight, but an answer from the department head said
that nobody else could be spared at the moment and
that "ID photographs should be sufficient . . . this is
a completely unofficial contact."

We looked through the available stuff that would
indicate that the group was investigating or was even
aware that Heffron and Small had been killed, but
there wasn't anything in the system yet. Not on the
files we'd copied, in any case.

I also found myself in the system: a report on my
face-to-face talk with Rosalind Welsh. "Subject is

approximately six feet tall and athletic," LuEllen read. ". . . in a pursuit, deliberately burned a car to destroy any biometric evidence. He is considered exceptionally dangerous, and may be traveling in the company of a young female accomplice."

"Must have seen you from the helicopter," I said.

"That athletic-and-dangerous shit makes me hot," LuEllen said.

"I can handle that," I said.

THE NIGHT BEFORE, LuEllen, in her moment of intimacy, had told me why she might quit stealing. This night, with the lights dimmed, I had a couple of fingers hooked inside the front elastic band of her underpants, and we were going through some kind of juvenile what-does-this-feel-like routine, when I absolutely geeked out.

I'm not a geek. I'm an ex-wrestler and an artist. But I gotta admit, I was easing her underpants down and the words just burped out of me: "Jesus Christ, it won't work."

"Won't work?" LuEllen pushed up on her elbows, confused, with a certain *tone* in her voice.

"Not that, dumb-ass," I said. It must have been churning around in the back of my brain. "This data search stuff won't work. They've got a fundamental problem. It won't work."

She yawned and asked, reluctantly, I thought, "Why not?"

"Suppose they get every database in the country hooked together and they start looking for patterns. Going through all the data, looking for terrorists, looking for criminals. Okay, got that?"

"Um." Her interest was under control.

I kept talking; like I said, geeking out. "Okay. Suppose this data-mining method has amazing capabilities. If it's ninety-five percent accurate—which is way, way more than anything I can even imagine—one person in twenty would still get past them. A false negative."

"So it's got holes." She was a little more interested.

"More than that. It'll also point a finger at one person in twenty who is absolutely innocent. If you ran it against, say, the population of the U.S., that's . . ." I did some figuring. "That's fifteen million false positives. Fifteen million people who you think might be guilty of something, but who are absolutely innocent. Victims of random error. Unless you take a closer look—surveillance, wiretaps, that sort of thing—there's no way to tell them apart from the real positives you get. No way at all."

"Fifteen million?"

"That's it. At ninety-five percent accuracy. Nothing is that accurate. I don't think anything ever will be. There's just too much fuzz and bad information in the system. How in the hell do you do hard surveillance on fifteen million people?"

"So it won't work."

"Nope." I flopped flat on my back. "Nothing they can do to make it work—not that they won't try. And they gotta have people smart enough to know it."

"Then why are they doing it?"

"Funding, probably. Jesus. This whole goddamn data-mining thing is another five-hundred-dollar hammer." I reached over and patted her on the leg. I was so *pleased*.

After a moment of silence, she said, "You're such a fuckin' romantic that sometimes I can't stand it."

13

LUELLEN HAD BEEN awake half the night, occasionally poking me to ask, "Are you still awake?" and then following with a disturbing question. Like "What are our chances?" and "Why do you think Carp cracked Bobby's computer?" and "Would Bobby really put the decryption codes on the same computer?"

"Our problem is," I groaned late in the night, "is that we really didn't know Bobby. We thought his security was almost perfect, but some low-rent federal *technician* figures out a way to get to him."

She pushed herself up on her elbows and was looking down at me in the dark. Somehow, she still had nice-smelling breath. "We know they're looking for us. Looking for you and me, I mean. Personally."

"They have been since the satellite heist," I said. "I never gave a shit before. We were covered."

"So what's going to happen?" she asked.

"Well, in the next three minutes, I'm going back to sleep. Unless you stick a finger in my ribs again. Christ, I almost pulled a muscle."

"Why do you think Carp cracked Bobby's computer?"

"Because I haven't seen anything, anywhere, about the Norwalk virus. That's the biggest thing he's done so far, and I can't find any trace of it in the DDC files."

WHEN WE FINALLY got up the next morning, LuEllen insisted that we get out the tarot cards. I dug out the card box and did a spread called the Celtic Cross, which I like because it combines simplicity and flexibility. The Hanged Man came up again, but this time, as the basis of the problem rather than the outcome. The outcome spot was taken by a card from the minor arcana, the King of Cups, in the reversed position.

"Is that bad?" she asked. She became very quiet and focused when I was doing a reading.

"It's ambiguous, just like the readings with the Hanged Man," I said, as I rewrapped the deck in the silk rag. "It can mean *treachery*, but that doesn't tell us a hell of a lot. Everything in this deal is treacherous."

"So are we stuck?"

"I think . . . I may have a really bad idea. Either that, or I'm a genius."

She looked at me skeptically. "What idea?"

"Remember when I went to see Rosalind Welsh? That moved some people around. I'm thinking . . . what if we go after Senator Krause? Face to face. Figure out where he lives, hit him sometime when he's alone, or maybe with only another guy or his wife."

A few minutes earlier, she'd run down the hall to get a bottle of orange juice, and now she stood drinking it, draining it, looking at me. She licked the last of the juice off her upper lip, and she said, "That sounds like a last resort."

"We don't have that many resorts left. And this DDC business scares the shit out of me. I can't believe that they're running a test on public officials—somebody in there is goofy. It's *already* out of control."

"So let's keep it as a last resort and figure out a couple of other resorts that we can go to first."

One thing we did, right away, was drive over to our wi-fi site and go online looking for Lemon. He wasn't around—Bobby had always been around, but then, Bobby was crippled—so we left a message telling him that Carp had killed two people, and that we were going to have to give up his name.

Carp is undergoing psychotic collapse, may kill more people. We will wait until we hear from you.

We had breakfast, and then went back online. Lemon had strayed, but not far. He was there when we went back:

Don't give up Carp name yet. Must get laptop.
Can't let feds get laptop. If they get laptop, we
could be done. I have been doing research on Carp
and find he has girlfriend Mary Griggs lives in
Arlington. Suggest check before giving up name.
Also searching possibility that he has been in con-
tact with old employer. Nothing yet. Check Ar-
lington and get back.

—*Lemon*

He appended a note with Griggs's address and phone number.

"Man, this Lemon guy has to understand that we're not cops," LuEllen said. "We can't kick down the door and bust somebody."

"He might not understand that," I said. "Half of these guys live on video games and never get out of their folks' basement."

"Carp got out."

"Yeah. But he's nuts. I think Lemon's right: we ought to see if we can spot him. He can't carry the laptop everywhere. If we can spot him, and we see him going out with Griggs, we can hit the apartment, or hit the car, grab the laptop, and call the feds in."

"I don't know," she said moodily. She shifted around in the car seat, looking over her shoulder. She was spooked by all the DDC stuff. "The whole feel of the thing is changing."

"Want out?"

"I want to see what you're gonna do. But this time, we take the gun."

I DIALED GRIGGS'S number. That seemed like an easy enough first step. The phone rang and I handed it to LuEllen, who listened for what seemed like a long time, and then said, "Hi, is, uh, Terry there?"

She asked with the voice women use when an unknown male answers the telephone of a female friend, a voice that seems to ask, rapist? lover? plumber? Then she listened for a moment and said, "Gee, I'm sorry. I don't know what I did, I'm just silly."

She got off and turned to me. "Guy's voice."

"So let's go take a peek."

"Didn't . . . mmm . . . sound like Carp. I only heard him for that one minute at Rachel's, but he seemed kinda squeaky. High-pitched. This guy had some hormones. His whole attitude was sorta . . . cool."

"I dunno," I said. And I didn't.

MARY GRIGGS LIVED in a small brick apartment building in the Ballston area of Arlington, an upwardly mobile neighborhood with a little rolling contour, a four-acre park in the middle of it, the whole thing almost as green as Longstreet. The day was insufferably

hot and humid. By contrast, the park looked pleasant
and cool, with big spreading trees and what I took to
be government workers sitting on the park benches
eating their bag lunches.

We left the car a block off the park, down toward a
busy street. LuEllen had spotted a deli as we went in,
and we stopped and got sandwiches—apparently the
source of the government sandwiches and white paper bags—carried our own lunches up the block and
across the street to the park, found a bench where we
could see the front of the Griggs apartment building,
and nibbled on the sandwiches. Off to our left, a woman
was lying on a blanket, reading a book. A bunch of kids
were sliding down a curvy slide at a playground, and
a park worker was changing a net at a beach-volleyball
court that featured real ankle-deep yellow sand.

Because I was carrying a gun, I'd worn a sport
coat, despite the heat, and had the revolver in the left
breast pocket. There might have been a little fullness
on that side, but nothing obvious. Still, I could feel
the weight hanging off my chest.

"That kind of building," LuEllen said, looking at
Griggs's apartment, "is the worst of all possibilities."

"Worse than a Saddle River jeweler's house with a
hundred-thousand-dollar alarm system?"

"In some ways," she said, launching into a burglar's analysis. "You have an insider in the jeweler's
house, so you eventually figure out a way to handle
the system. You've got somebody telling you when
the house will be more or less empty, and even if it's

not empty, you can spot the people still inside. But you get a place like this, people are coming and going all the time—nobody knows who'll be coming and going, or why. It's random. And the building is older so it's probably got relatively thin walls: if you have to break a door, somebody'll hear you. Or they'll see the damage. Plus, everybody inside probably recognizes strangers." She took a bite out of her sandwich and studied the building.

"Just don't tell me you'd go in over the roof," I said. She liked ropes and climbing.

"I was just thinking that was a possibility," she admitted. "You avoid a lot of issues that way. And look at the windows. They're the old-style windows that open, with a twist-lock. You poke a hole through the glass, twist the lock, slide it up, and you're in. You don't meet anybody in the hallways, you don't have to break any doors. No visible damage."

"Of course, you have to get on the roof."

"That can be done." She studied it some more. A guy in a funny old-fashioned snap-brimmed hat strolled by, led by a bulldog on a leash. The guy took a good look at LuEllen; the bulldog sniffed what I assumed was a bed of pansies—they looked like the African violets in Strom's sink from the day before, but in lighter colors, and with more variety—and then lifted a leg and peed on them.

I was following them on their path through the park when I saw the guy with the binoculars. I casually turned back to LuEllen and said, "If you look past the back of my head, you'll see a guy in a blue shirt looking at us with binoculars. Either that, or he's looking at a really low bird."

She turned toward me and laughed, threw back her head, and said, "I see him. Yup. Who is it? Somebody tagged us? How did that happen? So now what? We run?"

"Maybe not run, but we go. I'll wad up the sandwich bag and walk over to the trash can to throw it in, and you can sit here. Then I'll call you over, like I'm looking at something. That'll get us a hundred feet toward the car."

"I hope he doesn't have a camera. I hope he doesn't have a long lens. I hope he doesn't have our faces."

"Just binoculars so far," I said. When people look at you with binoculars, or shoot your picture with a long lens, they unconsciously take a particular position that gives them away. A guy looking at you with binoculars, for example, will have his arms and hands in almost a perfect triangle, elbows out, fists meeting in front of his eyes. Photographers, on the other hand, scrunch their arms together as they support the camera and lens, and their faces are completely obscured by the camera body. When you see either one of them, you won't mistake the positions for anything else.

I got up, took LuEllen's bag, made a little show of scrunching it up. She pulled her feet onto the park bench, while I strolled toward the trash basket. I dumped the bag, did a double take at something, then waved LuEllen over.

She got up and strolled toward me. I was looking at her, and past her. The guy with the binoculars was gone. "We better hurry," I told her when she came up. "He's out of sight."

She nodded and we turned, walked a little way toward the edge of the park, and then I turned and walked backward with her, saying, "Yadda yadda yadda yadda," so that I appeared to be talking with her, but still couldn't pick up the guy with the binoculars. "Okay," I said. "Time to move faster."

She nodded and we both started jogging down the diagonal sidewalk to the corner, the car a block farther on. At the cross street I looked back at the park, but didn't see anything—and then Carp broke out of a little copse of trees a scant seventy yards away. He was running fast, for as big as he was, a pair of binoculars dangling from his neck, and he had a gun in one hand.

"He's coming," I said. "It's Carp and he's got the gun." LuEllen looked the same way and we broke into a hard run. Carp was about as close to us as we were to the car. He hip-checked a Cadillac in the street as we ran down the sidewalk toward the car, and I said, "We're gonna slow down getting in and getting started." I pulled the car keys out of my pants pocket and handed them to her. "You drive. If he opens up on us, I'll slow him down."

She didn't say anything: that would have been a waste of time. She was moving, breaking off the sidewalk to run between two parked cars, then up the street toward the driver's side of our car. Carp broke around the corner deli when we were still twenty yards away from it. Then LuEllen was inside and I dragged open the passenger-side door, slipping the revolver out of my jacket pocket, and she shouted, "Get in," and Carp, now forty yards away, slowed to a walk, brought his weapon up, and fired at me.

I wasn't aware of the slugs going by—you can actually hear them go by if you're far enough from the blast of the gun, a whip-snap sound. That's if you're not preoccupied by something else, like shooting back. I was shooting back, carefully, taking my time, aiming everything into a tree next to him. I could see people far down the street, and while I didn't think the .38 would reach that far, I didn't want to kill some old lady or her dog.

I fired four shots and suddenly he stopped shooting, looked at his gun, looked at me. I took a step toward him and he turned and ran back around the corner.

I jumped in the car and said, "Go," and LuEllen ripped out of the parking space and we were down the street, fast for the first hundred yards, down to the corner, then we were around the corner and away. As we went, I was looking out the rear window. He was gone.

"You shot at him," LuEllen said in her calmest voice, which she uses only when she's intensely cranked.

"Not exactly. I shot an elm tree to death. Can't shoot him until we get the laptop. Sure as shit slowed him down, though."

"You're okay?"

"Never touched me," I said. "He fired every shot he had, I think. Six shots, probably. It's not like doing *Quake* in your basement."

"Jesus."

"He was too far away," I said. "Too freaked out. I was trying to be careful to hit the tree and I was shaking like a leaf."

"You're still shaking like a leaf. You're talking about a hundred miles an hour." She started to laugh. "I don't think anybody saw us. All those people sitting in the park, and when I looked back there was nobody down the street or on the street. I don't think anybody saw us. And we were right in the middle of everything."

"Fuckin' crazy," I said. "If somebody saw him running with that gun . . . Wouldn't have got a good look at us, anyway."

She laughed some more, started driving too fast and I had to slow her down. "What a rush," she said. "What a rush."

14

WE DROVE A half-mile or so, taking it easy, watching for anything that was moving fast. Three or four minutes out, I turned LuEllen around and we went back into the neighborhood, looking for the Corolla. We didn't find it, nor did we see Carp again. Life went on around the park—there were no cops, no people standing around scratching their heads. We both turned toward a running body, but it was a kid, having a good time. We'd given a gunfight, and nobody came.

"Let's go to a zoo or something," LuEllen said. She was manic, her eyes sparkling, her cheeks pink. "Let's go on a hike. Let's go for a run. Let's do *something*. We gotta get out of that hotel room. I can't think in there anymore."

"Maybe we could, uh ..." I was struck by a thought.

After a moment LuEllen said, "What?"

I looked out the car window at a large woman in a poppy-orange blouse, leading, on a leash, a dog the size of a biscuit. "Just drive, don't talk to me."

I kicked the seat back as far as it would go, put an arm over my eyes, and tried to work it out. Doing the numbers. Thinking about the tarot, about the King of Cups reversed. At some point LuEllen asked, "You all right?" I could feel the wheels bumping along the road, feel us rolling to a stop at a light—feel LuEllen looking at me.

Five minutes, doing the numbers, and then Lu-Ellen said, "C'mon, Kidd. What happened? You're not having a stroke?"

I exhaled, cranked the seat back upright, and looked out the window. We were at a little business intersection and I could see the Washington Monument ahead and off to the left, a white arrow against the blue sky. Nice day. "That motherfucker."

"*Who?*"

"Carp is Lemon."

We sat halfway through a red light before she noticed. As we went through, she said, "Tell me."

"We get a note out of the blue—doesn't have to be from Bobby, just has to be from somebody who knows Bobby is dead. Doesn't demand contact, just allows us to make it on our terms, so that we feel safe. Guides us into Washington. John's black and

I'm white, and the two guys who went to his apartment . . ."

"Black and white."

"And it was almost dark, and he was waiting for us, a black-and-white pair. He knew we'd be coming because he gave us the address, and he knew at that point that we weren't from the government, because we'd responded to his e-mail. He knew we were Bobby's pals because we told him so. He knew we'd check the address he gave us, to see if it was really Carp's. We did. It's the same technique he used to get Bobby. It's like fly-fishing. You throw the fly out there, let it drift, wait for a strike."

"But he—"

"Yeah. His big mistake—this must have really mind-fucked him—was that he didn't know that there were two groups looking for him, that there were two black-and-white pairs. He must've thought that if two unknown people from Minnesota and wherever else got shot in a bad neighborhood, who could connect it to his apartment? But he kills a couple of government guys who were going to his apartment, so now . . ."

"He's screwed."

"Well. Maybe they can't prove it. He was wearing that wig; he'll have been reported as a blond."

She thought about it for a minute. "And he didn't know John was shot. . . ."

"Right. He didn't know that for sure. He was already running when he pulled the trigger. And if he slowed down when he realized he wasn't being chased, and circled back and looked at the car, he would have seen John walking out and getting in with the rest of us. And that's where he got the tag number off the car."

"Then, after the miss at his apartment, after he sees in the paper that he got the wrong guys, he sets us up," she finished. She thought about it for a moment and then said, "Ah, shit."

"Yeah. Maybe I'm wrong. But I'd say it's at least ten to one that Carp and Lemon are the same guy."

"We were chumps."

"That's not the major problem. I mean, we're not dead, anyway. The major problem is, he contacted me. By name. He knows who I am."

I was looking at her, and she turned her head and I saw something like fear in her eyes. "That's . . . doesn't get any worse than that."

"Not this side of being dead. But we've gotta get back online. I can check this."

THE STATE OF Minnesota allows anyone to check anyone else's license plate, but requires you to identify yourself before the information is released. Your name is then put on the file, and the person whose plate you pulled is notified. That's if you go in the front door. I never did, and I didn't think Carp—Lemon—would be likely to go in the front door, either. But . . .

"How can you tell?" LuEllen said, peering at the laptop screen as I went online and dialed into the DMV.

"There's a counter. You'd really have to tear up a system to beat it." I got the plate database, checked my tag number. My name and address came up. The counter said the information had been accessed the night of the collision at Rachel Willowby's apartment.

"There it is," I said. "He had to have seen the car at Rachel's place. That's the only way he could have known." It was a queer feeling. I'd been so careful, for so long, so unbelievably, unhealthily careful, that to have somebody crack my cover was like having your house burglarized.

"That fucker. He set us up." A hint of admiration in her voice? She snapped her fingers as she remembered the tarot connection. "That was the tarot card. Remember? That was the—"

"King of Cups, reversed. Yeah, that popped into my head back at the park. Coincidence jumps up and bites you on the ass."

"You been bit on the ass so many times you're lucky to have an ass left," she snorted. "When are you gonna believe? You're some kind of fuckin' gypsy spook or something."

"No. No." I shook my head. "No, it's just superstition. But it's . . . interesting."

"What do we do?"

"Maybe what he did to us," I said slowly. "I gotta think about it. He doesn't know that we know."

"What if he looks at your DMV records again and sees that somebody else has checked them. He'll know it was you, and he'll know why."

"We're not dealing with a sure thing," I said. "It's all murky. Let's go walk around the Mall and see if we can figure something out."

WE FIGURED SOMETHING out, all right. What we figured out took an hour of talk—argument— working over the problem of the DDC group, the existence of the laptop and what that might mean, and the fact that Carp had identified me.

Our strategy unwound like this:

LuEllen asked a simple question: "Why don't we just call him up and make a deal? Find out what he wants? We know that he killed Bobby and we could give the FBI a trail that leads to him—Baird saw him, and so did Rachel. We've got a big stick."

"So does he. He knows who I am."

"Right. So you should be safe with each other's information. We call him up, tell him we want to look at the laptop—nothing more, we just want to look at it, meet at some safe, open place and make sure there's nothing on it that incriminates us. After that, we walk away."

There was an objection to that idea. I said, "You're saying we let him get away with killing Bobby."

"Not because I want to."

"And if we go online and try to make a deal, we

give away our edge," I said. "We know Lemon is Carp, and he doesn't know we know."

"So what? So we know his exact name and the type of car he has and even the license number, but there are about a billion people in Washington. How are we gonna find him in this mess?"

I was still unhappy with the idea. "What if he doesn't even know what he's got on us? He might not know yet, given the size of Bobby's files. He might be willing to make a deal now, then find out something big, and decide to go with it."

"With the murder rap hanging over him?"

"That's exactly it. Suppose he found out what we did with the Keyhole satellites. He could use the information to deal his way out of a murder charge. I *know* the government deals down murder charges. You see it in the papers, some killer disappears into the Witness Protection Program, and the next thing you know, he's your Little League coach."

"Damnit."

"The goddamn laptop is a bomb," I said. "We gotta get it."

WE WORRIED ABOUT that for a while. "Look," I said, "we gotta wonder why he came to Washington at all. To make a deal with somebody? To get his job back? He might still be hoping to do that, if nobody can prove he did the killings at the apartment. And shit, the way things run in Washington these days, not being proven guilty is considered the same as being proven innocent."

"Well, that's what the letters in his laptop say—he's trying to get back in with Krause."

"What if we went online and told Lemon that Senator Krause wants to make a deal with Carp. What if we throw *that* fly out on the water?"

Once we got that going, other bits and pieces started falling into place, but it was all tentative, all guesswork, and all dangerous. LuEllen embroidered on the idea, and concluded, "It's doable—but the whole idea depends on us spotting Carp first. And on where Krause lives. If he lives downtown in a big apartment complex, the Watergate or somewhere like that, it won't work. Even if it's in a house, he could have big-time security, with his job."

"We can figure out a way to finesse the security. And Krause's been here for twenty years, he's gotta have a house," I said. "He shouldn't be too hard to find."

ONE OF THE keys to the hunt for Carp was the attack outside of Griggs's apartment. We wondered, why there? How did he know about the park? The park had been a perfect spot for an ambush—small enough that he could watch the whole thing from one place, with good protective contour, good concealing foliage, busy enough that he wouldn't be noticeable, quiet enough that he wouldn't be shooting through a crowd.

We went online to my pal in Montana, the government-files maven, and asked him to pull Carp's tax returns and check the addresses. We had an answer in twenty minutes: Carp had lived for a year in a house not more than a two-minute walk from the park. And more background: he'd apparently moved into the apartment in the District only six months earlier. Before that, he'd lived in an apartment complex in south Arlington.

We didn't think he'd dare go back to his own apartment after killing the two government guys, so it was possible that he knew the people in the house he'd lived in, and bagged out there, or that he had a friend somewhere down in that apartment complex and was hiding there. Either would explain both the park meeting place and his invisibility.

While my Montana friend was compiling the addresses, we did a quick check on Krause; he had a house in a northwestern suburb, as close as we could tell with our Washington map.

"So it's a possibility," I said. "The whole setup we talked about."

"If we can spot Carp's car. . . ."

WE KNEW CARP was driving a red Corolla. We knew the license number. He knew our car, and the

number. No problem: we went out to National and
rented a couple of cars, one from Hertz, one from
Avis on my Harry Olson Visa card and Wisconsin
driver's license. We still had the walkie-talkies from
New Orleans.

We started looking, driving separate cars, staying
in touch with the walkie-talkies.

THE HOUSE IN Ballston we crossed off immediately. The area seemed to be upgrading, and the
house where Carp once lived was being rehabbed and
was empty. Two carpenters were rebuilding the front
porch, and you could look straight through the place.
We headed down to south Arlington.

Fairlington is a few hundred acres of low two- and
three-story red-brick apartment buildings with white
window trimmings in a faux-federal style, spread
along narrow, quiet, two-lane streets overhung with
oaks; a pleasant enough place for new families just
getting started, and we saw a fair number of young
mothers out pushing baby strollers.

We thought Carp might be at the White Creek
complex, a U-shaped building with four white pil-
lars at the main entrance, and an asphalt parking
lot in the front. I cruised the parking lot, which
wouldn't hold many more than a hundred cars,
while LuEllen lingered up the block in another car.
No Corolla.

"You go around to the left, I'll go right," I told her.

"Roger. Over and out." She thought the walkie-talkies were fun.

IF WE DIDN'T find him in the first sweep through the complex, we'd agreed that we'd check a few more times—he might simply have gone out for lunch.

But he wasn't out.

LuEllen found the car fifteen minutes after we started looking for it. The Motorola beeped, I picked it up and said, "Yeah," and she said, "Got it."

WE WENT OUT to a sandwich place in a shopping center on King Street, got chicken-salad sandwiches. "We could just stick the gun in his ear and threaten to pull the trigger if he doesn't give us the laptop," LuEllen said.

"Two problems: we'd have to get close enough to him and we really might have to shoot him if we got that close. He's got that gun. And what if he doesn't have the laptop with him?"

"We'd only try it if he had it with him."

"Too many windows looking out at us, too many mothers on the street." I shook my head. "Let's go the other way. Even if we miss, we'll know where he's staying."

"Simple is usually best. This isn't simple."

"And this is fucking Washington," I said.

"Yeah-yeah," she said. "Finish your sandwich. Let's go look at Krause's house."

KRAUSE LIVED IN a leafy neighborhood northwest of the city of Washington proper, on the opposite side of Burning Tree Country Club from I-495. We drove past the club entrance five minutes before we cruised his house. The landscape was wooded and rolling, the streets smooth and quiet and curved and rich. His house sat above the street, with a hundred-foot black-topped driveway and a three-car garage.

"When?" she asked.

"This evening," I said.

"How do we know he'll be in?"

"It's Sunday night. He could be out playing golf, and then have some friends over, but he ought to be home sometime in between—say, six o'clock. Dinnertime."

"How about a FedEx shirt?"

"We can fake it," I said.

"Somebody might see your face."

"Can't help it."

She said, "I just went to eighty percent on the Lu-Ellen scare-o-meter."

THE WHOLE THING was complicated to talk about, but the actual *doing* was fairly quick. We needed to get very close to Krause very quickly, and without scaring him. Once we were close, he wouldn't have a choice about talking—but getting within conversational distance of a major Washington politician, alone, was not a sure thing.

We went downtown and rifled a FedEx box, taking several cardboard letter-size envelopes and the bigger, sacklike envelopes. Then we stopped at an art store where I bought a jar of black poster paint, a watercolor brush, and an X-Acto knife. I bought a black golf shirt at a department store, and a black baseball cap from a sports shop two doors down the street.

Years before, we once had needed a full-face mask, and found one, of former President Bill Clinton, at a novelty store. To LuEllen's delight, the store was still there, and open, and she bought another one just like the first. The great thing about the Clinton mask was that it was Caucasian flesh-colored, and from more than a dozen feet away it might be mistaken for an actual face.

We took all the supplies back to the hotel and up to LuEllen's room.

On the back of the cardboard FedEx envelope we found a logo just about the right size for a shirt. We cut it out with the X-Acto knife, and LuEllen sewed it above the pocket on the golf shirt, tacking it on with three stitches of black thread from her sewing kit.

"Good from six feet," she said, looking critically at the shirt. "If a cop stops us to give us a ticket, you can tear it off."

"Can't have any cops," I said. "We'll have to do the plates when we get close to Krause's, but they wouldn't fool a cop."

"Gonna be some cops in that neighborhood," she said.

"We need five minutes," I told her. "Give me five minutes with the guy."

"We could call him on the phone."

"He wouldn't believe us. We've got one chance at it."

While we were talking, we cut another logo out of one of the FedEx bags, and we put that one on the baseball cap. "Who knows what a FedEx uniform looks like, anyway?" LuEllen said. "You just look at the logo, right? You just look at the box the guy's carrying."

Before we headed to Krause's place, we went out on the hotel line—this was nothing sensitive, just a Google search—and found a half-dozen pictures of Krause. Took a long look: he had sandy hair, a narrow face, a long nose, a rounded chin. He looked English, upper-class English.

WE CRUISED KRAUSE'S house at five o'clock, driving my rental car. High summer and still full daylight. That was a particular problem, because we couldn't see any signs of life—no lights, no movement, all garage doors closed. We cruised it at five-thirty and at six, at six-thirty and at seven. In between, we found an elementary school with a deep turn-in.

That's where we'd do the painting, if Krause ever showed.

"Maybe he's not home," LuEllen suggested, when we went by at seven. The house was still dark; and now the sun was going down. "A lot of these guys go back to their home states on weekends, right?"

"That should have been mentioned on one of the schedules," I said. "It wasn't . . . and he's not up for reelection for four years."

THE HOUSE SHOWED lights at seven-thirty and I headed back to the school yard. "You ready for this?" LuEllen asked.

"Let's just do it," I said. We pulled into the turn-in, and I got out and did a quick touch-up on the front license plate with the black poster paint—changed an H to an M, a 7 to a 1, made a 6 out of a 5. When I was done, I screwed the tops back on the paint bottles and put them in a plastic bag in the trunk. I pulled the Clinton mask over my face, held in place by a rubber band stretched around my head, above my ears. Once it was on, I rolled it up onto my forehead, so that when I was wearing the ball cap, the roll of the plastic mask was obscured by the bill.

"Ready," I said, when I got back in the car.

LuEllen was in the backseat. "You know what you're gonna say?" she asked nervously. We'd rehearsed the possibilities all the way over.

"Yup." I yawned, as nervous as she was.

FOR ALL THE sweat and preparation, we got this:

I pulled all the way into Krause's driveway, LuEllen lying down in the backseat. Once I was inside, she'd move up to the driver's seat and get ready for a fast exit. I got out of the car, carrying a FedEx package full of newspapers and my Sony laptop, with the screen lit up. We thought that looked sort of like one of the FedEx delivery slates. If Krause's wife came to the door, I would politely ask for her husband. If she wanted to take the package, I'd refuse, and say that I would come back the next day. If that didn't get him, we'd leave.

If Krause came to the door, I'd turn away as soon as I saw him, duck my head and pull the mask over my face, and show him the gun. I'd taken all the shells out, because if he did something weird, I didn't want to wind up shooting him. Unfortunately, when you take the shells out of a revolver, the person who the gun is pointed at can see the empty cylinders. I'd have to be careful, show him only the side of the gun.

MOST OF THE working-out stuff wasn't necessary. I walked to the front steps, rang the doorbell, and a minute later saw Krause walking toward the door. He was wearing shorts and a madras shirt instead of his usual blue shirt, but his long face was unmistakable.

As he came to the door, I turned my face away.

The hand with the FedEx package was visible from the doorway, along with the lit-up computer screen; I pulled the Bill Clinton mask down. As I heard the door open, I realized that we were losing just a bit of the light—not quite twilight, but the sunlight was dimming.

The door opened and the senator said, querulously, "FedEx?"

I turned toward him and he shrank back, seeing the face.

I put the gun up but said, quietly, "I'm not going to hurt you. Shut up and don't move. I need five minutes of talk and then I'm going to get out of here." I was holding the door open with my foot, still had the package and the laptop in the other hand.

He took another step back and looked over his shoulder, looked back at me, and I said, "I'm going to save your career if you give me five minutes. If you start screaming, I'm gonna run, and it'll be the worst decision you ever made."

He said, "FedEx?"

"No. Listen to me. Do you know the shooting in Jackson, Mississippi, of the black man, where the cross was burned?"

"Yes," he said tentatively. He looked back over his shoulder again. He thought about running, but knew he wouldn't make it.

"The man who was killed was Bobby. Do you know who I'm talking about? The hacker Bobby?"

He frowned. Now, for the first time, he thought of

something other than escape. "I saw it on the news, but they didn't say anything about a hacker."

"But you've heard of Bobby?"

"I've heard of him, but I—"

"Did you know that two men from your DDC group were killed yesterday?"

"Who are you?" He was a politician, trying to take the offensive; and he had heard.

I cut him off. "Bill Clinton. Listen, one of your former staff members at the Intelligence Committee, James Carp, killed Bobby—murdered him, beat in his head, and stole a laptop with information that could hurt me and other of Bobby's friends. Then he killed your people, while they were looking for him. He used information from the laptop—*listen to me*—to do all of the political hits of the past week, all the so-called Bobby stuff. The daughter of the senator from Illinois, the military execution, the Norwalk virus, the Bole-blackface story . . . there are at least thirty more stories ready to go. We think a lot of the stuff was taken out of your DDC group."

"*What?*"

Now I had his attention. I repeated myself, and added, "What in God's name ever possessed you to run total background security probes on other members of Congress? Do you think there's any chance your career will survive? What do you think your chances are of not going to prison?"

"I think you're . . ." He looked at the gun. "Sir, I'm not sure that you are fully, uh, aware . . ."

"I'm not nuts," I said. I looked past him. "Is there anybody else home?"

He hesitated, then said, "Not at the moment. My wife . . . should be home momentarily."

"I don't want to frighten your wife. But if there's a telephone close by, you could make a call to someone who would tell you that I'm a reliable, mmm, source. There's a Rosalind Welsh at the NSA."

"I don't know her." He backed away a couple of steps, and I followed him inside.

"Maybe you can introduce yourself," I said. "I'm going to let you make the call, but if you have a panic code, or something, I'll probably figure it out, and I'll be gone. I'll be gone from here before anyone can get here, anyway, so there's no point in trying to yell for help—and if you do, you might not find out the rest of what I'm going to tell you."

"You said Jimmy Carp killed this boy . . . this, uh, man in Jackson."

"Murdered him. According to your FBI investigation, he beat in his head with an oxygen tank. Bobby was crippled and in a wheelchair and couldn't defend himself."

"I saw the story. You're sure it was Carp?"

"Yes. Not only that, he probably would have killed a little girl if we hadn't stopped him, and he definitely killed your two men. Set them up and shot them down outside his apartment."

"Sonofabitch." Now he was worried.

"The whole thing started when he was doing

research for your committee on Bobby. Now he's got Bobby's laptop and he's decoding stuff from it. He's got something with your name on it."

His eyes narrowed, and his head tipped skeptically. "My name? Like what? I've never done anything."

"Other people might not see it that way," I said. "Now the woman at the NSA, she's one of their top security people."

I followed him down a hallway, past a coat closet, past a living room entrance, and finally to a big kitchen with a phone on the wall. The kitchen smelled like bread and peanut butter. I didn't give him Welsh's number and he didn't ask for it. Instead, he dialed a number out of his head and when the phone was answered at the other end, he said, "This is me. There's a woman at the NSA named Rosalind Welsh. She's in their security branch. I need her home phone number right now. Instantly. Call me back."

He hung up and said, "There wasn't any panic code. What's Carp got on me?"

"I don't know everything he may have—or may not have—but he knows all about your bank loans from Hedgecoe Bank. What he actually has is scanned documents with your signature on them. I'm not a banker, but it seems like you got extraordinarily good terms, without collateral except for the stock you were buying. In fact, from the paper on the computer, it looks like the loans made you rich. You borrow big chunks of cash during the nineties, drop it into the stock market, Amazon, AOL, that whole crowd . . . you got to be a multimillionaire, right?"

"Nothing wrong with it," he snapped. "Nothing wrong. Just good business. I paid all the money back, with interest."

"Yeah, but how many ordinary guys could get a two-percent loan in 1990, with no collateral, and use it to speculate?" I looked at him, and answered the question: "None. You pulled a million bucks out of thin air, used it to make, what? Five million? Ten?"

"It was just . . ."

"You know where the money came from?"

"I knew some people on the board of directors," he said hoarsely. "They know me and my reputation."

"From the Saudis. From the Saudi Arabians."

"What?"

"The Saudis are the money behind the bank, and you were running the Senate energy committee at the time. Unfortunately, it was some of the same Saudis who funded bin Laden. This does not look good, huh? Especially not now, post nine-eleven." We were staring at each other in the now-gathering gloom; the phone rang to break the spell.

He picked it up, listened, wrote on a message pad, said, "Thanks," and, "Talk to you about it later." He hung up, grunted. "Cell phone, supposed to be full-time," and dialed a number. It must have rung a couple of times, and when it was answered, he said, "This is Senator Krause. Is this Rosalind Welsh? Yes.

I need to ask you a question. Would you prefer to call me back at my house, with your directory, to confirm who I am? Okay. I see. Mmm. Then this is the question. What can you tell me about . . ." He looked at me, and I tapped the mask. "Bill Clinton."

Another pause.

"Yes, a mask. Is he . . . mmm, reliable?" I was already edging toward the door. He listened for another few seconds, then said, "Thank you. I'll be back in touch."

He looked at me and said, "The recommendation wasn't the best."

"But do you think I'm lying about Carp?"

"No, no." A car pulled into the driveway, lights playing across the front of the house. "That's my wife," he said. I heard the garage door going up.

"I've got to run anyway. Welsh will have her NSA people on the way. I just wanted to let you know the quality of what's out there. But I guess we'll find out if you're telling the truth if the word gets out."

"No, no, that word can't get out," he said hastily.

"Give me your phone number. A cell phone. I'm going to call you tonight with a proposition that may get us all out of this mess."

He gave me a number and we heard a door opening in the back. I repeated the phone number to him, and backed out the door. "Don't follow us. Don't try to spot the car. Just let us go, and maybe we can save your ass."

But he said, "Wait. What was that you said about research on Congress?"

"I can't believe you don't know about that," I said.

"I don't know what you're talking about."

"Then you may be genuinely fucked," I said. "There are people in your group who are doing deep background research on a whole bunch of congressmen, on cabinet officers . . . all kinds of people. Heavyweights. And I mean *deep* background research, including surveillance. They have compiled a series of what I could only call blackmail files."

"That's not right," he said. He wasn't quite whining.

"Bullshit. Ask around. But I'd be very, very careful about who I asked."

He was still deep in the house when I headed out toward my car. I heard his wife call to him, and then I was in the driveway and out to the car and backing down the hill, lights still off.

In the street, LuEllen asked, "How did it go?"

"It went. Let's find a place where I can wipe the license plate, just in case." I threw the Clinton mask in the backseat, and she took us out of the neighborhood.

15

WE CALLED KRAUSE from Gettysburg, Pennsylvania—now that the NSA was in it, we wanted to be away from anywhere that might have a tight federal law-enforcement presence, where they could move on us quickly. If we'd called from one of the big Washington-area malls, there was a 95 percent chance that we'd have been okay. That means that you get caught one time in twenty, which is too often. We're willing to take one time in a thousand.

In any case, we called Krause from a highway rest stop, and he answered on the third ring. "Yes?"

"Senator Krause, this is Bill Clinton. Do you want to talk?"

"Yes. I've, uh, talked with my staff director. He does liaison with the working group. He says he'll check on what you told me, but says he doesn't know anything about it. I'm afraid he's lying. There's more going on than I know about. I could see it."

"He has a problem, though," I said. "He can't cover forever because some of the files are already out there. We've got some, Carp has some, we don't know what Bobby might have gotten before he was killed."

"You said you might have an idea about how to handle this."

"Yeah. But before we get to that, let me tell you again. You've got to be careful. Really careful. There's some strange stuff going on."

"You can't think . . . I mean, that there would be any physical danger."

"I do think that. Three people are dead, murdered. Two of those people were apparently trying to jump Carp without any . . . regular authority. They were intelligence people, for Christ's sakes. Somebody has freaked out and we don't know who."

"I can make some arrangements."

"If you want, I could call with a threat. Make it sound Middle Eastern."

"No, no, no. Let me handle it," he said. "Now, your idea."

"WE—OUR GROUP—have two limited objectives," I said. "We want to kill Bobby's computer and we want Carp punished for murdering Bobby. That's all. If Bobby's laptop is destroyed, that solves our problem and solves part of yours. That's one less wild card running around out there. Of course, you still have to deal with your working group."

"What about the stuff you have? That's still a problem."

"If you talk some more with Rosalind Welsh, she'll tell you that we are discreet as long as we're not fucked with. I don't want the FBI coming after me—they might find me. Once we've got Carp in hand, and the laptop, you'll never hear from me again. Besides, we don't have much. Carp, on the other hand, has about fifty huge files. He has used a small fraction of only one, and that's the one I've got."

"Fifty?"

"That's right. He hasn't used one percent of what he's got."

"Oh my God."

"WE THINK WE can get to Carp, without him knowing it," I said. "Sort of, mmm, through a third person. We could tell him that you want to make a deal. That you'll cover for him in exchange for neutralizing the Bobby laptop. We know he's broke and desperate and probably homeless, and we think he's crazy—so he might go for it. We think you might be able to set up a meeting."

"And then what?"

"You're the politician, Senator. Negotiate with him. Try to bring him in. I wouldn't try to grab him, though. He's crazy, but he's smart. If he agrees to a meeting, he'll set up some way to get out. And there's too much of a chance that he'll have set up a time bomb on the laptop."

"*What?*"

"You know, an information bomb. You grab him, he does nothing but keep his mouth shut, and twelve hours later, the computer dumps everything to CNN. That's simple enough to do. All you need is a motel room with a telephone, and a few lines of computer code."

"Goddamnit."

"You've got to do *something*," I said. "Right now, he's completely out of control. If you go after him with the FBI, the laptop is going to become public property, and you're toast. If you can talk to him, face-to-face, you should be able to deal with him. Somehow."

"I've got to think about this. How would you convince him to get in touch with me?"

"We're not exactly sure we can. I don't want to explain it to you, because it would give something away. But we think we can get him to call . . . to get in touch."

"Okay. You do that, and I'll think about it."

WE DID NOTHING overnight, except make a stop at a Home Depot to pick up a couple of bronze plumb bobs; and talk about it.

If we called at night, we thought, Carp might do

something like set up a middle-of-the-night meeting somewhere, and that would make him much harder to track. Better to do it in daylight.

As we lay awake in bed, LuEllen said, "Every move you make, you act like you think Krause is gonna pull something smart. That he's gonna double-cross us."

"I'd bet on it," I said. "That's why we don't get involved with any exchange. Let them work it out. If we can get the laptop, that's all we want."

"There are a lot of assumptions buried in that—that Carp takes the Corolla, that he takes the laptop and leaves it in the Corolla, that he tries to figure out something clever."

"It's more than just hope," I said. "He has to believe that nobody's figured out the Corolla—nobody official, anyway—or they would have grabbed him already. He can't leave the laptop with anybody, because if he *is* busted, and it makes television, then his friend, whoever he's staying with, would have no choice but to turn it in. If he didn't, then he'd go down with Carp. So Carp can't trust anybody, but he can sort of trust the car."

WE GOT UP the next morning at seven o'clock, had a quick breakfast, drove out to our wi-fi building, and went online to Lemon.

We have been monitoring Sen. Krause. He is talking to his staff director about making a deal with

*Carp, so we think Carp may have contacted him
and Krause is disposed to deal. Do you have *any-
thing* more on Carp location? Anything would
help? If not, we may abandon Washington.*

Twenty minutes later we got:

*Nothing more. Sorry. Will check everything, will
monitor Krause if I can. Stay in touch.*

"He never asks what happened at Griggs's place,"
LuEllen said. "Because he *knows* what happened."

"And he sort of kisses us off. He's gonna call
Krause," I said.

TEN MINUTES LATER, we were staked out two
blocks apart, on opposite ends of Carp's parking lot,
in the two rental cars. LuEllen had pointed me at the
Corolla, and I'd cruised it once, just to make sure I
had it. Then we settled down to watch.

WE WAITED THREE hours, staying in touch with
the walkie-talkies. I had a couple of books in the car,
the *Times*, the *Post*, and the *Wall Street Journal*, and
LuEllen had some papers and a stack of magazines.
Still, it got hot, even with the car windows down. I
worried about attracting attention, just sitting there
doing nothing, but nobody even glanced my way.

LuEllen spotted a cop car coming from her end of the block, ducked before it got to her, called me, and I rolled up the window and slid down out of sight until it was safely past. That was the only cop we saw.

We had two false alarms, heavyset men walking into Carp's parking lot carrying briefcases. Sitting there waiting, I had time to think about how out-of-shape Americans were getting: a few thin people walked by, but it seemed that seventy or eighty per-cent of the people I saw were overweight, sometimes grossly overweight.

I watched a short woman who might have weighed two hundred fifty pounds making her way down the sidewalk with a shopping bag, and wondered if she had any thought or care of what she was doing to her heart—that she might as well have been walking around town carrying a half-dozen car batteries. Then LuEllen beeped: "Wake up, bright eyes."

And here was Jimmy James Carp, pushing a moun-tain bike across the parking lot; a black nylon brief-case hung by his side, on a shoulder strap. He opened the car door, popped the trunk from inside, had a little trouble taking the front wheel off the bike, then put the wheel and the rest of the bike in the car trunk, along with the briefcase. A moment later, he rolled out of the parking lot and LuEllen called, "Coming your way."

I went out ahead of him to the first big cross street and took a left toward Washington. He was a half-dozen cars behind me, also in the right-turn lane.

He followed me obediently around the corner, and I
called and said, "On Quaker."

LuEllen: "I saw him turn. I'll be around in a sec."
Then: "I'm around, I've got him."

I accelerated, putting more cars between us, but
we were coming to a freeway access. I didn't want to
go on before him, so I pulled into a Wendy's parking
lot and drove around the building just in time to see
him go by the entrance. LuEllen was still on him and
I pulled out behind her. We were both behind him
now, and we followed him onto I-395 and headed
north.

"Slow way down," LuEllen called to me. "He's going about forty-five. I think he's looking for people
going slow behind him. I'm trying to fade back."

I slowed down to forty, and LuEllen faded on him,
and he got off I-395 and swung between the Penta-
gon and Arlington cemetery, along the Potomac and
then across a bridge toward the Lincoln Memorial.
Just across the river, he dropped off the highway onto
a riverside street and headed north. I caught a street
sign that said Rock Creek Parkway.

FOR THE FIRST mile or two, there was enough
traffic to cover us. Carp was still moving slowly, but
maybe, I thought, that was the way he drove. We went
up the river, past people in rowing shells, past a single
sailboat heading upstream under power, and then into
the ravine that was the lower end of Rock Creek Park.

Traffic disappeared, and before long, I was the next car behind Carp.

"I'm gonna have to get out," I called to LuEllen. "I'm getting off at the next street. You stay back as far as you can."

"Okay."

Rock Creek Park must be several miles long; it's the designated body-dumping spot for the Washington metro area. The lower end of the park is a narrow, steep-sided, heavily wooded ravine. In places, the boulder-filled creek runs precisely through the middle of it, with the road pinned to one side, and a hiking or jogging trail on the other. As I went past a narrow wooden footbridge across the creek, I began to get an inkling of Carp's thinking, of why he'd taken a mountain bike with him. If he were ambushed in here by people in cars, and he were on the bike, he'd be able to outrun anyone on foot, and go where no car ever could. I wondered if he'd considered the fact that bullets can move even faster over rough terrain than mountain bikes.

A side street was coming; I switched on my right-turn signal and took it. As soon as I was out of sight of Carp, I did a U-turn and saw LuEllen go by. I fell in behind, keeping pace, but well back, always in touch with LuEllen by radio.

We wound farther into the park, and it got wilder and deeper. The cross streets were infrequent, and if Carp stopped to look at trailing traffic, he might bust us.

LuEllen called. "He turned, he's getting out of the park. I gotta keep going or he'll spot me."

"I've got him," I said.

I followed him up the side of the ravine, on a narrow blacktopped street that suddenly got wider and merged with a busier street; lost him for a minute, then saw the Corolla turn right, fifteen or twenty cars ahead of me, onto Sixteenth Street. I charged up the hill, beeped impatiently at a car ahead of me—got the finger from the driver—turned right, and then timidly followed Carp a couple of blocks to a park.

As I called and gave directions to LuEllen, Carp turned into a street that led across the park to what looked like a small stadium. I stopped in front of a Presbyterian church, idled by the curb, and watched him drive toward the stadium. I was about to follow when he pulled into a parking spot.

"He's parking," I told LuEllen. Two minutes later, she pulled in behind me. A baseball diamond sat right on the corner, with soccer fields on the other side, and then tennis courts, and then the parking lot where Carp was getting the bike out of the car.

"Let's watch some baseball," I said to LuEllen on the walkie-talkie, and we both got out and walked over to the ball diamond, where a group of parents were sitting on a berm along the third-base line, watching their small children play T-ball.

We found a grassy spot and from there watched Carp assemble the mountain bike behind the Corolla.

When he was done, he rode it once, in a practiced way, around the parking lot. He seemed too big for the machine, but he rode it with a confidence that suggested that Jimmy James Carp had talents we didn't know of. A second later, the bike having been tested, he went back to the car, pulled on a long-billed black fishing cap, then slammed and locked the door.

He didn't have the briefcase with him.

"I'm gone," LuEllen said. She'd try to stay with him. We both got up, both dusted the seat of our pants, and walked back to the cars. She did a quick U-turn and then went down the street beside the church and did another, so she was pointing back toward the park. Whichever way Carp went, she could follow, as long as he didn't cut cross-country.

I watched Jimmy James pedal by, take a left, and head back to the street that had taken us up out of the park. LuEllen dropped in behind him, and I went after the Corolla.

ON THE FRONT seat of my car, I had a plumb bob. Plumb bobs are one of the oldest surveying tools in the world, and were undoubtedly used to help build the pyramids. Basically, the modern version is a slender brass cone, with a sharp stainless-steel point. A long piece of string attaches to the precise center of the blunt end of the cone, and when you let the plumb bob dangle, and the pendulum movement subsides, the string makes a perfect vertical line.

That's useful if you're making a pyramid foundation.

Which I wasn't. I'd pulled the string off and had thrown it away, leaving myself with a heavy brass cone with a sharp steel point. I pulled into a parking spot next to Carp's car and called LuEllen.

She came back, "He's headed back into the park, down the hill. I'm not gonna get out of the car, but I could lose him. . . . I can still see him. . . . Do the car now."

"Doing the car," I said.

I got out of my car, carrying the plumb bob. Stepping up to the driver's-side window on the Corolla, I put the point of the plumb bob on the glass, just outside the inner door lock. I hit the blunt end of the plumb bob with the heel of my other hand, and the steel point poked easily through the glass with almost no sound at all, or obvious motion on my part.

I pulled the plumb bob out of the hole, stuck my finger through the glass, popped the lock. Inside the car, I took a few seconds to find the trunk latch: found it, popped the trunk, took the briefcase out. I couldn't help myself: I looked inside, and there, just where it was supposed to be, was an IBM laptop.

"Excellent," I said to myself as I got back in my car. "Kidd, you are a fuckin' genius."

THEN LUELLEN CALLED. Her voice was jerky, screeching, and for the first time I'd ever heard it, afraid: "Kidd, I'm in trouble here. I'm in trouble, Kidd. This is a trap, this is a trap. Carp's running on the bike. They're stopping cars. I'm gonna try to get out, oh, Jesus, Kidd. *Get out. Get out, get out, wipe your car, dump your car, I'm gonna try to run.*"

Two minutes later, I got a last call: "Kidd, if you can hear me . . ."

"I gotcha." I sounded calm to my own ears, but my heart was in my mouth.

"It was a trap. They're sweeping the park, there must be thirty of them," she said. "They spotted me watching him, they blocked me out, they got the car. I don't know if they got him, or not, I saw him heading into the woods on the bike." She was breathing heavily, but no longer sounded frightened. "I'm on foot, in the woods, but they're all around here, they're gonna get me. I ditched all my ID, buried it, they've got nothing on me. I'm gonna throw the walkie-talkie in a minute. Get me out. Get me out, Kidd. Don't leave me."

And she was gone. I sat with the radio pressed to my ear, listening for anything. Nothing came.

16

I KEPT REMEMBERING the exact timbre of her voice: "Get me out, Kidd." I'd never heard that out-of-control note in LuEllen's voice before, and it was deeply disturbing, the kind of disturbing you get when you think your heart has just stopped.

Besides, this didn't happen. We didn't get caught. We were too good.

Not counting what she described as youthful experimentation at local department stores, LuEllen had been a professional thief for fifteen years, had worked five or six times a year during that time, sixty or seventy jobs, without ever taking a fall. She'd never been fingerprinted, and had been photographed only once, as far as we knew, and that was by me. I'd never been suspected—not by the cops, anyway. We'd managed to live outside the system, invisible.

Now they had her. Or somebody did. I didn't
know who Krause had gotten cranked up, but it had
to be one of the intelligence agencies—I doubted
he'd risk the FBI, where his control would be limited.
Anyway, LuEllen was no longer invisible. They were
probably fingerprinting her, photographing her. Hell,
they may have been working on her with a cattle
prod; these weren't cops.

WHEN LUELLEN'S RADIO went down, I got in
the car and steamed back to the hotel, frantic to
get there; but not so frantic that I ran red lights or
broke the speed limit. I had to get there in a hurry,
not get stopped by the cops. The problem was, if they
had her car, they'd have my fake ID, and eventually
they'd have my rental car, too. A little while after that,
they'd have my hotel room, which was on the same
credit card. Because they didn't have her ID, they
wouldn't have her room. Not for a while. If they put
her on TV, then all bets were off.

I was back at the hotel in fifteen minutes and drove
the car to the most crowded part of the parking ramp.
I meticulously wiped the interior, and left it. With
any luck, it might sit there for a few days before anybody noticed. Then I headed upstairs, to the room
I'd rented, but which I hadn't used, wiped anything I
might possibly have touched, recovered my bags, and
carried them up to the room LuEllen had rented.

Wiping her room took an hour. When I was done,

I stripped the sheets off the bed—DNA analysis has made all of us crooks a little paranoid—and stuffed them into one of my suitcases, and checked out the back door.

Twenty minutes later, I was checking into a hotel across the street from the White House, under my own name, with my own credit card. I'd been there before, when I was in Washington on business. It was one of my favorite hotels in the world, and LuEllen knew it.

AS SOON AS I was set up, I headed toward what Washington calls the downtown, and called Krause from a mall. He answered, a little cocky and maybe a little wary: "Yes?"

"Senator Krause, this is Bill Clinton." Some of the fear leaked into my voice, and that little show of weakness pissed me off.

Krause picked up on it, of course; that's what politicians do. "We have your friend," Krause said, in the congenial voice of a man who's looking at four aces. "We think it would be best if you came in now. If you come in, we are prepared—" He was either reading a written statement, or he'd memorized the speech.

I cut in, not quite shouting: "Shut up, motherfucker. *Shut up*. Listen to this: Every half hour that my friend is held, I'm going to dump another congressman or senator. I'm going to do the first three right now. *Right now*. No bargaining. *But it's not quite*

free of charge, asshole. When I do each one, I will call
that guy's office, and I will tell them that their dis-
grace was organized by you. You and your information surveillance office. I will send them proof. After
the first three are done, which should be in a couple
of hours, I will give you a chance to free my friend, if
you haven't already. If you haven't, I'll start doing
more of them. If you don't release her at all, a good
chunk of Congress will be down the drain by this
evening, and they'll all know who to blame. Someplace along the way, I'll do you. Good-bye."

   "Wait—"

   I hung up and left, to look for a few clean phones
and a new wi-fi site.

KRAUSE WAS A negotiator, like all people in his
job. Therefore, no negotiation. The choice had to be
stark: release LuEllen, or face ruin. If I let him negotiate, he might talk *himself* into the proposition that
sooner or later I'd cave in. And I wouldn't—I'd never
cave.

   LuEllen and I had talked about this possibility, in
somewhat different contexts. Giving them two people, instead of one, never made sense. That was behind all the talk of whether LuEllen should have left
the current job, the hunt for the laptop. There hadn't
been any desperate need for her to stay on, but she
had stayed, for too long, because she'd been enjoying

herself. That was a mistake, but there was no point in compounding it.

To get her back, I had to keep the pressure on Krause. I could do that, I thought, with the photo file from the first laptop. The question was, could I push Krause over the edge before they got something definitive on LuEllen?

IN THE MEANTIME, I found another phone and called John.

"They got LuEllen—the government did, Krause," I told him. "I'm trying to get her back, but we might need a railroad out of the country."

"I can give you Mexico if you need it."

"Get something set up. I don't know what's going to happen." I told him, briefly, about the ambush in the park.

"Forgive me for saying it, but you don't sound all that smart."

"We didn't think they'd stop everyone in the park," I snapped back. Then: "Sorry. You're right. I think that's another reason I'm so pissed. I feel stupid."

"But you don't think they got Carp."

"I don't think so, but I don't know. Just something about the way he went into it. I think he knew more about the park than they did. I'll find out soon enough."

"If LuEllen ditched her ID like she said, and they haven't found it, then I don't know what they could do," John said. This was the law-office John. "What can they charge her with? If she's tough enough to keep her mouth shut, they won't know who she is, or what she does. What can they do with her?"

"Stick a cattle prod somewhere and keep asking questions. These are intelligence guys, and they're desperate," I said.

"You don't think she's tough enough?"

"Not tough enough forever. Nobody is. But I think she's tough enough to hang on until I get her out. And I will."

"Call me when you know," John said.

EXCEPT FOR CLIENTS who were buying my polling software, I never paid much attention to elective politics. Politicians always seemed about as differentiated as Daffy and Donald, the Ducks, and you have to ask yourself, would you send Daffy Duck to Washington to set policy on medical care or nuclear waste? I just hope I'm dead before the entire unholy scheme—created by politicians, lawyers, and our new class of media courtiers—blows up in our faces.

End of rant. I personally knew nothing at all about the three victims I picked to hammer Krause. All I knew was that they were crooks, which was no surprise, and they all had quite a bit of clout in the government.

The three were Congressmen Frank Marsh from Connecticut and Clark Deering from Oregon, and Senator Marvin Brock from Missouri.

Marsh ran the House Armed Services Committee, which annually handed out a couple hundred billions in military pork. Deering was the second-ranking Republican on the House Appropriations Committee, which handled most of the rest of the economy. Brock ran the Senate Agricultural Committee, which might have been not so big a deal if Krause hadn't been from Nebraska.

I GOT ONLINE and checked all three networks, and both CNN and Fox News, and made lists of names of working producers. I started calling from a series of phones I found by walking around downtown. I'd call each Washington bureau and start asking for producers until I got one on the phone. I never did get one for CBS, but I got the rest of them. Like so, with Fox:

"This is John Torres."

"I'm calling for Bobby," I said. "*The* Bobby. We're releasing files on two more congressmen and a senator. We need e-mail addresses. We expect to release within half an hour."

"How do we know you're from Bobby?"

"Look at the files. You don't like them, throw them away. What's one more piece of spam in your mailbox?"

Five-second pause. Then, "Right. Send them to . . ."

I SET UP with my wi-fi can across the street from the Department of the Interior, which had so many possible connections that it took a while to sort them out. I wanted a fast line—I got it; the government always goes first class—because the files I was sending were big. They were essentially scanned-in pictures, rather than text files. That is, they contained text, but instead of a tight little stream of numbers and letters, they were reproductions of photocopies, or in some cases, actual photographs.

Marsh, the first congressman, had been running a whole series of nickel-and-dime scams, mostly involving travel. He traveled by private jet, like a movie star, and paid for it out of his own pocket, the equivalent of a first-class fare. That's a cheap ticket for a chartered plane, but he always claimed that he was simply "riding along" with corporate people. What was not visible in the government accounts was that his wife and family, including two grown daughters and their husbands, traveled with him, but invisibly, all paid by two large defense corporations. That was thoroughly documented, and was bad enough.

The killer was the château in the South of France, which he had apparently been given as a gift by a French military hardware conglomerate. Superficially, the deal looked like a purchase, rather than a gift, but if you had the right set of documents, the reality was clear enough. The congressman had neglected to tell anyone about his good fortune; not even the IRS. But we had the deed and we had a nice picture of his wife working in their pretty French garden.

With Deering, the other congressman, it was strictly sex. We had pictures of him with half a dozen different women, none of whom looked like virgins, all of them far too young. Names, dates, times, and places. The photographs looked like the product of professional surveillance. He'd be charmed by that.

Brock's situation was more intricate. All of his investments were made on his Senate salary—he had no family money—and supposedly were controlled by a blind trust. But the trust was placed with an investment company that had a tight relationship with a huge private commodities corporation.

Agricultural commodities—like wheat, corn, sugar, cocoa, and orange juice—are bought and sold by two different kinds of buyers. The first are speculators, who are betting on the price moves the commodities will make in the future. The amount of rain in Iowa in June can send corn prices all over the place, depending on whether it's too little or too much or just right. Really smart, tough, fast speculators can get rich. Most go broke.

The second type of buyer is the big commodity-using corporation, which sells the wheat or corn, or buys it to make pizza or pancake flour. They're not speculating—they're using futures contracts to stabilize the prices they will get or spend on the commodities.

Brock's investment company routinely handled the futures contracts for the commodities corporation, as a way of stabilizing future prices. But the trustees for Brock's account, handled through the same firm, were speculating with Brock's money. And doing it brilliantly. Too brilliantly. They won virtually all of their speculative bets, and had run a few tens of thousands of dollars into nearly fifteen million, tax paid.

The trustees won all their bets because, according to our xeroxed account returns, the commodities company was quietly picking up Brock's losing bets and replacing them with winning bets of their own. Because it was all handled inside the same investment firm, all the scheme needed was a few adjustments in a computerized account. And Brock had all the paperwork and paid all the taxes.

Nice. Invisible. Illegal.

And fifteen million was such a large, juicy, fat, ridiculous, greedy amount, that when the word got out, Brock would be screwed.

I PUT THE word out and gave Krause credit for developing the information. I thought about calling each official's office separately. Instead, I re-sent the files I'd sent to the networks to each man's executive assistant. I included the Krause note. Whether he let

LuEllen go or not, Krause was in trouble with his peers and the party.

As I worked the wi-fi connection, I'd been staring at the back of the Interior Department building, a wall of some kind of undistinguished gray stone. I thought later that if I had to describe it to someone, I would have said that it looks like the Ministry of Truth in Orwell's *1984*.

But then, I may have been overwrought.

I CALLED KRAUSE at three o'clock in the afternoon and he said—no calm reason this time, but with real fear on his side, choking down a scream— "Stop it! Stop it! We let her go, she's just fine, we're not following her, we're not surveilling her. We let her go."

"I don't think surveilling's a word," I said.

"What? What? What do you mean—"

"I mean if I don't hear from her in six hours, I start again," I said. "I've got three more ready to go and one of them might be you."

"I told you, we let her go, you asshole. We let her go." Yes: real fear. Almost too much. Had something happened I didn't know about? That I'd never know about?

"Did you get your boy Carp?"

"No. He had that bike. You shithead, you've done more damage than you can possibly understand."

"You better get Carp," I said. "Whether or not

you turned my friend loose, we're gonna publicly put this killing on your guy, if you don't do something about him pretty quick."

"We'll get him—we're going to the FBI."

"I'll give you a couple of days. If you get him and you stay off our backs, you won't be hearing from us again. If we hear from you again, we'll drop the bomb."

I hung up, found a deli, bought thirty dollars' worth of food and drink, and headed back to the hotel. I spent the rest of the day and the evening lying on my bed, or sitting at the desk, poking at the computer I'd taken out of Carp's car. I was afraid to leave the room. At six o'clock, the first stuff about Deering, Marsh, and Brock started to leak onto the news, CNN, and Fox at first, and then ABC. There were no details, only teasers about how "more powerful Washington legislators may be entangled in the growing Bobby scandal that has rocked Washington for a week."

Good enough; the TV boys were checking out the documents. I wondered if Bobby would be pleased. As far as I knew, he'd never used any of the blackmail stuff himself—but then I didn't know where all the continuing Washington scandals came from, and I didn't know what might have been done quietly, as pressure, rather than as a direct attack.

WAITING. GOING FROM TV to computer and back. I finally got out the tarot deck and did a spread.

I took a while to frame a question about LuEllen, and when I did, came up with the Two of Cups. That was interesting, but didn't give me any hint of what might happen in the next few hours.

And I thought, *Jesus, Kidd, you're doing a gypsy reading, as if you believe in this shit*. That says something about my level of stress.

Before I put the cards away—my little man, the leprechaun-like id-character that everyone carries in the back of his head—was laughing at me, but I did a reading on my own future. Just killing time. Came up with the King of Swords, which told me nothing I might not suspect even without the cards.

Not entirely bad, but not entirely good, either. But self-psychoanalysis is not what I needed. Or, rather, I may have needed it, but it wasn't what I so desperately wanted. What I wanted I got at eleven o'clock; I almost ruptured an appendix getting to the phone.

"YEAH," I SAID. LuEllen had known where I'd be; and she'd call me through a hotel switchboard, so there wouldn't be anything on my cell phone.

"It's me," she said. She sounded tired. "I'm near that narrow lane, the one we used to check for tails the last time we were here. The airplane time. You remember? I don't want to say the name. Nobody could have followed me this far. I went to a Goodwill store and bought clothes and dumped all of my stuff, every stitch, and my shoes, so I'm not bugged."

"Are you okay?"

"Mmm. Physically. Otherwise, I'm pretty screwed up. They put me in a room and every once in a while, somebody would come in and ask a question. I didn't say one fuckin' word to them. Then they came and got me, put me in a car, drove around for a while, gave me a hundred dollars, dropped me off, and told me to get lost. I don't know where I was in the room, it was like an office building, but I don't know where."

"They got your car?"

"Yes. They'll have my prints. I didn't see anybody take a picture. They . . . they weren't real cops. They were something else. I thought maybe Army—some of them had those funny white-sidewall haircuts."

"Okay. So I'll cruise the lane in exactly twenty minutes. You got your watch?"

"No, I dumped everything. But I know twenty minutes."

"You come in at the same time I do, so you're moving. I'll flick the lights when I come into the street."

"See you." She really did sound beat.

I GOT HER twenty minutes later, on a narrow one-way lane that we'd once used to make sure that nobody was behind us. I went into the lane slowly, blinked my lights, and crawled through, worried sick that she wouldn't be there.

She was. She stepped out from behind some kind of evergreen, next to a low stone wall and a garbage can, and held up her hand and I slowed and she got in.

"You look like you just got out of *Vogue*," I said.

"Shut up and drive," she said. I was still wound tight as a grandfather clock, afraid that a black federal car would suddenly block the way, and guys with guns would come parachuting out of the trees.

But they didn't. Six blocks down the road and around a few corners, and she said, "Pull over."

"What?" I looked in all the mirrors and saw nothing.

"I need a squeeze," she said. "Really bad."

I pulled over and we spent a little time just squeezing each other, though modern cars aren't built for it. Christ, I'd been worried. I'd been so worried. . . .

"You got me back," she said.

17

LuEllen disappeared into the bathroom, taking her cosmetics bag with her, leaving the Goodwill clothes on the floor. She said she expected to be in there awhile. I gathered up the clothes and stuffed them in a sack. We could drop them somewhere the next day.

With the bathwater running in the background, with LuEllen home and well, I went back to Bobby's computer, the laptop I'd taken from Carp's car. I'd been poking at it during the afternoon, while I waited to hear from LuEllen. What I'd found was curious.

The files that had been on Carp's computer, the blackmail files, were there, all right, as were the encrypted files. But some of the encrypted files had been decrypted. He'd made notes: *This from File 23,*

Indexed as MRG Cleanup: and there was the Norwalk virus file.

The question that plagued me was, how had he decrypted it? Where had he gotten the decryption keys? Bobby's laptop had the encryption program right there, out front, and it was a good, solid commercial program that would essentially produce an uncrackable file.

From the bathroom, LuEllen said, "Oh, Jesus," and I looked up, then rolled off the bed, went to the bathroom door, and poked my head inside.

"What was that?"

"My ass hitting the hot water. Close the door, you're letting the cold air in." I took a longer lingering look before I backed out. She'd put some bubble bath in the water, and it smelled good; and some pink parts were poking out of the bubbles, fairly artfully, I thought. She said, "Your look is lingering."

"I wanted to make sure you were physically okay," I said.

"What do you think?"

"I'll need a closer look." I shut the door.

BACK TO THE laptop. The thing had an abnormally huge hard drive. And the files were large, I could see that much. From Carp's note, I knew that one, or part of one, was an index.

Was it possible that Bobby had hidden the keys

somewhere in the computer itself, and that Carp had found them?

I began tearing the laptop apart, a boring and ultimately fruitless activity. The problem was the size of the files—they were just too big. What I was doing was like walking through a library looking for a particular sentence, without knowing what book it was in. Yet Carp had done it. Was he that much smarter than I was?

Leaving behind the mystery files, I looked through some nonencrypted utility programs that Bobby had stashed in a corner. They had esoteric names like *Whodat* and *Whatsis* and *Dogabone* and *Bandersnatch*, a bunch of fishhooks for various jobs that Bobby had needed done. I had the same kind of collection in my laptop, with the same kind of names.

I transferred *Whodat* to my laptop and pulled it apart, and found a search program that looked for names. That's all it did; but it was nicely written, and would be very fast. I had encountered circumstances where it would be useful, like searching a company's database for memos to or from a particular person. *Whatsis* was a big library of electronic circuits. If you had a big enough circuit diagram, you could import it into *Whatsis* and *Whatsis* would give you a list of machines that you might be looking at, that used that precise circuit.

Dogabone was a modification of an old program I'd written myself, years ago, which would find programs

in one place and put them in another. I still had the
same program on my computer, but my original was
called *Fetcher*, which is where I suppose Bobby got
the *Dogabone*. The next program, *Bandersnatch*, was
meant to be left in a remote computer, where it
would watch whatever file you attached it to. When
that file was manipulated, *Bandersnatch* would immediately make a copy of the manipulated file, change
its name, and re-store it. So Bobby could go into an
outside computer, and if he encountered an encrypted file, he could attach *Bandersnatch* to it. When
it was manipulated—that is, decrypted—*Bandersnatch*
would copy and store it. Bobby could then come back
and retrieve the file without ever having the decryption key.

I thought about that until LuEllen emerged from
the bathroom, and then I stopped thinking about it
for a while.

"WHAT DO YOU think we should do?" she asked
late in the night. We were tangled up in the sheets of
the big king-sized bed. We each had a bottle of Dos
Equis.

"I've been thinking about that since they took
you," I said. "I had nothing else to do but talk on the
phone and wait . . . and I did some tarot readings
that were all over the place. And I think you should
go on home. Lay low. If you stay with me, you become dangerous to both of us."

"Tell me how," she said.

"Because I may do something that would attract some attention—not much, but some. If they see you, then they know that they've got the right guy. And they'll know who I am, and then they might be able to get back to you. I mean, get all the way back to the real you."

"What're you gonna do?"

"I want Carp punished. And I want this Deep Data Correlation program stopped. I'm thinking of going to Bob—Congressman Bob. He's in the DDC file. I'm not sure he could blow up the program, but he's got his hand on a lot of government money. If nothing else, he might be able to starve it to death. In any case, he'd be pretty damn interested in what they've got on him."

"Bad?"

"A little questionable dealing here and there. Bob did some favors that were a little too enthusiastic. They don't have him nailed down, but you get the impression that if they pushed hard enough, they might get him."

"So you tell Bob . . ."

"I tell him that I've dealt some code with a guy who's involved in some big hassle with the government. That this guy knew I'd worked with Bob and asked me to pass the file on."

"That's pretty thin ice."

"Yeah, but there's no way to prove anything else happened. I'm a painter, for Christ's sakes."

She sighed. "I'll get a plane out tomorrow morning."

"That'd be good," I said.

We were silent for a while, and then she said, "If they really dug into you about the e-mail file, they'd ask how come you got to Washington before you got the e-mail file."

"No, they won't. I e-mailed the file to myself a couple days ago. I sorta thought this might be coming."

"You didn't tell me?" One eyebrow went up.

"I figured you'd squeal like a piggy," I said. "There was the possibility that I'd never need to do it, so why mention it and put up with all the squealing?"

"Ah, jeez," she said. "You want another Two-X?"

LUELLEN HAD DUMPED her ID, but it hadn't been the real LuEllen anyway. She carried a backup behind the lining of a lockable jewelry case in her luggage, along with a few credit cards, a Sam's Club card, and a membership card to the Museum of Modern Art.

She wore her hair short as a matter of course, and carried two very good wigs as a regular part of her wardrobe. We bought her a new wallet the next day, along with a new purse and a ton of the usual crap that women carry around with them. We were at National at eleven o'clock. I kissed her good-bye in the car, then trailed her, at a little distance, into the airport. There was no trouble at all. The razor-sharp security made her take off her shoes, because they had steel shanks in the heels, but it never occurred to anyone that the pretty blonde might be wearing a wig. She looked nothing like she had in the park.

She turned on the other side of the security line and nodded at me, a quick eye-lock and a nod, and then she was gone, a small, well-dressed woman carrying a medium-sized purse, maybe somebody doing business for a nonprofit, or a congressman's aide going home.

BEFORE LEAVING WITH LuEllen for the airport, I'd called Congressman Wayne Bob at the number he'd given me for the casino research. When he answered, I said, "This is Kidd. Congressman, I gotta see you today. This is a no-shit, honest-to-God emergency. It has to do with all this corruption stuff on TV. You need to talk to me."

"Am I gonna be on?" he blurted.

"I don't know. I don't think so, but you could be. They've got a file on you, and it goes into a deal with Whit Dickens. You know a Whit Dickens?"

You could almost hear him lick his lips, and he said, "Maybe."

I said, "I could explain better if we could get off in a corner somewhere."

"Where?" he asked.

"How about the Hay-Adams?"

"Good. How about two forty-five? I'll get us a cranny."

"See you then."

THE THING ABOUT the Hay-Adams is that politicians wander in and out of it all the time, every day, virtually every hour; and the restaurant has lots of little nooks and crannies, where you can have intense conversations without being seen or overheard. Even better, I could get from my room to the restaurant in a couple of minutes.

I got to the restaurant at 2:45 on the dot. A waiter took me back to the reserved cranny, gave me a glass of ice water and a menu, and a minute later came back to say that Bob was running ten minutes late. I ordered a Dos Equis and drank ice water and beer and read the Post until 2:55, when Bob came around the corner.

Bob was short and too heavy in a masculine, pink, southern way. He had a florid, short-nosed face and a belly, white haystack hair, and a perpetual smile. He was sweating with the summer heat when he slid into the booth across from me; he was wearing a blue-striped seersucker suit, which you're only allowed to wear if you come from the South, and a pinkie ring with a deep blue oval stone, and he looked pretty good in all of it. He was about fifty, I thought, and his pale blue eyes were worried. Bob was kind to old people, children, and dogs, but had a reputation for striking like a rattlesnake if you pissed him off.

"What's shakin'?" he asked. Before I could answer, he pointed a pistol finger at a waiter, and then tipped his thumb into his mouth. The waiter nodded and disappeared. "Universal signal for a Beefeater's martini, up, with two olives and ice-cold."

I dug into my pocket and found a printout of the documents that had been compiled against Bob. I passed it to him. He read it once, then again, more carefully, then put the paper on the table, folded it four times, into a small square, and stuck it into his pocket. "Could cause me some trouble," he said thoughtfully. He looked me over. "Where's it coming from?"

"Frank Krause. Your friendly neighborhood senator."

He took a moment to think about that, and then a single wrinkle appeared in his forehead. "Frank Krause? I saw something on TV about Frank Marsh, they said something about Krause."

"That's what I'm talking about," I said.

"How are you mixed up in it?"

"There's a guy I know only on the Internet. He's apparently involved in some kind of hassle with Krause. Anyway, he says that Krause has got a rat's-nest interagency intelligence operation going, and one of the things that they're testing is called Deep Data Correlation. The basic concept was supposed to be that they could look at an ocean of data and figure out from that who might be bad guys. Terrorists."

"Is that bad?" The waiter came back with a martini,

waited, with me, until Bob nodded. The waiter went away and I continued.

"Not if that was what was happening. But there are some fundamental problems with that kind of data mining," I said. I explained the numbers problem. "So essentially, what they were trying to do is impossible. *But*—if you come at it from the other end, starting with a name, then going after associated data, you can develop some pretty powerful tools."

"Wait a minute," Bob said. "You're saying that instead of looking at the data, and finding suspects, they find a suspect, and then mine the data to support the suspicion."

"Yeah. Except, of course, that you've got to identify a target first. With terrorists, identifying the target is the whole problem. That's the hard part. If they'd been a private company, say, hired to find techniques that would identify terrorists, they'd have concluded that data mining was a waste of time. But they're not in a private company. They're with the government. So they apparently said to themselves, 'Well, data mining won't work, but we've got this great research tool, let's just check it out on a few targets.'"

"They chose me?" He looked floridly earnest, but not all that surprised.

"Bob," I said, "I gotta trust you, I think, but honest to God, we've occasionally given each other reason to think that neither one of us might not be . . ."

I shrugged, and he finished the sentence for me. ". . . as close to God as our mothers might wish."

"Exactly," I said. "So I'm gonna show you something. But if you tie me to it, or mention it to anyone that you heard it from me, I'm gonna shove it up your ass sideways."

He smiled. "That's the kinda deal I understand." His smile vanished like a turned-off light, and he looked at me over the rim of his martini glass as he finished the drink, his eyes cold as ice. "They won't hear about you from me; you got my word."

I took my laptop off the seat beside me, turned it on, waited until it was up, then called up the file. I turned it toward him and said, "You can page through it with the Page Down key."

He started paging through, stopping occasionally to mutter, "Just saw this one on TV . . . Krause is doing this? . . . Jesus, I didn't know this guy was queer, I was just peeing in the next stall to him . . . *Landford Hewes* took a half-million out of Mejico Rico? Holy shit, he's supposed to be Mr. Clean . . . Oh man: Davy Fergusson, he's a friend of mine and so is Tina, and this says he beats the shit out of her. Look at the mouse on that woman, and the hometown cops bailed him out without a word."

He was slack-jawed, fascinated.

"You gotta think about this," I said. "This use of their data-mining tool is inevitable. It's the perfect weapon to use against elected politicians. I mean, I might not care if they find out that I've been renting porno videos or getting blow jobs from seventeen-year-old boy hookers in the local park, but a politician would. Imagine what would happen if this capability got into the hands of lobbyists. We'd be at the mercy of any special interest willing to use it."

"Umm . . ." he said. He took thirty minutes to work through the file. "If you're making mental notes, don't bother," I said. "I got the whole thing on a CD for you. I'm giving them to you."

He looked up. "What for? There's a lotta horse-power here."

"Not for me," I said. "I'm a painter. Just being around this shit scares me to death. But this DDC stuff scares me, too. I thought if you had the informa-tion, you could talk to some of the people there . . ." I nodded at the laptop.

Again, he finished my sentence for me: ". . . and shove it up Krause's ass sideways?"

"Something like that. I don't care so much about Krause as this group he's got working for them. It's not right. It won't catch terrorists; all it can be used for is blackmail."

"It *ain't* right," he agreed. "You got that CD?"

I took it out of my pocket and passed it to him. "We are now two of the most powerful people in this whole fuckin' capital of the world," he said, looking at his reflection in the CD. "You and me, and we're sitting here in a hotel booth drinking a martini and a beer and I'm looking at my face in a record."

I couldn't think of a quip, so I said, stupidly, "Makes you think, huh?"

18

AFTER ANOTHER AFTERNOON and night in Washington, and a span of boring computer digging, I carefully checked out of the hotel—that is, I got my bags and took a cab to National, went inside, then back outside, and took another cab to a department store adjoining the parking structure where I'd left my car. I walked through the store to the car, and two minutes later was on my way to St. Paul, looking over my shoulder all the time.

Washington to St. Paul by car is two killer days, or three easy ones. I decided to take three. I'd get enough ideas while driving the car that I'd want to get out and crank on the computer for a while. Motels are good for that: nothing but silence, give or take the odd house-keeper. I had my cell phone plugged into the car's inverter, hoping that LuEllen would finally feel safe enough to call. As the hills and mountains of Pennsylvania rolled by, the phone remained silent.

At three o'clock, I stopped at a convenience store, bought a half-dozen Diet Cokes, then pulled into a Ramada Inn just off I-76 south of Youngstown, Ohio. I got a no-smoking room on the second floor and plugged in for more boring computer diddling.

I was getting nowhere; I got so desperate that I dug out the tarot cards, did a series of spreads, and figured out nothing at all. The cards were disorganized, random, trivial.

How had Carp done it? That's what I needed to know. How had he found the keys? I went to the bed, lay down, and put a pillow over my eyes. Instead of random digging at the machine, let's look at Carp, I thought. What did Carp do?

After worrying about it for a while, a thought popped into my head. An encryption *key* would consist of characters that you can see on a keyboard, because, on occasion, folks had to manually type them, and not everybody knows how to get to the alternate character sets on a keyboard. An encrypted *file,* on the other hand, usually includes all the characters that a computer can generate, including many that are not represented on a keyboard. If I were to write a search program that looked for strings of letters and numbers that were visible on the keyboard, but contained none of the other, hidden characters . . . then, if the keys were hidden in the huge files, maybe I could pull them out.

Hell, it was a start, and writing a little software program would keep my brain from turning to cheddar. I pulled out my own notebook, where I had my software tool kit, and spent a quarter-hour or so creating the search program. The coding was interspersed with a few minutes watching CNN, a few more watching the Weather Channel, and maybe a moment or two of self-doubt, a feeling that I was wasting my time. When I finished, instead of transferring the program via disk, I got a cable out of my briefcase and hooked my laptop to Bobby's, to transfer the program.

And the minute I did, Bobby's laptop began running the *Dogabone* program, trying to fetch something from my laptop; and it did it as my laptop was transferring the search program. If I hadn't been able to see his laptop, I would never have known that he was searching mine.

Huh.

THE SEARCH PROGRAM found nothing in the encrypted files, no long strings of out-front characters. But as I sat on the bed, watching the machines talk . . .

After we grabbed Carp's laptop back in Louisiana, he'd only had Bobby's laptop to work with. He'd been going online with me, as Lemon, and who else? Who else that Bobby knew?

I could think of only one person: Rachel Willowby.

Rachel Willowby, who had gotten a free computer from Bobby. Ten minutes later, I was calling John from a pay phone in a strip shopping mall. "John, where's Rachel?"

"She went down to the library with Marvel," he said. "What's up?"

"I need to go online for a minute with Rachel's notebook. Is it there? Or did she take it with her?"

"She takes it everywhere. That's why she's at the library—they got it fixed so she can plug into their ethernet and she can get a fast line free. She's in heaven."

"Got a phone number for the library?"

I TALKED TO the Longstreet librarian, told her it was urgent, and she went and found Rachel. "Hello?"

"Rachel, this is Kidd. You remember?"

"Sure. What's up?" She asked the question just like John; already picking up the family traits.

"I'm at a pay phone in Ohio. I need to go online with you for a minute. I've got a couple of phone numbers and some protocols for you. Give me your ethernet address and I'll be down to hook up with you in a couple of minutes."

"All right." She was enthusiastic. More phone numbers were always good.

TWO MINUTES LATER, I hooked up with Rachel, using Bobby's laptop, and watched the *Doga-*

bone program go straight into her. Five seconds later, I had fifty short blocks of numbers and letters that looked like nothing more than computer keys. Sonofabitch. Bobby had hidden his keys with the little computer kids, scattered anonymously all over the country.

Now I had them. Just like Christmas. I talked with Rachel for a few seconds, then transferred a couple of good phone numbers for her to look at. They were big, semisecure computers where she wouldn't get caught, but would have a lot to explore. And they'd keep her from thinking too hard about why I'd wanted to go online with her.

Back at the hotel, I got busy with Bobby's laptop. The keys were in the same order as the files, so opening the files was no problem. I sat at the shaky little motel table and started scanning through what Bobby had accumulated over the years.

Forty-five of the fifty files contained text documents on topics that interested Bobby—biographies and photos of hundreds of people, along with what were apparently confidential assessments of many of those people, made by law enforcement and intelligence agencies. Out of curiosity, I looked and found one on me, though it wasn't much more than a standard FBI file, listing my military service, my technical specialties, and a few additional random notes: ". . . currently self-employed as a fine arts painter."

AH, BUT THE other five files.

These were the keys to the kingdom.

Here were the routings and codes that would get you into almost any computer database in the world. I won't list the stuff, but it is this simple: Bobby had access to almost everything, everywhere. He'd been around as a phone phreak in the CP/M and early DOS days, had fiddled with Commodores and Z80s and all that. He'd been in the early networked computers before anybody thought about online security, and he'd been building trapdoors and secret entrances all along.

As they'd grown, and shifted, and evolved, he'd grown right along with them.

There are, undoubtedly, some serious databases that he couldn't get at—computers that had been isolated from any phone service; computers where, to download information, you had to accept the information on disk or on paper, handed to you by a guy who checked your credentials in person and got a signed receipt for the disk.

But those computers are damned few. It's just too inconvenient. If the director of the CIA wants to look at something on his desktop, he doesn't want to have to go down in the basement to look at it. He wants it in his office. And if he looked at it on his desktop, then Bobby could look at it too. Because Bobby was everywhere.

I scanned through the information in the last five files, and thought three things.

First, when Wayne Bob had looked at that single

disk of information and commented that we were now two of the most powerful people in Washington, he may have been right, but that disk was a child's trinket compared to Bobby's laptop.

Second, it occurred to me that I was now the Invisible Man—I could go anywhere, and see almost anything, and probably do quite a bit to people I didn't like.

And third, I thought, *You're in a lot of trouble now, Kidd.*

AFTER CONSIDERING IT for a while, I transferred the encryption keys to my own notebook, so I wouldn't have to re-fetch them from Rachel every time I wanted to look at Bobby's files. I had a good-sized hard disk myself, and hid them in the clutter. Still, if the feds got their hands on it, and knew what they were looking for, they'd find the keys. I'd find a better hiding place as soon as I got home.

Home . . . What if Carp had called Krause back, had given him my name and my license plate number, and some thugs were waiting in my apartment to take me down? I got paranoid thinking about it, and finally called the old lady who lived downstairs from me—a painter, and a good one, who took care of the cat when I was gone—to check on the apartment and to tell her I was on my way back.

"Means nothing to me. You can stay away as long

as you want." She loudly crunched on a carrot stick or piece of celery, and said while she was chewing, "I put the cat through the garbage disposal two days ago, the stinky thing, and stole your Whistler. What else do you have that I need?"

"How about a real sense of humor?" I suggested.

She was ragging on me, which was good: she knew everything that happened in the apartment building, so there probably weren't any thugs waiting on the landing.

THE REST OF the evening was spent systematically going through the last five files, figuring out exactly what was there. An index helped, but the entries were often cryptic in themselves—just a couple of words or initials that Bobby would recognize.

At one o'clock in the morning, I popped an Ambien to take me down, and got six hours of good sleep. Sometime before nine o'clock the next morning, I was again crossing the rolling green landscape of Ohio, heading toward I-80, which would take me into Chicago.

I hadn't thought much about Carp—what he might be doing—since I'd last seen him on his bicycle outside Rock Creek Park. He was in hiding, I thought. I'd also lost track of the murder investigation in Jackson, which I resolved to check into that night. If the feds didn't winkle him out pretty soon, I'd start messaging the FBI myself.

At ten o'clock, or a little after, I stopped at a Dairy Queen to get an ice-cream cone. I was leaning against the car's front fender, munching the dipped-chocolate coating off the ice cream, when I heard the phone ring in the car. LuEllen.

I scrambled to get inside without dripping ice cream on the upholstery, got the phone, and punched it up. "Yeah?"

Child's voice, shaky, and thin, as if she were some distance from the phone's mouthpiece: "Mr. Kidd? He took me on the way to the liberry."

"What?"

"He took me on the way to the liberry. He wants Bobby's laptop."

Shit. Not LuEllen. It was Rachel. "Where are you, honey? What're—"

"Kidd? This is James Carp."

Like getting whacked in the forehead. "Carp?"

"I assume you're the one who took the laptop out of my car. Pretty smart. I want it back. I'll trade you."

"What're you talking about?"

"The laptop. And Rachel, here. I've got her, and I'm going to keep her until I get the laptop. But there's a deadline. I assume you're still in Washington. I want you down here near this place, Longstreet, as soon as you can get here. Tonight? Tonight, I think."

"I'm not in Washington," I said. "I can't get there tonight. I'm in my car in the middle of nowhere."

"Then get somewhere," he snapped. His voice had a high, squeaky quality, as though it were on the edge of cracking; as though *he* were on the edge of cracking. "I'll tell you this. This is what I'm going to do. I'm gonna stick this girl so far out in the woods that you'll never find her. Out in the wilderness. I'm gonna chain her to a tree. If you fuck with me, I'll never go back, and you'll never find out where she is."

"I'll get you the laptop, but I can't get there tonight," I said. My voice was scared, and I didn't care if it showed; maybe it was better that it showed. And I was lying like a motherfucker, trying to buy time. "I'm way up in West Virginia. I can get there maybe tomorrow afternoon. Honest to God, I'm out in the sticks. I'll get to an airport, try to find a flight that'll get me into Memphis, and I'll get a car from there. But don't put her out in the woods. If you put her out in the woods and she dies, you'll get the death penalty. You still might be clear with the cops."

"Oh, bullshit. They know I killed Bobby. The only thing that'll get me clear is that laptop, and the files. If I have that, they'll talk. They'll let me go off somewhere and play with myself. Otherwise, I'm toast. You try to jump me, I swear to God I'll put a gun in my mouth and little miss black girl here will rot under a tree in the middle of a swamp."

"Don't do that. Don't do that," I said, as urgently as I could.

"Fuck you. I'll talk to you again tomorrow."

He was gone.

———

I CALLED JOHN. "I just got a phone call from James Carp. He's there in Longstreet and he says he's got Rachel. Have you seen her?"

"Rachel?" He was sputtering like I had. "Rachel? She just left here half an hour ago, walking down to the library."

"I talked to a little girl, just for a moment. Sounded like Rachel. She said he got her on the way to the library, goddamnit, John, I think he got her, you gotta check."

"Call you back," he rasped, and he was gone.

I HAD PASSED Cleveland on I-80. As soon as John was off the phone, I turned around and headed back, my laptop propped against the steering wheel. I pulled up Microsoft's Streets and Trips program. Cleveland International was on my side of the metro area, fortunately, and I was able to take I-480 right back in. As soon as I figured out where I was going, I called directory assistance and got phone numbers for four charter air services. I was probably sixteen hours from Longstreet by road, close to a thousand miles. But maybe I could get a plane into Greenville.

The first place I called at Cleveland International was basically an air ambulance service. The woman who answered the phone recommended another service, whose number I didn't have, but who she said was most likely to have a plane free quickly.

I called, and got a man's quiet voice. "Rogers Air Transport."

"I need to get a plane to Greenville, Mississippi, in the next couple of hours," I said, and my voice reflected it. "Do you have one, or do you know where I could get one?"

"What do you want, exactly?"

"To get down there as fast as I can. I've got a family emergency."

"Well, uh, I can get you a Lear into Greenville, have you down there in a couple of hours or a little more. But, uh, it won't be cheap."

"How much?"

"Mm, I'd have to figure it." There was a moment of silence, and I had the feeling that he was staring at the ceiling, rather than running an accounting program. He came back. "About forty-five hundred. That's if I don't have to hang around down there." He sounded apologetic.

"I'll take it," I said. "I'm on the way to your place now. I'm maybe thirty or forty miles out. You won't have to hang around, I'll fly back commercial to pick up my car."

"About payment, uh, we require—"

"You can have it any way you want it," I said. "Cash, check, or credit card."

"Cash would be fine."

ROGERS AIR TRANSPORT had its worldwide headquarters in a cream-colored metal pole barn that served as both hangar and office. I parked in front, dug my stash cash out of the trunk, got one bag with clothes and another that had all three laptops, and carried them around to the office, which smelled pleasantly of aviation gas and hot oil, and was empty.

"Hello?" I called. Nothing. A side door led out of the office, and I stuck my head out and saw a red-headed man walking toward me. He wore denim overalls and a train engineer's hat, and was wiping his hands on a rag. "Mr. Kidd?" he asked cheerfully.

"Yes."

"I'm Jim Rogers." He stuck out a hand and I shook it. "We're ready if you are."

"My car's outside."

"It'll be okay there until you can get back. I hope it's nothing terrible down in Greenville."

"It's bad enough," I said. I wasn't going to be able to avoid saying something. "My dad's had a heart attack. They're gonna try to fix things, but nobody knows what's going to happen."

"Aw, too bad," he said. A woman came around the corner, mid-thirties with smile lines around her eyes, a good tan, a ponytail, and a flight suit.

"This is Marcia, our copilot," Rogers said.

"I'm his old lady," Marcia said. "You ready?"

Jim's eyes sort of drifted—I had the feeling he wasn't the most dynamic of executives, though he might have been a hell of a guy—and I said, "Oh, yeah, better give you this," and handed him forty-five hundred from my stash cash. He took it and nodded, not asking the obvious question, which I answered anyway. "I was up here buying pottery," I said. "Lucky for me, a lot of those places only take cash."

"Lucky," he agreed.

JIM ROGERS WAS a garrulous guy, and his wife smiled a lot and nodded at him. They took turns flying the plane, and Rogers talked us down to Greenville. Airplane stories, mostly—he'd been a bush pilot in Ontario for a few years. That was fine with me: I nodded and told him a couple of Ontario fly-fishing stories, and no real information was exchanged. I called John on his cell phone as we were passing near Louisville, and he told me that nobody could find Rachel.

"Sounds bad," I said, without thinking. Jim and Marcia glanced at each other, misinterpreting it.

"Get your ass down here," John said.

"I'll be in Greenville in a little more than two hours," I said.

When I rang off, Marcia said, "More trouble."

"Pretty tense situation," I said.

"Gotta pray for the best."

John was waiting when we got there. He grabbed

my bag with his good arm and started off to his car, while I shook hands with Jim and Marcia; I think they thought John was my faithful retainer, me being white, John being black, and all of us being in Greenville.

John and I were on our way to Longstreet by 3:30. John was as grim as I'd ever seen him. "He's a crazy man," he said. And, quietly nuts himself, "I'm gonna kill him."

19

WE PULLED INTO Longstreet after six, still bright daylight, and brutally hot. People tended to stay off the streets with these temperatures, and the downtown strip had that cheap-science-fiction-movie vacancy, the emptiness that makes you think the residents are off having their brains eaten by aliens. Two yellow dogs, sitting in the awning shade in front of the Hardware Hank, were doing nothing but staying alive.

Marvel had been roaming the town in her car, methodically, street by street, looking for Rachel and for Carp's red Corolla. She found neither. John called her when we were a mile out of town and she pulled into their short driveway just a few seconds ahead of us.

Marvel watched us park, and when I got out of the

car she stepped over to me, looked up, and asked, "What's going on, Kidd? What'd you do?"

"It's all part of the same thing that got Bobby killed and John shot," I said. "Bobby's goddamn laptop turns out to be worth its weight in plutonium, and Carp's crazy to get it."

"Then give it to him," she said. "Get Rachel back."

"We're gonna get Rachel," John said from behind her. "We're gonna get her, one way or another."

Marvel almost got launched again, spinning around. "You, Mr. Shot-in-the-Arm bigshot spook secret agent—"

"Shut up," he said, and walked into the house. Marvel's mouth snapped shut, and a moment later tears started. I'd never seen John speak to her in anything like the tone, even without the words. She hurried after him and I stood in the yard with my bag full of computers, feeling like the world's leading asshole for just being a part of it.

THEY DIDN'T TAKE long to make up, and spent the next hour taking care of each other—which didn't prevent some hard talk. "Call the cops," Marvel was saying. "We've got four guys down there at the police station that we can count on. We get them going . . ."

But John was shaking his head. "Don't you see? It's all tangled together. We can't tell anyone anything, or it unrolls. The next thing we know, we've got wall-to-wall feds in the front room. We can get her back, but *we* have to do it."

Nobody said, *"If she's still alive."*

JOHN HAD MENTIONED during the ride from Greenville that his kids were staying with their grand-mother overnight, and maybe for a couple of nights, to clear out some space. I didn't ask what he meant by that, the *space* comment, because we were talking about three things at once, but an hour after we got in, a couple of black guys arrived at the house. They were not particularly big or prepossessing, but you probably wouldn't want to fight either of them. They were smart, and smiling, and said hello to John and gave hugs to Marvel, and went back to a third bed-room like they'd been there before.

A half hour after the first two guys arrived, an-other two came in. Two more arrived before mid-night. More talk, a few bottles of beer, lots of ice water and Cokes for three of them who were former alkies:

"They could just be ditched in a hotel or motel anywhere up and down the highway."

"Fat white guy with a beard and a little black girl? A real little black girl? I don't think so, he doesn't want to be noticed and Rachel's smart, she'll holler her head off first chance she gets."

". . . got the same problem with any kidnapping, how do you trust each other to make the trade?"

"The other question is, is this laptop worth saving?"

"It's not the laptop, man. It's Bobby and all the rest of it."

"Cut our losses."

"Can't cut Rachel."

"That's not what I meant."

DURING THE COURSE of the conversation, I told them about the last time I'd seen Carp, as he rode off on his mountain bike to make the deal with Krause. They all listened carefully, and then one of them, Kevin, said, "So he'll try something tricky with us, too. Maybe the bike, maybe something else."

I said, "When I talk to him tomorrow, I'll make the point that we've *all* got trouble if this trade caves in. *We've* got trouble because he knows my name, some of what we've done, and our association with Bobby. So we can't go to the cops. And he's got trouble because we know he killed those two guys at his apartment, and he killed Bobby, and he can't go to the cops. I'll tell him we just want Rachel back and I'll trade the laptop because I can't get into the laptop anyway."

"The question is, where does he make the trade?" asked a man called Richard. "What's the tricky thing that he's gonna do? We've got five cars, and we all got cell phones, so we can talk, but if he sees us chasing him, and he's got something tricky going, and shakes us, what do we do? Then we're really fucked."

We argued about that for a while, and with all the talk of tricks, a thought popped into my head. "John, do you have a decent map?"

He had a county map, and one of the other guys had a big Rand McNally map book, and together they worked well enough. We spread them out on the kitchen table and the others gathered around as I pulled my finger down the curlicue of the Mississippi.

"Look at this. This could be the trick. If he has me go to someplace pretty far north or south of town . . . and if he bought a canoe or a boat, or stole one, or rented one . . . If he leaves his car on the other side of the river, paddles across, meets me, gets the laptop, and then paddles back to his car . . . we'd never catch him. We'd all be stuck over here, on the wrong side. If he takes us twenty miles downriver, it'd take the best part of an hour just to get back to the bridge and down the other side where he was."

"How long you think to paddle across?" one of the guys asked, tapping his finger on the blue line of the river. "I don't know shit about canoes."

"If he knows what he's doing, ten minutes," I said. "Two minutes in a powerboat." I pointed at a couple of narrow points, where the river looked like it was no more than a half-mile across. "He wouldn't pick one of the wider parts. And he'd get himself all set before he calls us."

"That'd be a good trick, the river thing," John said, "if it's not too obvious."

"I can't think of anything else. If he tries the bicycle thing . . . he'd still have to get to his car sooner or later. And when I think about it, around here, I believe he will try to do the exchange out in the countryside. If he just does the bike, we could figure out where the car has to be. Not that many roads. We could choke him off almost anywhere."

By one o'clock in the morning, we'd worked out a plan. We'd put two cars on each side of the river, each a few miles north or south of town. When Carp got me moving to a rendezvous, the cars on my side would move toward the meeting point, hanging a few miles off. The cars on the other side of the river would run parallel to us.

At the rendezvous, if he ran us around to more spots, the cars would maintain the interval. Once I met Carp, if he was on foot, or on his bike, or near the river, the people in the cars would look at his location as I called it in, and figure out where he'd most likely park his car.

"I'm not going to give him the actual files—I mean, they'll be the actual files, but they'll be re-encrypted so his keys won't work," I said. "He won't be able to tell the difference until he actually tries to open them. By then, we'll know if he double-crossed us on Rachel."

Marvel objected. "But you'd have double-crossed him first. What if he kills Rachel because of it?"

"He's gotta have the laptop with the files or he's done," I said. "If we double-cross him and he double-crosses us, and he manages to get away from us . . . he'll call us back. He's gotta have the files. But if he has both the files and the keys, and he's still got Rachel—then he can do whatever he wants."

"No computer files are worth that much," Marvel said. "Not worth a child."

"People have already died for this one—three people that we know of, and he tried to kill us," I said. "Carp is nuts. You think killing Rachel, getting rid of her as a witness . . . you think that would bother him?"

After a couple moments of silence, I got my stuff together and said good night. Marvel had gone off to the kitchen and was banging silverware around, although she hadn't cooked anything. Before I left, I stopped and said to her, "I'm sorry about this mess—I can't tell you how sorry I am. We'll get her back."

"You better get her back," Marvel said. As I stepped away, she added, "She was only here for what, a week? But she fit in with the family. And now, where is she? Some crazy guy's got her."

"But that really wasn't us. The crazy guy was talking to her before we ever met her," I said.

"You don't feel like any of this is . . . our fault?"

I exhaled, wagged my head, and said, "Yeah. Some of it is. I feel like shit. But . . . we'll get her."

She patted me once on the back as I went out, on down to the motel. In the motel room, I transferred the critical files and the keys to my own notebook, then re-encrypted the files on Bobby's computer, deriving new keys, which I erased. No one, including me, could now open the files on Bobby's laptop.

I took two Ambien and got six hours of bad sleep. Rachel's face kept floating up out of the dark; I didn't want to think about her with Carp.

THE NEXT MORNING, on the way back to John's, my cell phone rang. The day before, I'd been expecting LuEllen to call, and got Carp. This time I was expecting Carp, and got LuEllen.

"You about back?" she asked, without even a *hello*.

I took a second to recalibrate on the voice. "I'm in Longstreet," I said. "We've got a big Carp problem."

"Oh, no."

I worry about talking on cell phones—they're radios of a kind—but I gave her a slightly cleaned-up version of what had happened. She was silent, and then said, "You're gonna handle it."

"Best we can," I said.

"There's nothing I can do."

"Not that I can think of. Are you okay?"

"I'm paranoid. Honest to God, I'm paranoid. I'm afraid to go to shopping centers because of that face-recognition stuff. There are cameras everywhere you look."

"I'll talk to you about it when I get back," I said. "Where're you going to be?"

"I was thinking . . . your place."

"You know where the key is."

"You don't mind?"

"Nope. I'm flattered. I gotta get off this phone because Carp might call—but I'll call you when we're done here."

"I'll wait."

JOHN, MARVEL, AND I sat around in the living room, watching television, for better than three hours, with no contact. Marvel didn't entirely believe in air-conditioning, so all the windows and doors were open; they had a small vegetable garden out back, with a dense twenty-by-twenty-foot patch of sweet corn, and I could smell the corn in the warm air filtering in across their back porch. John's friends were already out on the highways on either side of the river, both north and south, waiting. I kept looking at the river maps, trying to figure the odds.

Here's the thing about the river, down South. After a catastrophic flood back in the late 1920s, the lower Mississippi was penned up behind levees. The levees weren't built right at the water line, but followed the tops of the riverbanks, often hundreds of yards back from the normal high-water mark. A few towns, at major crossing points, remained open to the river, but most of the towns shut the Mississippi away.

If you travel south along the Mississippi through Arkansas, Mississippi, or Louisiana, you'll hardly ever see the river, though you may only be a few hundred feet away for tens and dozens of miles. Conversely, if you're traveling on the river itself, you may see the rooftops of any number of small towns over the distant levees, but you can't get to them without walking through tangled, overgrown floodplain, marsh, bog, and backwater.

And if you ever need to find a poisonous snake in a hurry—rattlesnake, copperhead, cottonmouth—the strip between the levee and the water, anywhere between Memphis and New Orleans, is just the spot.

MAYBE I WAS crazy about this river-crossing thing. I was sure it would occur to him, but if he thought about it long enough, it would also occur to him that he'd be a sitting duck for a powerboat, out there in the middle of the river. By eleven o'clock, I'd convinced myself that he wouldn't try crossing the river: he'd get himself lost in the woods, instead. Maybe try cutting cross-country on that trail bike. As far as we knew, he didn't have the money to try anything more sophisticated.

My phone rang. We looked at it as though it might be a cottonmouth, and it rang a second time, and I snatched it off the end table where it was sitting. "Yeah?"

"You in Longstreet?"

"Just got here," I said. "I'm beat, I can barely see. If we're gonna do this, let's do it."

"You got the laptop?"

"Yes. But I got a couple of things to tell you. We think you might be planning to double-cross us on the girl. We're gonna give you the laptop, but don't double-cross us. You don't know exactly what you've gotten into with us, but if you hurt Rachel, we'll find you, and you won't be given a free phone call. We'll cut your fuckin' head off. You understand that?"

"Fuck you. Bring the laptop."

"Look, there's no point in a double-cross."

"I've thought of all that. So listen: You know where Universal is?"

"Universal? What is it?"

"It's a town, fifteen miles south of Longstreet. A cafe, a gas station, a feed store. Ask your friends."

I looked at John. "A town called Universal?"

He nodded. "Down south."

I went back to Carp: "Okay. They know where it is."

"Go down there. Stay off your cell phone. If you leave right now, you should be there in about twenty-one minutes, from your friend's door. I will call you on your cell phone in twenty-one minutes."

"Rachel . . ."

"I'll tell you about Rachel next time I call." And he was gone.

BEFORE I GOT out of there, John pointed to the town on the map. "There's a whole line of hills off there, all tree-covered. I'll bet he's up in the woods, where he can look right down into the town. And look at this—just a little south of there is one of the river's narrow spots, where it goes around Cutter's Bend, and the highway on the other side runs close. He's gonna do the river trick."

"I gotta go," I said. "You get everybody ready. Marvel, I'm gonna need your cell phone."

She gave me the phone, but asked, "Why?"

"Because I want to be able to talk to you guys while I'm talking to him on my cell. I want you to be able to hear what I'm saying to him. I'll call John on your phone when I'm a few miles out, and keep talking while I go in and wait for him to call on my phone."

We were out the door as I explained, and I got in the car and waved. John was already talking on his phone, bringing the guys who'd gone north back into the action.

THE HIGHWAY SOUTH from Longstreet has been featured in blues, jazz, country, and even rock tunes, from musicians running up and down the river between Memphis and New Orleans, stopping off in Baton Rouge, Natchez, Vicksburg, Greenville, and Helena. The highway's an old one, a cracked patchwork of tarmac and concrete, with lots of wiggles—half of them, it seems, known as "dead man's curve" by the locals—and mostly used for short runs, since they put in I-55 to the east.

I wasn't alone on the highway, when I headed south, but the nearest car in front of me was a half-mile away, and there was nobody in my rearview. Every minute or so, I passed cars coming the opposite direction, which meant that two-mile spacing might be typical.

The day was hot: August in the Delta. Heat waves and six-foot mirages hung over the roadway. A line of low hills ran parallel to the river, but well back from it, at Longstreet; but as I got farther south, the river and highway turned into the hills, tightening the valley. Ten miles south of Longstreet, the bottoms of the hills came right down to the road. The levee was a half-mile away, with a few narrow farm fields—cotton and beans—using up the space between the road and the levee. I called John on Marvel's cell phone, got him, then dropped the cell phone onto the seat between my legs where I could talk down into it. "Just coming into Universal now," I said, a few minutes later. "No call yet."

Universal was a dusty spot in the road, three buildings and an old postwar galvanized steel Quonset hut that appeared to have been long abandoned. The Quonset hut had a small sign on its side, the name of its maker, apparently—Universal—which answered one question I had about the place. I pulled into the parking area in front of the Universal Cafe, and my cell phone rang. "Got a call," I said to the phone between my legs.

I picked up my own phone and clicked it on. Carp:

"Get the laptop and start walking down the highway."

"Walking down the highway?" I repeated, mostly for John. "Listen, James, we gotta get something straight. I'm not going to put myself where you can kill me and get the laptop *and* keep Rachel. I'm not walking anywhere."

"I'm not going to kill you, for Christ's sakes." He squeaked, sounding exasperated.

"I'm sorry, James, I can't trust you. Tell me where to go and leave the laptop, and I'll do it."

"Your girl is already chained out in the woods. Nobody'll ever find her—just some hunter ten years from now will find a skeleton chained to a tree."

"And somebody will find your goddamn head in a wastebasket," I said. "I wasn't kidding about that."

A moment of silence. Then: "Okay. Drive south some more. Slow. I'll tell you when to stop, I'll tell you where to put the laptop. I'll be watching you."

"What about Rachel?"

"Stay on the phone. Drive south. We'll handle this."

"How far south?" I asked for John's benefit.

"Not far."

"Okay. If it's not far." I drove south, thirty miles an hour. Thirty seconds, and he said, "Pull over on the right shoulder when you see the red flag tied to the bush on the left side. Just pull over."

I saw the red flag, a kerchief. I pulled over. "What now?"

"Look back the way you came." I looked and saw him pedaling his mountain bike along the left shoulder, talking into his cell phone. "You can see me. I'm not holding a gun. If you do anything to me, Rachel is gonna starve out there."

"All right, I can see you. I'm giving you the goddamn laptop," I snarled. "Just come and get it. You want me to get out now?" More for John.

"Get out."

"I'm getting out," I said.

THE SUN WAS blistering, but the day, this far out in the country, was absolutely silent except for far-away car sounds; I could smell the ragweed cooking in the sun. Carp was forty yards away from me, on the bike, not moving, but balanced on it. No chance to run him down. He held up a piece of paper and spoke into the phone. "Map of where Rachel is at. If you go there, and yell around, she'll call to you. I marked the old store where the path starts, you can't miss it."

I held up Bobby's laptop. "This is the laptop. What do you want to do?"

"Leave the laptop. Leave it on the side of the road. I'll look at it, and if it's right, I'll put the map down. If you do anything, I'll run, and you'll never hear from me again. And Rachel won't hear from you."

"Cut your fuckin' head off," I shouted into the phone.

"Yeah, yeah . . . leave the laptop."

———

I CROSSED THE highway and left the laptop on the side of the road, then crossed back and pulled away in the car, south for another forty or fifty yards. He slowly rode down the shoulder behind me, to the laptop. I'd turned the laptop on in the car. He picked it up, flipped open the top, looked at it, hit a few keys, then closed it and put the map on the shoulder, weighed down with a couple pieces of gravel. A car zipped past, the driver looking at us curiously; but he kept going.

Carp was on the bike again, and he rode away from me and said into the phone, "You can get the map." He sounded gleeful. The phone went dead, and as I watched, he took the bike off the road, down the short slope of the shoulder and onto what must have been a path that ran down to the levee, across the end of one of the farm fields. I picked up Marvel's phone.

"He's left the map, and he's off the road riding down to the levee. I'm about a half-mile south of Universal. He's doing the river thing."

"We're closing on the other side. We're coming in on the other side," John said back.

I BACKED ALONG the shoulder until I was opposite the map, then walked over and picked it up. As I did, Carp crossed the levee and disappeared down the other side, into a forest of cottonwoods. From where I was standing, I could see a narrow path through the weeds, leading down to the levee. Local fishermen, I thought.

The map consisted of two pieces of paper: A Xerox of a road map, pinpointing a crossroads ten miles west of Longstreet, and a little south, probably fifteen road miles from where I was. The second piece was a hand-drawn map starting at the crossroads. There was a square, with the notation, "old abandoned schoolhouse," and another, with an arrow, that said, "power-line easement back into the woods." It appeared that the map would take you about a mile and a half off-road. The thing looked so good I began to believe that we were gonna get Rachel back.

"I got the map," I called to John.

"He's got a boat. The guys on the other side can see him, he's got a jon boat with a motor, he's putting the bike in the boat. They can't find his car. They say they don't see a car over there."

"Gotta be there somewhere. Watch him, he may have a gun."

"How about Rachel?"

"He said she's chained up in the woods. I got a map. I'm going."

"Where?"

I told him, and I heard him talking with Marvel, and he said, "Fifteen minutes. We'll see you there."

I HAD TO go four miles north before I could get a crossroad out of the valley that would take me west toward Rachel. On the way, John called. "He's running down the river, he's not coming across."

"Shit. What's he doing? Can the guys still see him?"

"They can see him, but they don't know where he's going. He's on their side, just under the levee."

"Must've hid the car somewhere that wasn't straight across," I suggested.

"They're still on him, and Marvel and I are on the way out to you."

A MOMENT LATER, he called again. "Shit. He's crossed back over the river. That's his second trick, that's his second trick. He faked us out. He's leaving the boat, he's getting out of the boat, he's on the bike."

I could hear him shouting into a second cell phone. "Gotta stay with him. Henry, get back south, get back south, his car's gotta be down there somewhere. Kevin, you go on down toward Greenville, get moving. . . . I know, I know . . . but that's the only way you're gonna get ahead of him if he keeps going south. . . . I know."

Henry was the driver of the car that had been south of me. He'd closed in when the trade took place, and when Carp crossed the river, had started back to Longstreet, and the Longstreet bridge. Now Carp was south of him, and nobody was south of Carp, and on the same side of the river.

"We're gonna lose him," I shouted into the phone, helpfully.

"No, no, no," John shouted back.

Then I heard him on the other phone, just his side of the conversation. "You see it? You see it? Get down south, keep going, Henry, keep going." And to me: "Henry spotted the Corolla. Carp's not there yet. Henry's going on ahead."

Okay. Now we had Carp between two cars. Two cars with smart guys. I couldn't hear it, but I assumed that they were tagging him.

In the meantime, I closed on the crossroads where Rachel was—two left turns, to get me around a lopsided net of gravel roads, into the old abandoned schoolhouse.

John and Marvel were already there, sitting in their car, looking at their map. I stopped, got out, jogged to John's driver's-side window, the sun burning down on my shoulders. "Let me see the map," John said.

I gave him the map. It was all very clear: we were at the right spot. We squabbled about it for a minute, quacking like a gaggle of geese, but that did no good.

There was no schoolhouse. There was no power line going back into the woods.

There was nothing but a burning hot gravel crossroads, with cotton fields stretching away on all four corners, stretching away forever. The kind of crossroads where Robert Johnson sold his soul to the devil.

20

WE WERE STANDING next to the car, triple-checking the map we'd been given by Carp with our own maps, when John's cell phone rang. He listened for a minute, then said, "Twenty minutes," and hung up.

To Marvel, he said, "I'm going with Kidd. You go on back to the house in case somebody calls about Rachel."

"What's going on?" she asked.

"Nothing, yet. But it looks like this tailing job might take some help. He's gonna spot our people if they can't switch out more often. You go on."

Something was up, and Marvel knew it. She squinted at him, and seemed about to say something, but he shook his head and she said, "All right."

"Don't do anything stupid, like try to follow us," he said. "We need you back at the house."

———

TWO MINUTES LATER, she'd gone one way and
we another, at right angles to each other, and even
from a mile away, we could see the plume of gravel
dust she left behind her as she headed back into Longstreet.

"He's at the RayMar Motel in Bradentown," John
told me. "He's in his room, so he's gonna be cracking
the laptop pretty soon. We've got two cars on him
now and another two coming in."

"How far?"

He looked at his watch. "If we're not lazy about it,
we can be there in half an hour."

"What's the layout like?"

"One-level mom-and-pop, an office at one end and
then a long string of rooms in a straight line. Not
busy. I don't know the people that run it, but black
folks stay there—no color line, so we won't be too
noticeable."

A HALF-HOUR LATER, we were still not there
and my phone rang. I dreaded picking it up, but had
no choice.

"You motherfucker," Carp shouted. "You cheated
me." You could hear the spit flying.

"We've just been at the crossroads, James, so don't
tell me about cheating. I can tell you where to get a
set of keys—and I would have done it if we'd found

Rachel—but now . . . I'd say your head's in trouble. You remember what I told you."

"I want the fuckin' keys," he shouted. "You want the girl back, you better cough 'em up."

"Are you still close to Universal?" I asked.

"Never mind where I am," he said. He was slowing down now. "How are we gonna do this? I don't want the kid to die, I got nothing against her, but I'll leave her out there if I don't get the keys."

"Can't figure out a way to trust you, James."

"I'll tell you—"

"I'll tell *you*, James," I said. "I'm still out here in the woods. I've been driving around, hoping I was at the wrong place, hoping I'd find that abandoned schoolhouse. I'm gonna hang up now and see if I can think of something. It's gonna have to be something weird."

"She's out in the woods, on a chain," he said.

"Call me back in half an hour," I said.

FIVE MINUTES LATER, we were parked down the block from the RayMar, in front of the Bradentown Bakery. Bradentown was just as hot as Longstreet, and smaller. Nothing stirred under the midday sun. I got out, went inside the bakery, and bought two Diet Cokes and two apple strudels, mostly to keep the cashier behind her counter. Back outside, I found two of John's friends in the backseat of the car.

"We got it figured out," Henry said to John. "If you want to go in, we can get him."

"He has a gun," I said.

"We can be on top of him in three seconds," Henry said. "We need somebody to go into the office and talk to the clerk while we go in."

They all looked at me, and I shook my head. "I need to talk to Carp. I need to hear what he says. One of the other guys'll have to talk with the clerk."

They did a quick eyeball vote and John finally said, "Kidd's okay. Let's get Terry to talk to the clerk. He's a bullshit artist." The other two glanced at each other and Henry nodded and took a cell phone out of his pocket. "Terry, you're going in to talk to the clerk. Park right in front where he can see your car, and don't touch anything when you get inside. Uh-huh. Uh-huh. Whatever, you make it up."

He hung up and nodded to John. "We're good."

I said, "His room doesn't connect to another one, does it?"

Henry said, "Nope. None of them connect."

TERRY TOOK A few minutes to get organized, and then we saw his car pull in to the RayMar. We backed out of our parking space, and as soon as Terry went through the motel's office door, we started down the block. Another car, an old Chevy, pulled into the parking lot a few doors from the end of the line of motel rooms.

"He's in the second room from the end," Henry

said. "Pull in right next to Bob's car, the Chevy, and wait."

Henry and the other guy—I never knew his name—got out and walked over to Bob's Chevy, and Bob got out one side, and a guy named Rote on the other. Bob was holding a heavy sledgehammer at his side. I wanted to say something about a safety chain on the door, but before I could, John muttered, "Rote's got the bolt cutters."

The four guys knew what they were doing. In fact, they looked a lot like cops; the night before, they'd even talked like cops. Bob got lined up on the door, taking his time, being quiet, while Henry and the others blocked the view from the street and the office. When Bob was ready, he nodded, and Rote showed a big pair of bolt cutters. The bolt cutters turned out to be unnecessary, because when Bob hit the door, there was a single loud whack like a car accident, the door flew open—no chain, or at least, no chain that held—and the four men went straight into the room.

I was a step behind them. Carp had been sitting on his bed, typing on a laptop, and when we came through he hurled himself at a nightstand on the opposite side of the bed, where a big military-style Beretta sat under the lamp. He almost made it; his hand was six inches from the gun when Bob landed on him, then Rote, and they had him by the neck, dragging him across the bed, and he screamed once and Rote hit him in the nose with a closed fist and his nose broke and he stopped screaming and started to gag; then the door was shut and he was on the floor, three guys on him.

"Roll him over," John said.

They controlled him—I thought *cops* again—and rolled him, and Rote sat on his chest while John knelt next to his head. "Where is she?" he asked.

Carp's eyes were wild, and his torso was shaking under Rote's weight, from adrenaline. But he choked out, "Fuck you. Go ahead and kill me, motherfucker. You'll be killing the kid, too."

Rote stuck the heel of his hand on Carp's lips, and pressed his jaw open; he pressed down harder until his fist filled Carp's mouth. John looked at Carp for five seconds, then dug in his pocket and took a red Swiss Army knife out. He chose one of the blades, looked down at Carp, and said, "I'm gonna ask you one question. If you don't answer it, I'm gonna cut your nose off. Then I'm gonna cut your eyes out. Here's the question. What town is Rachel closest to? Universal? Longstreet? That crossroads? Here in Bradentown? Which town? Don't have to tell us where, just which town she's closest to."

Rote pulled his hand out of Carp's mouth. Carp gasped for air, groaned, and then said, "I don't care if you kill me, I'm not gonna tell you where she is. You cocksuckers, you cocksuckers."

John leaned forward with the knife. "I'm gonna cut your nose off," he said. "In ten seconds, your nose gonna be gone. Nobody's gonna put that nose back on." He was talking quietly, but his face was a stone; he was scaring the shit out of me. "So answer my question. Not where she is, just what town she's closest to."

Carp stared at him for six of those seconds, then finally spat out, "Universal. If you'd really given me the keys, I would have told you."

John turned to me and said, "Get back up there."

"I need to—"

"Just get back up there," he said impatiently. To the others, "Let's move him. Terry's gonna be running out of bullshit."

ROTE HANDED ME the bolt cutters, said, "For the chain, if there is one," and that was the last I saw of John's friends. John was running things now, and I got in the car and did what he told me: I headed up to Universal.

GETTING THERE TOOK a while. Driving at the speed limit, watching the yellow lines, scared to death that a cop might stop me for anything. Saw no cops; Universal was as dead as ever.

Fifteen minutes after I got there, I was sitting in a booth in the cafe, one of two customers. The other guy looked like a farmer, and he was eating pie at the far end of the line of booths, reading the local newspaper. I was picking at a BLT and a plate of fries—I wasn't hungry, but I needed a reason to wait there—and Marvel arrived.

I saw her get out of her car in the parking lot, and she looked at me through the window. As she came in, the counter lady said, "Hello, Miz Marvel," and Marvel smiled and asked, "How are things?" Then she turned as if checking out the rest of the cafe, spotted me, did a double take, and said, "Say, aren't you Mr. Barnes from the highway department?"

"Yup. And you're the mayor of Longstreet."

"Can I join you? I've been meaning to call you about the bridge approach lanes."

"I was afraid of that," I said. I made a gesture to the seat opposite. Marvel asked the counter lady for a Coke and a piece of apple pie, and came and sat across from me. We talked about the bridge until she got her pie, and then, when the counter lady went to talk to the other customer, Marvel leaned forward and said, "John called. We're waiting. He said he'd call again on my phone."

"Where are they?"

She shrugged. "I don't think we want to know too much about it." She looked suddenly bleak. "I love that man. I know he's done some things in the past and I love him anyway. But I haven't seen him like this. He scared me this morning."

"He scared me this afternoon," I said. I spotted the cafe lady coming with a carafe of Diet Coke, and added, "But if there's no way you can push the mill-age rate, I really can't see the state sequestering the money long enough for you to make it up through the regular road revenue."

"There's gotta be some loose money somewhere," Marvel said. "It shouldn't be up to the taxpayers in Longstreet alone to take care of that bridge. People use it for hundreds of miles around."

"You'll have to talk to the legislature about that," I said.

We went on like that for ten minutes, and were running out of bullshit. Then John called, and Marvel's dark eyes lit up; she got a map out of her purse and said, "Yes, I see. Yes, I see. Okay. I'll go now."

She hung up and said to me, "I've got to go. I hope to see you at the public hearings this fall. Any help you can give us with the regional supervisor would be welcome."

"Got to go myself," I said. I dropped a couple of bucks on the table, and we paid our bills separately at the cash register. I lingered, talking a minute with the cashier, buying a couple bottles of Dasani water, and let Marvel get outside. She was headed south on the highway when I got in my car. I caught her a minute later, and she took us, moving fast, south down the highway for six miles, then turned away from the river and took us about five more miles back into the countryside.

She pulled to the shoulder at a dusty crossroads that looked a little like the one we'd been at a few hours before—except this one was in rougher country, small cut-up fields spreading away from three-quarters of the crossroads, with a steep wooded hill on the other quarter.

At the bottom of the hill was an abandoned wood-frame building with a fading sign that said "Charm Township Hall." Marvel got out of her car and said, "We're supposed to use the map from this morning, but the old town hall is the abandoned school."

I nodded and said, "There should be a trail on the side of the building."

I got the bolt cutters and the two Dasani bottles, and we found a trail right where it should have been, and headed up into the woods. "Watch for snakes," Marvel said as I led off.

THERE WERE NO snakes. The trail got narrower but was always visible, as we went up the hill. It was half game trail, and maybe used by hunters in the spring and the fall, I thought, guys going into the woods. We spooked three does a quarter-mile back and watched them bounce off ahead of us.

A half-mile in, Marvel said, "You think we've gone a mile yet?"

"No. Half-mile, maybe."

"Carp told John it was a mile. He said he checked it with a GPS. A mile in a straight line."

"Ten more minutes, on this trail," I said, "if we don't lose the trail."

We went on, getting hotter and hotter by the step. There was good leafy overhead, but the air was so hot that even the shade didn't account for much; both of us had sweated through our shirts by the time we were at the top of the hill. The path continued just below the crest—a good sign of a deer trail—and after a few more minutes, I said, "We gotta be close."

The woods were thick, and brush was piled up beside the trail. We couldn't see more than fifty feet in any direction. Marvel tilted her head back and screamed, "RACHEL!"

Nothing.

"RACHEL."

And faintly, "He-e-e-el-l-l-lppp."

SHE WAS A noisy little kid, with a fine set of lungs. We found her, another two hundred yards along the trail, in a little open patch of grass. She was standing next to a tree, laptop under her arm, a skinny girl with big eyes, wearing a blue, flowered blouse and jean shorts, a chain around her waist, closed with a padlock. The other end of the chain was wrapped around a two-foot-thick tree, also padlocked. Just like Carp had said; a chilly breeze swept through my soul, as I realized that he would have left her there.

Marvel ran the last hundred feet, fell down, bruised herself, popped back onto her feet, and closed in and grabbed Rachel and lifted her up, and started crying, and Rachel looked at me and said, "I got bugs all over me," and she began to cry, and I took the laptop from her, and between gasps she said, "Jimmy James hurt me. Jimmy James hurt me. Jimmy . . ."

I caught on with the first word; Marvel didn't, not right away. She was just cooing, "We can fix it, honey, we can fix it, you're okay now, where'd he hurt you?"

Rachel started sobbing again and screwed the heels of her hands into her eyes and then looked at Marvel and said "He made me do it with him. He *hurt* me."

Marvel said, "Oh, Jesus. Oh, baby . . ." She looked at me; she was horrified. So was I.

The bolt cutters took care of the chain. Rachel was heavy, and Marvel not that big, but she carried the kid out anyway. I offered to help, but Rachel shook her head and Marvel said, "Better not," and I figured that maybe Rachel didn't want to have much to do with anybody male. Not for a while.

"I was afraid the motherfucker might take my laptop," Rachel told me over Marvel's shoulder. And a minute later, "I had to pee in the woods."

HALFWAY DOWN THE hill, I called John. "Got her."

"Thank God. I'll see you back in Longstreet. She okay?"

"Not exactly," I said. Pause, and he knew.

"See you back in Longstreet," he said.

"What about Carp?"

"See you back in Longstreet."

I didn't ask again.

21

AT THE TOP of a gentle rise that begins at a rambling country highway—a highway that might be in New England—Mansard Penders had built himself a two-million-dollar arts-and-crafts house. The porch looks over a sweeping lawn, a stone fence, the highway, and his forest. He owns the forest, twenty thousand acres of plantation pine, with some mixed hardwoods, in the Rufus Chamblee Bend of the Mississippi River above Mansardville, Louisiana.

A messy, English-style cottage garden twists along gravel paths on the back and sides of the house. The garden was created by Florence Penders, and has all the color of Monet's garden at Giverny. But while Monet's garden is confined in beds, Flo's garden sprawls and scampers and climbs, flaring up in the spring, muting a bit in June and July, roaring back in

the summer: red, white, and yellow roses, pink hol-
lyhocks and chrysanthemums, flaming gladioli, deep
blue irises, scarlet poppies, cornflowers and larkspur,
orange cockscomb, red and purple dahlias.

From anywhere among the flowers, you can see
the river twisting below like a blue-steel snake. Sometimes, when the wind is right, you can smell the dead
fish and mud of it, and on stormy days, you'll see the
weather rolling in from the west.

Inside the house, in the west wing, is a study with
walnut walls and bookcases. Walnut is a dark wood
with a touch of gray; the room is brightened by
clerestory windows, arts-and-crafts lamps, and several thousand hardcover books with bright, varie-
gated dustcovers.

Five oil paintings will hang in a band on one wall,
on the theme of The River, with books both above
and below. Mansard Penders is paying me three hundred and fifty thousand dollars to do the paintings.

As part of the deal, Manny had insisted on the
right to specify the sites of the paintings, although
not the details of them. After looking at the sites, I
accepted. My dealer, who thinks I'm an asshole, and
who was sure I'd turn the offer down, went out for a
large whiskey and soda, or maybe two, and, I suspect,
to a snug little whorehouse down by the river in New
Orleans.

God bless him. He puts up with a lot.

I WORKED ON the preliminary oil sketches for most of September, trying to get it all just right. I was dreaming about them every night; I wanted them to glow from the walls, to hold the colors of the river, and to stand up to the house.

But some nights, I'd wake up in the motel, in the middle of a painting dream, and when I couldn't get back to sleep—I can never get back to sleep anymore—I'd wander over to my laptop, load the Bobby files, read and think and work.

One thing I worked out: Bobby had penetrated the DDC. Some of the files on the laptop certainly came from there. It's also possible that he was directly in touch with Carp—maybe that's why Carp was so confident about flicking that little fly out there, about dragging Rachel in front of Bobby's computer eyes.

AS FOR JIMMY James Carp, he was gone and he wouldn't be back.

John and his friends had split up, going their own ways, after we got Rachel back. When John arrived at the house, he was grim as the reaper himself. He said, "Hi," in a quiet voice, when he came through the living room, and I nodded toward the bathroom. Marvel and Rachel had been inside for the best part of an hour. I could hear them talking and sometimes, crying.

John knocked on the door, talked with them for a

minute, then came back into the living room. "That jerk," he said. He was calm enough. He went to the refrigerator and got out a beer and popped the top. "You want one of these?"

"Yeah, I'll take one," I said. The beer tasted pretty good, cold and spiky against the heat. "She'll be okay," I said. "Marvel will fix her."

"She might grow up to be okay, but she's not okay right now," he said, tipping the bottle up.

"How did you get Carp to tell you where she was?"

"He made the mistake of thinking death was the worst thing that could happen to him," John said. I opened my mouth to ask another question, but he tipped the bottle toward me and said, "Don't ask, okay? Those guys you saw . . ."

"What guys?"

He nodded. "Exactly."

He took another calm pull on the bottle, looked at it, and then screamed, "That motherfucker," and he pitched the bottle right through one of the plate-glass windows on the front of the house, which blew out as though it had been hit by a bomb.

Marvel came wide-eyed out of the bathroom: "What was that?"

"Window broke," John said.

All right.

THAT EVENING, AS the sun was going down—and after we'd gone to the hardware store for glass and putty and I showed John how easy it is to replace a window—John, Marvel, Rachel, and I headed for Memphis, all jammed into John's car. They dropped me at the airport, where I caught a plane back to Cleveland, to retrieve my car. They went on to see a doctor, not George, but a lady friend of George's, who'd give Rachel a complete exam. Nobody said anything about it, but if Rachel had been made pregnant . . .

That'd be just about the final little chip of horror in the story. The doctor would make sure that wouldn't happen.

On the way, Rachel confirmed what I thought but hadn't mentioned, about how Carp had found her. She'd been going to the Longstreet library with her laptop, and from there, she logged into her regular baby-hacker chat rooms with her baby-hacker name. If you knew what you were doing—and with most programs, it's really easy—you could track that back to her location.

LuEllen was at my apartment when I got back to St. Paul from Cleveland. I walked in the door and she called, "Kidd? In the kitchen." I dropped my bag in the hallway and found her eating a toasted bagel with cream cheese. The red cat was sitting on the kitchen counter, next to her, licking his chops. Cream cheese was one of his favorites.

"So what happened?" she asked.

I told her. All of it.

"Fuck him," she said about Carp.

TWO DAYS LATER—this is while the DDC was still operating—I found her file in a DDC computer under the tag *Betty 47.* "Betty," as it turned out, was intelligence-speak for an unidentified female. The file contained partial fingerprints from her car and a dozen photographs taken by a concealed camera in the room where she'd been detained.

"They did a good job hiding the camera," LuEllen said. "I never saw a thing. And I looked."

"Some of the lenses are the size of pinheads," I said.

I downloaded the photographs, went out to the FBI files and picked up another dozen surveillance photos of a dark-haired woman named Harriet. With a few hours of tedious work in Photoshop, I replaced LuEllen's face with Harriet's, while leaving LuEllen's body and the room backgrounds. The fingerprints were replaced with a set picked at random from the FBI files.

Is she safe? I don't know. There may be hard copies, or optical-disk copies, of all the stuff on LuEllen. You can't get into somebody's desk drawer from a computer.

Am I safe? I don't know that, either. I do have reason to believe that they don't know who I am. Not yet, anyway—because if they did, they'd come through the door with an Abrams tank.

Before we went to sleep that night, LuEllen said, into the dark, "My real name is Lauren. My mother named me after Lauren Bacall."

She still hasn't told me her real last name; maybe we're getting to that.

CONGRESSMAN BOB HAD been busy with the CD I gave him, though not exactly saving the Republic. When the Bobby attacks suddenly stopped, most of the air went out of the other charges, too. The political counterattack started with a lot of media bullshit about *responsibility* and *McCarthyism* and *anonymous smears*, despite the black-and-white evidence for many of the charges.

The hottest charge, the supposed Norwalk virus experiment on San Francisco, cooled off when the governor of California, a possible presidential candidate in three years, congenially agreed that there wasn't much evidence to support the claim. Somebody, I thought, had gotten to him. With evidence from the DDC files? Who knows?

ONE POLITICIAN WHO did take a heavy hit was Frank Krause.

Like this: Two weeks after the Bobby attacks

ended, a UN deputy secretary-general got rolled on
the east end of Capitol Hill. At a previously sched-
uled press conference, somebody asked the President
about it. The President made a few comments about
the poor physical condition of the capital city—the
bad roads, the deteriorating building stock east of
Fourteenth Street—and suggested that America could
do better. A week later, the Senate majority leader
named Krause to head a special Senate Committee on
the Capitol, said that Krause would now be the Capitol Czar, and everybody shook hands and smiled.

Bob, in a mildly lubricated call a few days later, told
me that the Committee on the Capitol was the political equivalent of an isolation chamber. Krause could
remain a senator until his constituents realized that
he could no longer deliver the pork, but he wouldn't
have any real clout. He'd hurt too many colleagues.

The DDC itself disappeared. The initials did, anyway. They tried to hide it all away, but nothing hides
from the All-Seeing Bobby Eye. The Inter-Service Research Bureau is slowly gathering itself back together—
same people, different building. They work under the
guidance of the House Special Sub-Committee on
Coordination, Congressman Wayne Bob, chairman.

SO IN SEPTEMBER, after time to talk and do a bit
of contemplation, I went back to Louisiana and the
Penders project. I stopped in Longstreet and talked
with Marvel and John, and they were full of each

other again. Rachel was as deep into her laptop as ever. We didn't talk about Carp.

Lauren calls every night. She's at my place most of the time, now. The Minnesota weather had turned crappy; they got snow flurries on the fifteenth, she said. She grumbled about the shortness of the golf season and said she was planning to rent a place down in Palm Springs in January, February, and March.

I was invited.

"There's a golf club there, they've invited me to join."

"That was nice of them," I said. "Nonsexist."

"The downstroke is a nonsexist quarter-million dollars." A downstroke, she explained, was the up front membership fee.

"Ah. Maybe they're not liberals after all," I said.

"Maybe not. I've got the money. I'm thinking about it."

"A quarter-million dollars to chase a little white ball around a sod farm?"

"Hey—remember what I said about golf. . . . When are you coming back?"

"Another ten days or two weeks."

"Miss you," she said. "We could have a good time in Palm Springs."

California dreaming . . .

THEN ONE EVENING, the twenty-second of September, as I sat on a rickety motel chair among the fumes of the oil sketches drying against the wall, I got a note from Bobby. The note came into one of my alarmed dump sites. When I opened it, it scared the shit out of me—I felt the hair rise on the back of my neck, and I thought, *Carp.*

But it wasn't. It was Bobby:

Kidd:

As you probably know by now, I'm gone. I've waited this long to send the note just to be sure. I wanted to tell you how much I enjoyed working with you. Hell, it was a short life, but an interesting one, hey?

You're worried about my files, but you don't need to be. I didn't keep anything that could come back on any of my friends. Not a thing, encrypted or otherwise. That's all in my dead head.

I'm sorry I'm dead, because now I won't know how the world comes out. Hope *you* live long enough to find out. This was the best time to be alive, these past thirty years. What would I have done without computers? Say good-bye to Lauren for me . . . and if you don't know who that is, you'll figure it out sooner or later.

By the way, I've appended a list of databases and filenames that would be of use to you. Good luck, friend.

> *Bobby*
> *(Robert L. Fields, Jackson, Mississippi)*

I told Lauren about it that night, in our bedtime phone call. "You know who he is?" she asked. "He's the Hanged Man. Remember those tarot readings, right at the start of everything, where the Hanged Man came up? You said it was somebody in a state of suspension, between this and that. Bobby's like that. Dead, but not dead. Everything that's happened was because he was gone, but not entirely gone. Like Janis Joplin's song. And he's still doing stuff."

I thought about it, and rendered an opinion. "Horseshit," I said.

Now, at this moment, unable to sleep, I sit in the near-dark of the motel room, with nothing but the blue glow of the computer screen in front of me. The All-Seeing Bobby Eye goes into operation.

Bobby's files need maintenance. If they're not maintained, they'll erode, as passwords and protocols are changed, as trapdoors are found and closed, as databases are discontinued or transferred.

I don't know if I should bother. Maybe I should just put the laptop in the garbage; or better yet, toss it in the river. But there's so much here. There's knowledge, there's money, there's power. There's revenge. With those things, you can have almost anything else, too.

What do I want? I always wanted to be a painter,

and to do my work, and to be left alone. But with these files, you could change history.

What *do* I want?

I sit in the glow of the computer screen, and think, *Time to find out.*

Author's Note

JOHN SANDFORD conceived and wrote *The Hanged Man's Song*, but with serious help this time. The help came from Roswell Camp of St. Paul, Minnesota, and Emily Curtis of Los Angeles, California, who together provided geographical research assistance, filled me in on some technical aspects of computers and online life (Emily informed me that "online" is now officially one word, rather than "on line" or "on-line"), kept me straight on the logic of the story, provided editing and production services, and also provided the occasional adjective or noun where needed. In keeping with Strunk and White, most adverbs were eliminated.

JOHN SANDFORD

"If you haven't read Sandford yet, you
have been missing one of the great
summer-read novelists of all time."
—Stephen King

For a complete list of titles and to sign up for our
newsletter, please visit prh.com/JohnSandford